I0638933

Olawu

P. J. Leigh

Published by Brave Girls Press, 2023
Raleigh, NC

OLAWU

First edition. July 1, 2023.

Copyright © 2023 P. J. Leigh.

ISBN: 979-8988143802

Library of Congress Number: 2023910471

Written by P. J. Leigh.

Cover art by Bryn Threats

To the big, brown eyes watching me. You are my inspiration.

Author's Note

This story was inspired in part by the languages, histories, and culture of the Bantu peoples of East Africa. Some of those inspirations include the traditions of pre-colonial Tanzania (known as Tanganyika), Kenya, and other East African countries, as well as the history of the Dahomey Amazons, the Maasai tribes of Tanzania, and the conflicts between Mirambo of the Nyamwezi and the Tabora (1840-1884).

It's important to note that the cultures, tribes, and customs of East Africa were and still are very diverse. Pre-colonial East Africa had international trade which affected some customs and the availability of goods. Travel and migration patterns also had an effect on the cultural landscape, and many tribes spoke multiple languages or blended forms. Many people groups, even those in close proximity, held vastly different customs and ways of life.

This is a work of fiction. As such, I took a healthy dose of creative license in crafting Olawu's story. I hope you enjoy it. As there are words and sayings borrowed from the Zulu, Kiswahili, and Xhosa languages and cultures, a glossary of terms is included.

Thank you for reading!

Glossary

Primary languages

Kanakam – Zulu
Borimbe - Swahili
Oloko – Xhosa

Name Pronunciations

Olawu (oh lah woo)
Dikembe (dee kim bay)
Mbako (mm bah koh)
Ugami (ooh gah mee)
Fadhila (fah zeel la)
Batiko (bah tee koh)
Dhakiya (thah kee yah)
Pootagi (poo tah gee)
Dikebe (dee kay bee)
InDuna Dike (en doo na dee kay)
Kimani (kee mah nee)
Businge (boo sin gay)
Oloko (oh loh koh)
Basange (bah san gay)
Hondo (hahn doh)
Yero (yee roh)
Chief Umdaka (oom dah kah)

OLAWU

Kioli (kee yoh lee)
Chief Umfazi (oom fah zee)
Chausiku (chah see koo)
Bolanle (boh lahn lay)
Fayola (fay oh lah)
Kebe (kay bee)

Words and Phrases

Zulu
Amarabi – rabies

Hayi - no

Ibhubesi –lion or large cat

Induna – great leader

Inja – dog

Isilo esikhulu – monster

Isiphetho – the end

Isitshalo – plantain

Mama Induna – wife of the great leader

Sangoma – healer

Ubaba – father, plural obaba

Udokotela – doctor or physician

Umama – mother, plural omama

Umuntu inhlamvu engalungile – man of bad character

Unyana – son

Uxolo – peace

KiSwahili
Baba – father, plural akina baba

Babu – grandfather

Bibi – grandmother

Mama – mother, plural akina mama

Xhosa
Ekhaya – at home

Inja – dog

Inja ebomvu – red dog

Intaba – mountain

Intaka – vermin

Intlambo - valley

Inyoka – snake

Irhamncwa elibi – evil beast
Umama – mother, plural oomama
Umntu ngumtu ngabantu – Proverb meaning: a person is a person because of other people. (No man is an island)
Utata – father, plural ootata
Utatomkhulu – grandfather

Commonly Used Terms

Kaftan – similar to a robe, a pullover clothing item worn in African cultures
Kanga – square fabric worn around the chest or waist
Kitenge – a set of wraps that go around the waist, chest and shoulder, worn by Tanzanians and other east Africans
Mandazi – fried bread served in Kenya and Tanzania
Masika – the greater rain in Tanzania
Mchemsho - a special stew made in Tanzania
Msondo – a type of drum used in Swahili speaking cultures
Mvuli - the lesser rain in Tanzania
Ugali – a flour porridge made with corn, millet, or sorghum

Part One

Kanakam

Chapter One

Olawu did not understand why her umama wished for a boy. She and her sister, Ugami, did as their umama asked. They cleaned and cooked as she desired. They planted seeds in the garden. They sewed and mended their clothes, gathered water from the river, and buried their waste in the sand. All at their umama's word. Not once did Olawu waver. Not once did it seem to matter. Every night her umama prayed the same prayer. For God to bless her with a son.

God did bless her with another child. Kimani was a beautiful baby with shiny curls and fat fingers, silky black skin and light brown eyes with flecks of gold. Olawu adored her. She loved kissing her sweet cheeks and wrapping her tightly in kitenge cloth to hold her close. She sang lullabies to Kimani and told her stories of wise monkeys and greedy lions.

Umama cried many nights after Kimani's birth, but when Ubaba came home, he would always comfort her. Olawu loved her ubaba. He was tall and strong and smart. When he picked her up and lifted her high over his head, she felt like a princess.

She loved the way he smelled. Like sweat and medicine with a hint of copper. He always wore a white kaftan and cream-colored tunic when he worked. He was an udokotela, and his skills outmatched any healer. When Olawu grew big enough, he would let her tag along with him to the healing hut. She'd organize his herbs and medicines and lay out his instruments before surgery. She could not stay when patients were around, though she wanted to.

There were many rules in the village of Kanakam. Girls were not allowed to study the ways of healing, so Ubaba made her wait outside when someone entered the hut. Olawu did not like this rule, but she followed it.

Ubaba promised to teach her in secret so long as she obeyed. He taught her and her sisters to read and write, another thing girls were not allowed to do. Girls were not allowed to learn a trade or be an apprentice, or buy and sell at the market, or travel outside of their village without a male companion.

In Kanakam, there were three groups of people. The merchants owned cows and land and controlled the buying and selling in the market. Craftsmen were the second and included builders, potters, carpenters, and those with special skills.

The third group were the poorest in Kanakam. They were families with no resources, or more often, no men. They were not treated much better than the slaves captured by rival tribes in other places. These were called Pootagi in her village. And though women were not allowed to work for wages, Pootagi women would often do hard labor, working the crops for the merchants, herding cows, or performing other undesirable tasks in exchange for food.

Olawu did not give much thought to these things. She had Ubaba. He took care of her, Umama, and her sisters with so much love and kindness that the outside world did not matter. He sang songs to them so silly they drew laughs even from Umama. He was Olawu's sun and moon and stars; her hero. He never turned anyone away. Umama would chastise him when he would work for free, especially when he helped a Pootagi. Olawu had heard Umama scold him on many occasions.

"You know they cannot pay, Mbako," her umama would say.

"God would not allow me to sleep if I refused to help one of His children, Fadhila."

Umama would cluck at Ubaba's reply, but say no more, and Olawu would smile to herself, knowing that Ubaba had done the right thing. He always did the right thing. She vowed, one day, she would be just like him.

"OLAWU!"

Olawu pretended not to notice Batiko, looking handsome in a blue and gold kitenge with slacks, the uniform all boys wore as apprentices. He ran across the marketplace to greet her, but she turned her face from him, trying to hide her smile.

"Olawu? Wait!" He stepped in front of her, blocking her path on the dusty road.

"Ach! What is it, Tiko? I have laundry to take to the river." She flicked her eyes towards the basket she carried on her head.

"Let me take that for you."

He reached for the basket, but Olawu moved it out of his grasp. "Why? So you can tell all your friends that you carried Olawu's basket for her? Tch! I won't allow it."

Batiko laughed. "Come now, Olawu. Don't think so little of me. I just saw that you were carrying a heavy load and wanted to help you."

A young umama passed with her baby strapped to her back. She looked first at Batiko, then at Olawu before giggling and walking away. Batiko noticed her expression and grinned.

"I'm onto you, Tiko." Olawu huffed with narrowed eyes. "I can handle my own responsibility, so go away."

"Olawu, you're so stubborn. You should learn to be more like Ugami. She would never speak so crossly. Don't you know men do not like to marry such women?"

"And so what? What do I need to be married for?"

"So you will be taken care of, of course! Even though you have a sharp tongue, I still like you. I promise to take very good care of you when we're married."

Olawu snorted. "You seem so sure."

"No one else would marry such an ugly girl." He tipped the basket on her head and ran away, laughing.

"Ach! Batiko!" Olawu scowled as the basket fell to the ground. She raised her fist and chased after him, leaving her basket of laundry behind. "Come back here!"

"Try to catch me, first." Batiko grinned as he ran off, stomping through a half dozen rugs laid out with goods. He dodged two merchants repairing the gate for their sheep pen before skittering down the space between two huts. Olawu followed his trail of destruction, shouting a few brief apologies before taking off in earnest.

Batiko dodged a wall of bamboo and traveled its length before turning again. Olawu smirked and continued straight. She knew the market as well as any place. And she knew Batiko. He would try to lose her, then double back and head towards the potter's hut where he apprenticed. She'd cut him off near the jewel maker's cart.

Olawu ran past a row of men shouting as they haggled and bartered bags of millet for eggs and meat. She spotted Batiko as she crossed in front of the jewel maker, but his eyes were elsewhere and they were moving too fast. The two collided and tumbled before upsetting a small pen of guinea fowl. Feathers flew and hens scattered, hopping and squawking in every direction.

Batiko laughed and helped her up as the owner of the fowl came running towards them from down the road. "Come on, let's get out of here." He yanked her arm, but Olawu hesitated, looking instead at the broken pen.

"Ach! Tiko, why must you leave such a mess wherever you go? Help me gather the birds back together." Olawu began shooing them back into the pen. Her efforts were in vain, as the fowl easily escaped through the broken wood.

"Olawu, who cares about those stupid birds? Just run!"

She shook her head in dismay. "Ach, they make so much noise."

"Olawu, watch out!"

Batiko's warning came too late. The merchant grabbed Olawu by the arm and swung her around. "What do you think you are doing, eh? You think you can cause trouble like this, inja?"

Olawu's temper flared at the insult. How dare he call her a dog? She pulled her arm from his grip and shoved him back. "Ay! What gives you the right? Because I am a child you call me a dog?"

"Because you are a woman." The merchant snorted, then spat in her face. "You get out of here before I lose my temper."

Olawu stood speechless. Batiko looked from Olawu to the merchant and stepped forward. "Hayi! It was my fault. Please, do not act this way."

Spittle dripped down Olawu's nose and onto her chin. Her shock gave way to rage, and she glared at the merchant. "How dare you?" she shouted. "You spit in my face? I spit in yours!"

"Olawu, no!" Batiko reached for her, but she was too quick. She spat at the merchant.

Seconds later, she was on the ground, ears ringing. Batiko stood above her, silently shaking his head. Blood dripped from her nose. Fire engulfed the left side of her face. Dirt covered the right. The merchant smirked as he wiped his cheek with his sleeve. She had not even seen his fist.

Drums vibrated in the distance as a group of children danced in the dusty road. Olawu's heart pumped to the rhythm, building to a raging tempo. She pushed herself off the ground and wiped the blood from her nose.

"Is that the best you can do?"

Batiko's eyes grew wide. "Olawu."

She ignored him and took a step towards the merchant. "Do you think you are strong, hitting a girl? Eh?"

She hit the ground a second time. Her teeth chattered with this blow, and she tasted the blood from where she'd bitten her tongue. But she wasn't done yet.

Heart pulsing in her ears, she stood again. The merchant's eyes held a glint of pure hatred, but the third strike never came.

Ubaba held the merchant's fist. "Strike her again, and you will strike no more."

The merchant turned in surprise. "Mbako? Where did you . . ." He lowered his eyes. "Forgive me, Udokotela."

There were not three, but four groups of people in Kanakam. The Pootagi, the craftsmen, the merchants, and her Ubaba. His hands had healed many in Kanakam. From the lowliest Pootagi to the most powerful merchant. Even the pale foreigners from the eastern seas respected him.

Olawu grinned with bloody teeth. Her eyes danced over the merchant and landed on Ubaba, but his eyes held a hardness she found unfamiliar.

"Olawu, go home. Batiko, go to your work." Tiko did not need further prompting, but Olawu hesitated, confused by the anger in Ubaba's voice. "Olawu!" He barked a second time. She jumped at the sound and ran home. Past the jewel maker's cart, the merchant's rugs, and the laundry still sitting in the road.

She scraped her shoulders on the maze of bamboo surrounding their hut, but barely noticed. Ubaba was not one to speak harshly to her. His anger worried her more than the bruises forming on her face.

Chapter Two

Olawu winced as her sister pressed a damp cloth to her lip, shaking her head and sighing. "Go ahead and say it, Ugami."

Her sister sighed and stroked Olawu's soft, black hair. "You could have been really hurt, you know. Why must you provoke men so?"

"Why must they provoke me?" Olawu snapped, then winced again at the pain in her lip. Much softer she added, "He spit in my face, Ugami."

"You should have asked forgiveness and walked away. You bring shame to Ubaba acting this way." Olawu touched her swollen lip, and Ugami sighed. "Were you not afraid?"

"I was angry." She looked up at Ugami. Worry lines creased her young sister's brow. No man had ever struck Olawu before. She remembered Ubaba's face when he had stopped the merchant, and the worry that knotted her insides grew even more tangled. "Do you think Ubaba will still be upset when he comes home?"

"Ubaba is never angry for long. It is Umama you should fear."

"Ach!" She had nearly forgotten. Umama would be furious. Olawu already had a reputation for being outspoken, but spitting in a man's face would likely earn her a beating. Umama hated to hear her children's names on the lips of other women at the river. And Olawu's name came up much too often.

Perhaps Ubaba would save her once more before the night was done.

UBABA ARRIVED HOME haggard and hungry, but Olawu had prepared mchemsho for their evening meal. Umama and the others had already gone to sleep, but Ubaba took the time to go to each one and kiss them good night before returning to Olawu in the front room.

She sat on her knees and offered him the bowl of stewed vegetables and spices. Her backside ached from Umama's beating, but only a little. Umama had stopped after only three strikes with the bamboo stick, then sent her away to gather the laundry left in the road. She had expected much worse.

"Forgive me, Ubaba."

He took the stew and set it down on the table before gathering her into his arms. "Are you terribly hurt?" He sniffed and pulled away to look at her face, frowning at her bruises.

"No, Ubaba." She shook her head, alarmed by the tears in his eyes. He nodded and hugged her again. She had never seen Ubaba cry before.

"Olawu, you must take care. If I had not been passing by . . ." He did not finish, and shame poked at her insides. Ubaba was not angry. He was afraid. And not just him. Umama had been near tears as well when she beat her. Ugami had been right. She had caused her family to suffer.

"I'm sorry." Olawu sniffed. "I lost my temper."

"If a man loses his temper, he is forgiven for it. It is not so for you. Not in Kanakam. Your ubaba will forgive you, but you must promise to be careful. Mind your words and actions, especially in the market."

"I will." Olawu rested her head on his chest, listening to the sound of his heartbeat.

"As long as I have breath, I will protect you. And Umama, and Ugami, and Kimani. I love you all more than life itself."

"Try not to worry, Ubaba. If you had not come, Tiko would have helped me."

"Olawu." His eyes filled with sadness as he spoke. "Keep your distance from Batiko."

She shook her head, confused. "Tiko? Why?"

"I do not trust him."

"But Tiko is my friend. He teases me sometimes, but he is-"

"He is not fit for you."

Heat rose to her cheeks, and she shook her head again. "He is just a boy."

"He is nearly a man. And you are nearly a woman. He should have protected you from the merchant, but he chose to idly watch instead. Umuntu inhlamvu engalungile."

Ubaba thought him a man with bad character. "Should I not speak to him at all?" she asked.

He hesitated. "You may speak to him. But do not give him your heart. He is not worthy of it."

Olawu nodded. Though she did not understand, she trusted Ubaba.

Chapter Three

Olawu's fingers tingled with excitement as she crossed the road with Ubaba the next morning. She balanced a large basket of vegetables on her head. He carried a basket as well, grinning as though his were filled with gold. Her ubaba's smile was infectious and soon her face mirrored his, minus the bruises. It hurt when she smiled, but she hid it from him, not wishing him further distress. They were headed to the healing hut, but she did not know what they were doing. Ubaba had told her it was a surprise and would not say.

"Hold on, Olawu." He stilled her movement with his hand, pushing her back as a pair of riders passed down the road. Olawu watched them with curious eyes. They wore silky black tunics and dark brown kaftans. Four more riders passed. They continued down the main road, then beyond Olawu's sight. She wondered who they were and where they were headed. They did not often get visitors in Kanakam.

Ubaba waved her forward, and she followed him into the healing hut. He began arranging the vegetables on a table until they made out a human form. When he finished, he grinned at her and pulled her forward. "Today I will show you how to set a bone, Olawu."

She looked up at him, eyes shining. "Really? How?"

He pointed to the table. "I've been looking for vegetables that most closely imitate the sound and shape of bones, since you cannot work with me. But you have been studying, yes?"

"Yes!"

"Good! We will need to break many vegetables in order to give you good practice. Your umama will not be pleased, I think." His eyes twinkled with mischief.

"I promise to make good use of our practice and learn quickly." Olawu laughed as her ubaba wiped his brow in relief.

"Good girl! Let us start with the yam here. That is the most common injury in the village."

Olawu listened closely to her ubaba, snapping vegetables when he told her to, wrapping them just so, watching his every step, listening carefully to every word. They worked all afternoon without interruption. Thankfully there were no injuries in the village. When the last rays of twilight fell behind the mountains, he and Olawu headed home.

"We must not let the vegetables go to waste." Ubaba spoke solemnly as they made their way back to their hut. Theirs was the first one along the main road. Small shoots wrapped around the outside, creating a circle of safety from predators. A taller row of bamboo stood along one side, its match on the opposite end. It broke in the middle to make way for travelers coming in and out of Kanakam.

Olawu looked at her Ubaba in the waning light. Though his words were solemn, his eyes glowed with cheerfulness. "I shall remove all the wrappings and make sure they go into Umama's stew."

"Be sure not to miss any wrappings. Umama will be onto us, otherwise." He wiggled his eyebrows and Olawu laughed.

"Yes Ubaba."

"Mbako!" One of the village men approached just as they reached the outer wall surrounding their hut.

"Yes, Zulu?" Ubaba turned with worried eyes. "Is there an emergency?"

Zulu ran to her ubaba and placed his hand on his shoulder. "Chief Umdaka has called a meeting of the elders. Riders from the Dikebe tribe are here."

Ubaba cast a worried glance at her. "Go inside. Take care of the vegetables, and tell Umama I shall return."

"But-"

"Go on." He kissed her on the forehead. "Do not worry, my child." She nodded and walked towards the hut, but hid behind the bamboo to watch as the two men rushed towards Chief Umdaka's hut.

Chapter Four

Olawu wrung her hands with nervous energy as she waited for Ubaba to return. They had seen riders earlier today. Were they members of the Dikebe tribe? What did that mean? Was Kanakam safe? Olawu's head jerked up when her ubaba finally entered the hut.

"Ubaba!" She ran to him and hugged him. "Is everything alright? Are you hungry? I kept the stew warm for you." He nodded in thanks as she prepared him a bowl. "There's not a single wrapping in the stew, I promise! I saved a lot of them and put them under my bed so I can practice."

"Good girl, Olawu." He nodded absently. "Has Umama already gone to bed?"

"She just fell asleep." Olawu quietly watched him as he slurped his stew, offering him another bowl when he emptied the first.

"Thank you." He sounded tired.

"Are you not going to bed?" she asked.

He shook his head. "I do not think sleep will come tonight." He looked at her as she sat near the fire. "What about you, Olawu? Are you not tired?" She shook her head and he smiled. "If we will not sleep, then we should work, do you not agree?" She gave him a puzzled look. "Come!" Ubaba stood and lifted her from the floor.

"Where are we going?" she asked.

"Back to the healing hut. I have another surprise for you. I was going to wait, but I think you will do well with this task."

She smiled and followed him outside, her curiosity piqued. When they got to the healing hut, he lit candles and pulled out several balls of string, all in different colors. She helped him cut the string at various places, and they laid them out on the table.

"Olawu, do you remember the book I gave you with the diagrams? The one from the foreigners?"

Olawu nodded. She had only seen foreigners once in Kanakam. The pale-skinned visitors had been vexed by tsetse flies, and her ubaba had helped them. Ubaba had refused payment, but he'd gladly accepted their gifts of books and maps. "The one with the body systems?"

"That's the one. Now, look at the strings. Can you tell me what system this is?"

Olawu looked down at the strings, feeling confident. "Vascular."

He smiled. "Very good! Tonight, I will show you how the veins travel and what to do when they are severed. Come closer." She did as he instructed, watching his steady hands as they snipped and clamped the yarn. Her own hands trembled when he gave her his knife, as though she were really and truly cutting into human veins. They worked slowly and carefully as the night wore on. When the candles began to dim, Ubaba took her by the hand.

"Let's sit for a moment."

She sat next to him on the ground, leaning her head against his shoulder. He continued to hold her hand. It made her feel like a little girl again, safe and loved.

"Do not be alarmed when things begin to change."

She lifted her head and looked at him. Something had happened at the meeting of the elders. She could see it in his eyes. "Are we safe?" she asked.

"For now." He nodded. "But things will be different. Perhaps you will not notice them, at first. If we are lucky, you will not be affected at all."

Olawu's thoughts ran wild. What sort of changes would come to Kanakam? And why? "Who are the Dikebe?" she asked.

"The Dikebe have control of many of the villages surrounding the mountains and the valleys west of the river. They've been at war with the Oloko tribes to the east for many years. Our village has been mostly unaffected by their conflict, but InDuna Dike has taken an interest in Kanakam."

"Why?"

"He did not say."

"InDuna Dike is here?"

"Yes. He and his son are here."

"When will they leave?" Apprehension clawed at her stomach, and she squeezed her ubaba's hand.

"They will come and go. But members of the Dikebe tribe will stay in Kanakam, starting tonight."

Olawu absorbed the information. If Kanakam became part of the Dikebe tribe, what would that mean? Would they too be drawn into the conflict with the Oloko? She remembered the words of her umama, spoken long ago to her ubaba. They did not want war in Kanakam. They had no quarrel with the Oloko.

"Will we go to war?" she asked, fearful of the answer.

"I hope not, Olawu. But I do not know. We must pray to God for His protection."

Olawu nodded and bowed her head. She and her ubaba prayed for God to watch over Kanakam and all its people.

Chapter Five

Dikembe stared at the Kanak river. It flowed from north to south, through the Kanagari mountain ranges stretching east to west, then dipped into the valley below Kanakam. Dozens of Dikebe villages thrived in the grassy plains to the west, dependent on its waters. The Oloko tribes also depended on this river for survival. That would soon end.

"Dikembe!" He turned at the sound of his baba's voice. InDuna Dike stood perched atop the eastern wall of the recently constructed citadel. He waved Dikembe over, and Dikembe took another look at the river before climbing down from the hill.

It had taken a year to build the walls and outer gate of the citadel, but it was not quite finished yet. The tower still remained. Its construction would be the trickiest on the uneven terrain of the mountainside, but the end result would last for generations. Even unfinished, the massive stone walls were a stark contrast to the straw covered huts down in the village. Rows of bamboo stalks surrounded each hut. A weak deterrent for four footed predators, and no match for those who walked on two.

Dikembe made his way through the courtyard and up the stairs until he reached him. "InDuna Dike." He spoke his baba's title and bent down, placing both knees to the ground and lowering his head as he raised his crossed forearms. His baba crossed his forearms in kind and tapped them against him, signaling that he could rise.

"Chief Umdaka wishes for us to dine with him tonight." InDuna Dike wasted no words.

Dikembe did not hide his sneer. He cared little for the Chief of Kanakam, even less for the simpletons living here. After a year in Kanakam, he'd had his fill.

"We will accept his invitation. Dress appropriately."

Dikembe scowled. "Why must I dress at all? Chief Umdaka hardly wears anything over his stout belly. Perhaps we should dress in kind?"

"Do not joke, Dikembe. He dresses in his ceremonial garb whenever he meets us. We will bear it, for the sake of good will. With the citadel so close to completion, now is not the time to quarrel with the elders of Kanakam."

"And what if we do? Hondo and I alone could take the whole of the village. They are farmers and soft boys who've never tasted war."

"Even so."

Dikembe raised his right forearm and his baba mirrored the motion, tapping it gently. Dikembe walked away, holding in his frustrations.

"Oh, Dikembe?"

Dikembe turned. "Yes, InDuna?"

"Mama InDuna is in your room."

Dikembe's heart lifted at that. "She's here?"

He nodded. Dikembe smiled and rushed off, hardly noticing his baba's chuckle as he watched him run.

DIKEMBE WALKED INTO his room and immediately noticed the transformation. The once bare walls were now covered in richly woven tapestries. A pair of stone jaguars, the symbol of the Dikebe tribe, guarded a large fountain filled with blue lotus flowers. His simple slate bed was now dressed in fine linens. An ornately carved wooden table sat in the back of the room, and nestled comfortably in a tall stool was the most beautiful woman Dikembe had ever seen.

Her dark, smooth skin and light brown eyes matched his own. Her hair grew twice as long as his, braided well beyond the tail of her back and ornamented with gold clasps. She looked up at Dikembe and smiled.

"My son." She greeted him warmly. In a few steps he was beside her, embracing her, not wanting to let go. She was the very air he lived and breathed for. And he was the same to her. He had not seen her since his last visit to Borimbe.

"Mama!" The hardness in Dikembe's face melted away as he wrapped his arms around her. In front of his men and his baba, Dikembe was steady and unflinching. But with her, he was as vulnerable as a child.

"Dikembe, I suppose you've missed me?" She laughed. He answered by squeezing her tighter. "If you squeeze me any harder, I won't be able to breathe."

"I'm never letting you go," he teased, but he loosened his grip.

"Dikembe, come. You must look at this tapestry." She pointed to a large tapestry hanging over his bed. Four jaguars facing a large blue lotus flower were embroidered into the fabric. "Do you recognize it?"

"The one I've had since birth?" He turned to look at her.

She shook her head. "That one is still in Borimbe. I had this one made and brought it here so you could feel at home."

Dikembe swept the room with one eyebrow raised. "You brought all of this from Borimbe?"

She shrugged. "For my Dikembe, I would have moved the whole Borimbe market. Do you remember the spice cakes on the eastern side?"

"You brought some?"

"Check your table."

Dikembe rushed to the table, noticing the satchel laying on the top. He pulled at the strings, revealing the small cakes he'd loved since he was young. He smiled at her and showered her with kisses. "Mama, how do you do it?"

"Do what, my child?"

"Know just what I need when I need it?" He kissed her again. "You treat me so well. What can I do for you?"

"Nothing." She laughed. "Just be well, my son."

"So long as you are here, I cannot be otherwise." He embraced her again.

"Oh, Dikembe, you are too much!" His mama laughed, but then her breath caught, and she faltered. "Dikembe?" She spoke his name in a shallow breath.

"Mama?" Dikembe loosed his hold, and she nearly collapsed. "Mama!" He called her again with no response.

Chapter Six

Olawu slowly stirred the stew boiling in the pot. She wondered if Batiko would be at his auntie's hut. Ubaba had gone to deliver her baby. It was not likely that Batiko would be there, but it was possible.

Since he had finished his apprenticeship, she was less likely to see him roaming the marketplace. She had taken her ubaba's words to heart, but she still found herself looking for Batiko whenever she went out.

Heavy banging on the door startled her out of her musings. Olawu yelped as she tipped the spoon, splashing hot stew onto her arm.

"Ach! Who could that be?" She sighed and stomped over to the door, swinging it open with a huff. Her eyes traveled quickly over a rich, brown kaftan overlapped by a black and gold tunic and long, dark locs. A pair of light brown eyes glared with a frustration that matched her own. His lips moved and Olawu blinked, realizing that the words were for her.

"Aren't you listening, girl? Where is your udokotela? He's not at the healing hut, and he needs to come with me, now!"

"He's not here." Olawu finally spoke. "Why do you need him?"

"Have you not heard a word? Where is the udokotela? They said he lived across the road. This is where he lives, yes? Take me to him. Now!"

"He is delivering a baby." Olawu spoke in clipped tones. She did not like the way he looked at her. As if she were less than him.

"We must hurry!" The man growled.

"Why do you need him?" Olawu asked again. "Is there some emergency?"

"You test my patience, girl. Take me to the udokotela. That is an order!"

Olawu sighed and stepped back into the hut. "Ugami! Come watch the stew."

Ugami entered the front room, yawning sleepily. "Where are you going, Olawu?"

"To fetch Ubaba. Don't let it burn."

Olawu closed the door and began walking towards Auntie Morimbe's hut. She didn't bother to look back to see if the man followed. A few steps in, he grabbed her by the arm and pulled her around.

"Where are you going?" He snarled.

"To fetch my ubaba." Olawu tried to break his grip, but was unable to. He held her fast.

"We'll take my horse. It will be quicker." He pulled her back, but Olawu resisted when she saw the massive beast.

"It is not far, and I will do no such thing." Olawu scowled as she tried to free herself. He finally let her go, and she continued down the path through a row of huts. "Why do you need him?" she asked.

"It is my umama. She collapsed and is unwell."

"Was she in the sun for a long time today?"

"What business is that of yours?"

Olawu shrugged. "It was very hot in the village today. If she was not prepared for the heat, she could have suffered from dehydration. If that is the case, then you do not need my ubaba. Simply loosen her clothes, and give her ginger root tea-"

"Are you an udokotela? I was not aware that the uneducated girls of Kanakam were such experts in these matters."

Olawu swallowed a retort. "I have seen my ubaba do it many times. Place a cool, damp cloth on her forehead, loosen her clothes, and give her ginger root tea."

"I thought you said the home wasn't far?" He grunted.

"We're here." They stopped in front of a wooden door, and Olawu turned towards him. "What is your name?"

He seemed taken aback by the question, but he recovered quickly. "You may address me as InDuna Dikembe."

Recognition touched her thoughts, and she nodded. "Wait here." Olawu passed through the door, slamming it shut in Dikembe's face.

DIKEMBE MUTTERED A curse and stared at the closed door. Anxiety began to build in his stomach as the seconds ticked by. He could wait no longer. He raised his fist to bang on the door, but the girl opened it, stepping outside.

"He is nearly finished. He will clean up and come with you soon."

"This cannot wait." Dikembe scowled. "My umama needs the udokotela now!"

"Wait here." She went back inside, slamming the door in Dikembe's face a second time. Dikembe lost his patience and pushed open the door. Several faces looked up at him, including a sweat soaked woman lying on a cot with an infant in her arms.

Dikembe stared at the infant, clinging to its mama as it searched for nourishment. The woman held her child closely, weeping and thanking the udokotela.

"Thank you, Mbako! You saved my unyana. My sweet child." She kissed the infant over and over, rocking him in her arms. Dikembe pressed at the birthmark on his neck, struck by an old memory. There was something familiar about the udokotela.

OLAWU PRESSED A COLD cloth against Auntie Morimbe's head, then stroked the dark curls on her infant's head. "Rest well, Auntie Morimbe."

Her ubaba placed a comforting hand on the woman's shoulder. "Olawu will be with you now. You are in good hands." He looked at Olawu, then turned towards Dikembe, who stood at the doorway with his fingers pressed against his neck.

Her ubaba approached him. "I understand your umama is in need?"

"Yes." Dikembe cleared his throat. "Please, come with me to the citadel." Dikembe lowered his hand from his neck, revealing a birthmark in the shape of a lotus flower. Olawu glanced at it, then turned her attention back to Auntie Morimbe. She stroked her hair and spoke soothing words to her. Soon the woman began to drift off to sleep, and Olawu began cleaning up.

A thought struck her as she stood, and Olawu gasped.

"Olawu? Are you alright?" Auntie Morimbe asked in a tired voice. Olawu blinked and gave her a reassuring smile.

"I did not mean to startle you, Auntie. Do not worry about me. Rest now." Olawu continued with her tasks, troubled by the thoughts in her head.

Though the Dikebe warriors had been in Kanakam over a year now, she had not seen InDuna Dikembe until today. Her thoughts cleared, and she nodded to herself. She had seen that lotus flower before.

OLAWU REMEMBERED THE night clearly. Kimani was not yet born, and Olawu had just passed her eighth birthday. It had been unusually cold and she, Ugami, Umama and Ubaba had all slept in the front room near the fire. Someone stood at the door, screaming and banging against it. Ubaba had stepped outside. Umama had gone to the window to listen. Olawu had gone to the door, opening it just a crack.

A beautiful, dark-skinned woman stood facing Ubaba. Her braided hair kissed the base of her blue kanga, stained red at the chest where she clutched a young boy. Blood darkened his colorful kitenge, thanks to the black arrow buried in his chest. The woman's eyes were wide and frantic as she spoke.

"Please have mercy on us! If they find us, they will kill us!"

"What happened?" her ubaba asked, but the woman only repeated her desperate pleas. Umama walked out at the woman's words, pushing Olawu aside.

"Mbako!" Umama hissed. "Do not allow that woman into our home. That is an Oloko arrow. Kanakam has no part in the conflicts between the Oloko and Dikebe. If you help her, you will be inviting war into our home. Send her away!"

Ubaba looked at the woman with anguished eyes. "Perhaps if you try another?"

"I've knocked on every door. Please, my son is dying! The last person told me to come here. They said you were an udokotela. Please!"

"I'm sorry." Her ubaba hung his head. Olawu had never seen eyes so sad. When he turned back to their hut, he spotted her. They stared at each other for what felt like mere seconds. Then Ubaba did something she would never forget.

Ubaba turned back towards the woman and grabbed her son.

"Come inside. Quickly."

"Thank you! Thank you for your mercy." The woman followed him inside with a river of tears. Olawu followed Ubaba as Umama wailed against him. He placed the boy on a table in the front room, despite Umama's protests.

"Mbako, the blood! It will stain the table and the floor. He should not be here at all, and now you put him on our table? What are you thinking? Mbako, do not-"

Ubaba silenced her with a glance, then turned to Olawu. "Bring me my tools from the healing hut. Quickly. Fadhila, boil water."

Olawu nodded and raced away. When she returned, he had removed the arrow and was pressing a cloth against the wound. Long after Umama settled back into bed, Olawu watched him work. As he stitched the wound closed, Olawu pressed in close, studying every movement of his skilled hands.

Ubaba turned to the woman. "He'll need to rest a few days before he is moved, otherwise the bleeding may start again. You are safe here while he recovers."

The woman cried again, thanking him over and over. As night pressed into morning, only she and Olawu remained awake.

Olawu found herself drawn to the boy. He looked no more than a few years older than her. She touched one of his thick locs, pressing it between her fingers before releasing it. She looked at his chest wound, squinting as she tried to count his stitches. They were so small that they were hard to see against the boy's dark skin.

His umama placed her hand on Olawu's shoulder. "What is your name, child?" she asked.

"Olawu."

"Such a beautiful name. Thank you for watching over my Dikembe. You have your ubaba's kindness, I see."

Olawu smiled at the compliment and continued to stare at the boy, noting the rise and fall of his chest as he slept. That's when she noticed the small birthmark on his neck, shaped like a lotus flower. She had never seen anything like it.

"Olawu?" The woman called her name again. She unfastened a barrette from her hair and showed it to her. Olawu wondered at the design; a blue lotus flower made of glass, crusted with white crystals and blue gems with gold at the center. "There is nothing in this world I love more than my son. This barrette is the only one of its kind. I want you to have it."

Olawu shook her head.

"Because of you and your ubaba, I have the most precious thing I need. I am grateful to you. Please accept this as a token of my thanks?"

She nodded, and the woman fastened the barrette to her hair. Olawu had never parted with it.

Chapter Seven

Dikembe paced the halls of the citadel as he waited for the udokotela to finish examining Mama InDuna. Hondo stood near the door, watching him pace.

"She'll be fine, Dikembe."

Dikembe grunted. "Kanakam is filled with backwards, uneducated, superstitious fools, Hondo. This udokotela has a simpleton for a daughter. He may be no better. He may be giving her potions or chanting ridiculous words in order to heal her, instead of-"

The door opened and Mbako walked out.

"Mama InDuna will be alright. It seems the long journey from Borimbe and the heat put her in a state of dehydration. She's much better now after a cup of tea, though I told her she should continue to rest. You can go in to see her if you wish."

Dikembe nodded. "Thank you, Udokotela."

"You should thank my daughter. I did not wish to leave Auntie Morimbe, especially after such a hard labor, but she convinced me that she would take care of things in my absence. You see, she is a very compassionate simpleton, InDuna Dikembe."

Hondo tried to hide his grin as Dikembe cleared his throat.

"Udokotela!"

"Yes, InDuna?"

"Your daughter? What is her name?"

Mbako smiled. "Olawu."

"Please tell Olawu thank you on behalf of InDuna Dikembe. Hondo will see you out." Dikembe watched Hondo leave with Mbako, rubbing absently at his chest. He entered the room and cleared his throat, relieved to see Mama InDuna resting comfortably on his bed. A damp cloth lay across her forehead.

"Dikembe!" Her face lit up at the sight of him. "I'm sorry to cause so much trouble. I can see you were worried."

"Mama, you could never be trouble." He bent down on the ground and took her hand in his, kissing it gently. "Are you truly feeling better?"

"Much better!" She smiled and placed a hand on his cheek. "Do not worry, Dikembe. Your mama will be with you for many years to come."

Dikembe nodded, lowering his forehead to her hand.

"My poor son." She sighed. "I wished to only bring you happiness today. We've had our fill of grief and terror, and yet there is more grief and terror waiting for us tomorrow."

"I shall bear all of it alone if it means you are safe," Dikembe spoke solemnly.

"I believe you would if you could." She laughed, but Dikembe did not join her. She sat up, despite his protests, and kissed him on the forehead. "I'm fine. Now make your mama happy and try the spice cakes I brought."

"I care nothing for spice cakes." Dikembe spoke the words with a scowl, resting his head in her lap. "Only for you, Mama."

"I am grateful to have such a dutiful son. Now come, let us enjoy your spice cakes together."

OLAWU ABSENTLY CRUSHED the tomatoes in her hand and plopped them into the pot of stew simmering above the fire. Ubaba had not yet returned from the citadel, and Umama was fretting as she paced to and fro.

"Do not let it burn, Olawu." Umama glanced her way as she nibbled on her fingernails.

Olawu returned her attention to the pot. It was in no danger of burning, but she would not contradict her. "Yes, Umama." She sighed and stared at the fire. The flames were low. She would need to gather more firewood soon. Ugami and Kimani were outside hanging laundry. If Ubaba returned before dark he would do it. But he would be tired.

Olawu finished with the tomatoes and gave the pot a stir before heading outside. When she returned, Ubaba was home. She smiled as Umama nestled into Ubaba's lap. He stroked her hair and kissed her, and Olawu took a step back. She would have left entirely if she had not heard her name. She set down the firewood and took a quiet step forward.

"Olawu is not ready for such things, Fadhila." Ubaba sighed.

"Must you be so foolish, Mbako?" Umama scolded him, but her voice held no bite. "Olawu is not a child. She must find a husband soon. Do you think she will become Kanakam's udokotela when you are old? Do not look so surprised. I am not blind, Mbako. You must stop filling her head with such things, and leave her to me."

"There is no one here for her in Kanakam."

"What about Batiko? He has a good family, and everyone knows he likes her. Let us speak to his family and make arrangements."

Olawu smiled to herself. Batiko did like her, after all.

"No. Batiko is not suitable for her. There is no one here in Kanakam I would trust for her care."

"Then what do you suggest? She cannot survive in Kanakam without a husband."

Ubaba's eyes glistened as he leaned towards Umama. "When I cared for Mama InDuna today, she told me of Borimbe. They have opportunities for girls there that they do not have in Kanakam. Things are different there."

"And so what if they are different in Borimbe?" Umama sniffed. "We live in Kanakam."

"I thought, perhaps, Olawu could visit Borimbe?"

"But who would take her? She cannot go alone, and we need you here."

"I will ask Mama InDuna. Perhaps she can help us."

"But why would she? Eh, Olawu? What are you doing standing there?"

Olawu jumped as Umama spotted her in the doorway. "I was bringing firewood."

Olawu picked up the logs and placed them clumsily by the fire. She smiled briefly at Ubaba before bolting out of the hut. Heat pricked her neck as she ran towards the river. She dipped her feet into the cold water and sat by the bank, her thoughts swirling.

Was Borimbe truly different from Kanakam? Could she stand to be away from Umama and her sisters? From Ubaba?

She flicked her foot as a minnow passed beneath it, wondering if girls could be trained in Borimbe. Could she become an udokotela there? The thought was thrilling. Olawu laughed and lay her head on the grass. If anyone could convince Mama InDuna to help them, Ubaba could.

Chapter Eight

"Olawu, take this to your ubaba." Umama handed Olawu a large covered jar, and she opened it and sniffed. The spicy aroma of jollof rice tickled her nose and she smiled.

"Ubaba's favorite." She scooped a bit with her fingers, gaining an angry swat from Umama. "Where is he today?"

"At the citadel, tending to Mama InDuna. There were a dozen people in and out of the healing hut today, and as soon as he came home, he remembered that he promised to check on her today. He left without eating, and there's no telling when he'll be home before someone else needs him. Why can't he learn to just say no? Hm?"

Olawu shrugged. "Ubaba has a big heart, Umama. He would not be Ubaba if he were another way."

"Hmph." Umama scowled, but it did not reach her eyes. Olawu knew how proud she was of Ubaba. "Go now, Olawu, before it gets cold."

Olawu laughed as she left, toting the pot on her hip as she walked along the road.

"Olawu!"

She tried not to smile at the sound of Batiko's voice, but she had not seen him in weeks.

"Olawu, wait!" He ran to her with a huge grin on his face and a small covered basket in his hand. He stopped a few feet in front of her, extending the basket. "I bought these for you."

She stared at the basket. Ubaba told her not to give her heart to Batiko, but it would be impolite not to accept a gift, wouldn't it?

She accepted the basket and gave it a sniff. The smell of mandazi was unmistakable. She set down her jar and unwrapped the warm, fried dough. Her mouth curved upward, but she quickly stopped herself.

"Thank you, Batiko," she said coolly. "My ubaba and I will enjoy these with lunch."

"Your ubaba?" Batiko did not hide his disappointment. "But they are a gift from me to you, Olawu."

"If I can only accept the gift for myself, I cannot accept it." She handed the basket back to him, but he pushed it away.

"Fine. Do as you wish. But you should not treat me so. I do not have many possessions yet, but I will soon. By this time next year I will be trading in the markets of all the nearby villages. Think of it, Olawu. I will build you a hut bigger and better than the one your ubaba built for your umama."

Olawu snorted as she picked up her jar and continued on her way. "I hope you make the door big enough for your head to fit through, Tiko."

Batiko laughed as he matched her stride. "Was that so hard, Olawu? To smile for me? To call me by my nickname?" He moved closer to her, close enough for their arms to touch. "Promise you'll marry me?"

Heat rose to her cheeks, and she quickened her pace. "I need to get this to Ubaba."

Tiko picked up his pace as well. "I'll go with you. Where are you headed?"

Olawu gestured towards the citadel. It rested just outside of the village, near the top of the hill leading into the mountains. Platforms wrapped all around the tower as men continued to work on the walls.

Batiko grabbed her jar and held it out of reach, smiling and teasing as they continued down the main road.

"Have you seen your new baby cousin, yet?" Olawu asked.

"Yes! He looks just like my uncle. And thanks to your ubaba, he's alive and healthy. My umama said that his neck was wrapped in the cord. Is that true?" Olawu nodded. "Your ubaba is amazing, Olawu." Batiko returned the jar to her. His eyes met hers as their fingers touched. "You're amazing." He pulled Olawu towards him, kissing her roughly on the lips.

Olawu dropped the basket of mandazi and shoved him away with a scowl, raising her fist to strike him. An earth shattering crash stopped her.

They both turned towards the citadel. A plume of smoke swirled above the walls. One of the platforms surrounding the tower had vanished. Cold terror gripped Olawu's heart as she stared at the dust.

"Ubaba!" Olawu dropped the jar of jollof rice as she rushed towards the citadel. Batiko followed behind her, calling her name, but Olawu did not stop. She ran as fast as her legs would carry her, ignoring the squeezing of her chest and the burning of her eyes as tears and dust swept over them. She had to get to him. She needed to see him. She needed to know he was safe.

She ran past the end of the road and up the hill. At some point she lost one of her sandals, but she didn't care.

A group of men rounded the courtyard as she reached the outer walls of the citadel. They shouted as they ran down the hill, covered in dust. They carried a cot between them.

"Olawu!" She barely heard Batiko calling her as she climbed the steep hill.

"Chief Umdaka! Udokotela!"

Olawu's gut twisted as she heard the men's shouts. Were they carrying the chief? Were they looking for Ubaba? They should have seen him at the citadel. Where was he?

As soon as she reached the group, she began firing off questions. "What's going on? Please, tell me what happened? Where is my ubaba?"

Whether they did not hear or were not interested in answering, Olawu could not tell. They waved her out of the way as they continued to rush down the hill, crying for the udokotela. Perhaps Ubaba was in the village?

As the men passed, she caught sight of a cream-colored tunic. Her lips trembled and her heart quaked as she realized the men carried her ubaba down the hill. Time froze. But only for a moment.

"Where are you taking him?" she asked.

"Chief Umdaka!" The men continued to shout down the hill. She rushed into the group, tugging on arms and shouting to be heard.

"What is the matter with him? What happened?" She got no reply from the men. But Ubaba moved on the cot, and her heart leapt with hope.

He's alive!

She could not see him very well, there were too many men crowded around him. "What are his injuries?" Her question went unanswered, but she persisted. "What's wrong with him? Let me see him. I can help!"

She tugged on another man's arm, but he pushed her aside. Olawu followed them all the way to Chief Umdaka's hut, begging to see her ubaba. The men angled the cot through the maze of bamboo to Chief Umdaka's door, then carried him inside.

Olawu followed closely behind them, her questions frantic and pleading, but no one answered her. The door to Chief Umdaka's hut slammed shut in her face, leaving her standing by herself in the front yard.

Olawu stared at the closed door, then lunged forward. A hand wrapped around her wrist and jerked her away.

"Let me go!" She screamed in Batiko's face.

Batiko gasped in between breaths. "Olawu, what are you doing? You cannot enter the Chief's hut without permission."

"My ubaba is in there." She reached for the door again, heart pounding in fear, but again, Batiko pulled her away.

"Olawu! It does not matter if your ubaba is in there. If you enter the Chief's hut without invitation, you will be punished!"

"If I do not go in there, he could die. I'm the only one who can help him!" Olawu pleaded for understanding. "Chief Umdaka will not know what to do if Ubaba is bleeding on the inside. I must go to him!"

Olawu reached for the door a third time, but Batiko stopped her and dragged her away. "Stop it, Olawu. Stop it!" Batiko clamped strong hands around her wrists and shook her. "Who do you think you are? What do you know? You are barely a woman. What can you do for Mbako that these men cannot do? Stop talking nonsense."

"Let me go!" Olawu cried.

"No!" Batiko shook her again. "You will stay here, outside, until news of your ubaba is given. Do not enter the Chief's hut."

"I am warning you, Batiko." Olawu spoke through clenched teeth. "Let me go."

"Stop fighting with me." Batiko held fast to her wrists, digging his fingernails into her skin. Olawu kicked him in his softest place, and he buckled. She ran back to the Chief's hut, but a sharp pain in the back of her head thrust the wind and thought from her. She collapsed in a heap, blood trickling from the back of her head. Batiko dropped the brick in his hand and ran away as Olawu's world faded into darkness.

Chapter Nine

Olawu watched in a daze as men with painted faces carried Ubaba's body down the main road. His still form was laid out on a bamboo slat, wrapped in cloth. Neighbors and friends stood on either side of the road as they watched the men carrying him sing their songs of sorrow. Chief Umdaka stood at the front of the processional in his ceremonial garb. Olawu, her umama, and her sisters followed in the rear.

Umama was inconsolable and collapsed several times. Ugami was always the one to pick her up. Olawu did not have the strength to comfort anyone. When they reached the burial grounds across the Kanak River, the Chief, along with the other men who had carried Ubaba, did their traditional farewell dance around a blazing fire.

Umama wept. Ugami held Kimani's hand. Olawu stared at the flames. She stayed there in the burial grounds long past the cooling of the last ember. Ugami took their umama and Kimani home. Ubaba was buried in a hole and left there.

Her ubaba had died the way he had lived. Sacrificing for others. Doing the right thing. When the platform had collapsed near the citadel, he had pushed one of the workers out of the way. He couldn't bear to see another hurt. But for the first time in her life, Olawu questioned whether it was truly the right thing.

Did he not know the pain his death would cause? Olawu had always been so proud of him. But today she was angry. She felt guilty and selfish for feeling that way, but she could not help it. Her ubaba, her hero, was gone.

"Olawu?" A voice whispered from behind her. She clenched her fists as tears burned in her eyes. She would not let him see her cry. "Olawu, please talk to me."

Olawu swallowed and continued to stare at the ashes left by the fire.

"I'm sorry about your ubaba." Batiko sighed. "There was nothing to be done."

Olawu whirled around, flashing angry eyes at Batiko. "Nothing to be done? I could have saved him. He did not have to die. If I could have just seen him, told them what to do, my ubaba would be alive."

"Even if you could have saved him, who would listen to you, Olawu? You are not an udokotela. No woman has ever been, nor ever will be. Why can you not accept that? Eh? Accept your place in Kanakam."

Olawu turned away from him. "Leave."

Batiko sighed. "I am sorry, Olawu. I was only trying to protect you."

"I said leave!"

Olawu heard him sigh a second time. The sound of leaves against his sandals grew fainter until it finally disappeared. Only then did she allow her tears to fall.

Chapter Ten

Olawu wiped her face with the back of her arms as she continued to haul manure from the sheep pen. The smell was rancid, and her kanga was smeared with feces and dirt. She shooed away a stray lamb as it stomped around in the manure. The lamb dropped a few more pieces for her on the ground as it hopped back to its mama.

"Olawu!"

Olawu gritted her teeth and continued her work, focusing on the task in front of her.

"Olawu!"

Batiko spoke her name again, but again she ignored him. He stepped in front of her, careful to stay away from the piles of manure she shoveled outside of the pen.

"Olawu, why must you work so hard?" Batiko grabbed the shovel in her hand and held it still.

"Let go, Batiko." Olawu was tired. She had been up before dawn doing chores and favors for neighbors in exchange for grain and seed, and her day wasn't over yet. Nearly a year had passed since her ubaba's death, and they were barely getting by. She didn't have time for Batiko's taunting.

"I hate to see you this way, Olawu," Batiko crooned, stroking her face with his left hand. The hand used to wipe himself. Olawu frowned and pulled away, but Batiko only smirked. "You know that my umama would accept you as her daughter. You should treat me much better. If you do, perhaps I will marry you."

"I have work to do, Batiko."

He released the shovel. "You should be careful, Olawu. There's word an ibhubesi has been roaming near Kanakam. Merchants have found torn zebras on the road, and farmers have been losing sheep at night. Besides, women should not work in Kanakam. Especially women as beautiful as you. You are not as pretty as Ugami, but you are much more lively." Batiko curled a strand of her hair between his fingers and Olawu recoiled, batting his hand away.

"Do not speak of my sister in such a way, and do not speak of me. If my ubaba were alive he would not stand for such things!"

Batiko scoffed. "Olawu, wake up! Mbako is dead. He cannot protect you anymore. I can. If you keep refusing me, you will have no one to protect you."

"I do not need you to protect me," Olawu spat. "My ubaba would never have accepted you, and neither will I!"

Batiko's nostrils flared with rage. "I thought time would humble you, Olawu. But I see you have not learned your place. You'll change your tone when the Choosing comes."

"That has nothing to do with me." Olawu sniffed.

Batiko's laugh was filled with spite. "You speak as though you are above everyone. Olawu, you are Pootagi now. You do not have a choice. My umama told me your garden crops died before the rainy season arrived. If your family does not have a man to support you, you will starve. Do you think a man will come for Fadhila? She cannot even relieve herself without help. No one would want her. And what about Ugami? She could marry a craftsman, or maybe even a merchant, if you were not standing in her way. And all for what? Your pride? See how you cling to your pride when you starve."

"Enough!" Olawu flung a pile of manure at Batiko, splattering the top of his kitenge and his cheek.

Batiko frowned as he wiped the flecks from his face. "When the Choosing comes, and a lowlife jewel maker purchases you, I want you to remember this moment, Olawu."

"There will be no Choosing for me!" Olawu shouted. "I'm not a kitenge cloth to be handled, bought, and sold. And you, Batiko, will never have me."

"We shall see, Olawu. We shall see."

"HERE YOU ARE, OLAWU." Auntie Morimbe gave Olawu a small bag of grain and kissed her cheek. "I wish I could do more, but if my husband finds out we are still helping you . . ."

"I understand, Auntie. Thank you for your kindness." Olawu smiled at her, grateful that they could receive even a small amount.

"Your ubaba was such a good man. He saved my unyana, and I will never forget it." She placed a gentle hand on Olawu's face. "You remind me so much of him. Please take my advice? Marry my nephew, Batiko. He will give you a good life. Do not wait for the Choosing."

Olawu's mouth went dry. "This grain. Is it from Batiko?"

"Does it matter where it comes from, Olawu? Just take it and be grateful."

Olawu placed the grain back into her hands. "I cannot accept this."

Auntie Morimbe called out to her, but she walked away. Hot, angry tears streamed down her face, and she clenched her fists so hard they began to bleed. Her mind was a storm of thoughts as she made her way back to their hut. A commotion near the road cut into her thoughts and Olawu halted.

"Take him to Chief Umdaka! Quickly!"

Olawu's eyes followed the group of villagers until she spotted a young child. His face was mauled and bleeding. Instinct sent her feet running before her mind could catch up. The young boy's umama carried him, weeping as she ran with her relatives down the road.

"Auntie, what has happened to him?" Olawu asked the woman as she caught up to the group. She stared at the boy's face, a mess of tissue and bone. What could have done this?

"He went missing early this morning and was found near the river bank," one of the relatives explained, recognizing Olawu.

"Can I see him?" she asked. The boy was losing a lot of blood. If they did not act quickly, he would soon die.

"Move along, Olawu!" One of the men in the group pushed her back. "We do not have time for your questions."

"We must get him to Chief Umdaka." The first relative spoke softly, staring at Olawu. "If only your ubaba were here." The boy's umama wept harder at this. Olawu clenched her jaw to fend off her own tears. The child would be dead before they reached Chief Umdaka.

"Stop!" Olawu cried. "He is bleeding too much. You must stop the bleeding or he will die!"

"We must take him to Chief Umdaka!" the man repeated. "Do not stop! Chief Umdaka is his only hope!"

"What do you expect Chief Umdaka to do?" Olawu's temper rose. "He is not an udokotela. He is not even a healer. He knows nothing!"

"You know even less, inja!" The man snarled as he broke from the group. He shoved Olawu to the ground and spat near her foot. "You are not an udokotela. You are just a woman. If you do not want to end up like your umama, you should mind your own business."

Olawu recognized his face. This man had broken her umama for trying to buy food in the marketplace. She was certain he would gladly break her as well. Though her heart pounded with rage, Olawu remained in the dirt. The man spat again, this time in Olawu's face, before rejoining the group. Olawu's lip quivered as she watched him and the others disappear down the road. A year ago, she would have challenged him. But that was before Ubaba had died. Before Umama had been broken. Before Olawu had learned what it truly meant to be a woman in Kanakam.

OLAWU GREETED HER SISTERS with a weary smile as she entered the hut. Ugami returned the greeting as she rushed towards her.

"Did you get it?" Ugami asked, casting a skeptical glance at Olawu's empty hands.

"No." Olawu shook her head.

Ugami sighed, her expression bemused. "Did you not meet with Auntie Morimbe? She told me at the river that she would send us grain today."

"She did, but I gave it back."

Ugami gaped at her. "You gave it back? Why? We need that grain!"

"No, we don't. We'll get by without it."

"But Olawu-"

"There are some things more important than bread, Ugami."

"What could be more important than bread? Do you have too much pride to take grain now? Or does this have something to do with Batiko?"

"We cannot lose ourselves for a little food, Ugami. We'll find another way."

"What other way?" Ugami cried. "Ubaba is gone! Umama is crippled, thanks to you, and we have no one to help us. No one except Batiko and his family. Why not accept his offer and be done with it, Olawu? Why must our family go through hardship?"

"Do not speak back to me, Ugami!" Olawu snapped. "I am the eldest, and I've already decided. We will find another way."

"Can you not yield, just this once for your family? If you weren't so stubborn that merchant never would have hurt Umama."

"I did not know, Ugami!"

"Would it have made any difference if you had? Would you have minded your words? Held your tongue? Accepted his insults?" Olawu did not answer, and Ugami shook her head. "We will all be left to the Choosing because of you!"

"Olawu! Ugami!" They both turned at the sound of Umama's cries and rushed to her room.

"Umama? Are you alright?" Olawu asked, checking her dress for signs of soiling.

"Did we disturb you, Umama?" Ugami asked, stroking her hair.

"Girls, do not fight," Umama cried. "Please!"

"We're sorry, Umama," they replied in unison.

"Listen closely, my daughters. I have a brother who lives in Salimi. He has two sons and no suitable wives for them."

"Umama!" Olawu began to protest.

"Do not be so stubborn, child," her umama cried. "This is not the life your ubaba wished for you, Olawu. Nor for you, Ugami. We've been scraping by for nearly a year, beaten and abused by those we thought were our friends. I cannot bear to watch it any longer. I will send word to him to come for you and your sister. Perhaps he will take Kimani as well."

"What about you, Umama?" Ugami asked. "Will he take you in?"

"Do not worry about me." She cupped Ugami's face in her hands. "It is my job to take care of you. This is what I must do."

"No, Umama!" Olawu stood, her face as stony as rock. "Have you forgotten who your brother is? How my ubaba rescued you from him? Now you wish to send me and my sisters to him and his sons? No!"

"Olawu." Ugami chided.

"I would rather die than be sent to such a horrible man."

"We have no options." Umama sobbed. "If there were another way, don't you think I would take it? Please, Olawu, I cannot bear to see my children starve to death."

"They won't. I will find another way, Umama. I promise."

"The only other way is for you to marry Batiko," Ugami quipped.

Olawu shook her head. "Leave it to me, Umama. I will find another way. Do not send word to your brother."

Her umama nodded, though fear laced her gaze. But Olawu knew what she had to do.

Chapter Eleven

Olawu dressed herself by candlelight in her finest kaftan, a full length blue dress with gold embroidery. She had scrubbed herself from head to toe in the river once all of her chores were finished. She pulled out an old box kept in the corner of the room and opened it, careful not to disturb Ugami. A blue lotus barrette lay in the box, the golden center shining in the candlelight. She pinned it to the top of her hair, which was braided to one side in a single thick plait that extended well beyond the nape of her neck.

Olawu was not the same girl she was a year ago. Her foolishness had already cost her umama her legs. She would swallow her pride tonight for her family's sake.

Olawu sniffed and pressed her fingers to her eyes. Had her ubaba lived, things would have been different. She might be in Borimbe, under the watchful eye of Mama InDuna, or training with Ubaba. The people of Kanakam would not shove her aside if her ubaba were standing beside her. The child she saw in the road today might still be alive. Her umama would not have been broken because of Olawu's thoughtlessness.

If only she had held her tongue with the merchant that day. Olawu had not known Umama was buying food from him in secret. He'd taunted Olawu with lewd advances, and she in turn had rejected him. In front of the other merchants and all who were near. Olawu had walked away, thinking it ended with his sneer, but that was just the beginning.

When Umama went to his cart the next day, he pretended they had no agreement and exposed her crime. Women were not allowed to buy or sell at the market, and the merchants had beaten Fadhila until her legs were pulp, then left her there to crawl home. If Auntie Morimbe had not found Olawu by the river that day, her umama might not have survived.

Ubaba had warned her to mind her words and actions, but once again Olawu had spoken without thought. Ugami's words rung true. She was the cause of her family's suffering. But she would make it right.

Olawu blew out the candle and left the hut. She stared up at the citadel standing tall and bright. The top of that hill was her goal, and nothing would stop her from it.

Chapter Twelve

Dikembe stared at the maps laid out on his table. His lieutenant, Hondo, stood beside him, studying the topography of the mountain ranges surrounding Kanakam.

"There is vulnerability here." Hondo circled the area with his finger. "The Oloko tribes have been spotted to the east."

"How close?" Dikembe asked.

"They could reach Kanakam in a week's time. But their numbers are small. I suspect they are scouting groups."

Dikembe nodded. "The Oloko should not be underestimated, Hondo. They're dangerous, even in small numbers." Dikembe rubbed his chest, remembering the scars left behind by the Oloko. "They must not gain control of the river. Send Boku, Gamba, and Yero to the area. Once they've cleared the way we will join them."

"Yes, Dikembe." Hondo made to leave, but Dikembe stopped him.

"Hondo?"

"Yes, Dikembe?"

"No survivors."

"I understand." Hondo placed his forearm against Dikembe's and left the room. Dikembe watched him leave, then pulled out the plans for the Kanak River Dam. His baba had commissioned the plans to be drawn after their initial visit to Kanakam. Once the threat of the Oloko was eliminated, they could move forward with construction, though they would still need to be on guard.

Dikembe compared the plans for the dam with the locations marked on the maps, circling areas and making notations as he studied the topography. A commotion outside of the room caught his ear and he stood, hand instinctively going to the dagger at his side. His mouth twitched when he heard the lilt of an angry, feminine voice.

"Please! I must speak with InDuna Dikembe!"

"I will give you one final warning, inja. If you were not summoned, then you must leave!"

Dikembe smirked and walked slowly out of the room. He watched as just down the hall his guard, Ibawa, struggled to restrain the tiny, dark-skinned girl known as Olawu. She shifted to one side, but Ibawa grabbed her wrists and twisted her around. A moment later, Olawu was free and running down the hall towards Dikembe, a bewildered Ibawa at her heels.

Olawu's eyes met Dikembe's as he stood near the archway of his door. She flung herself to her knees, bowing low with her arms extended, even as Ibawa rushed towards her.

"InDuna Dikembe, I beg you! Please allow me to speak to you on an urgent matter!"

"Be silent, inja!" Ibawa snarled as he hauled Olawu to her feet.

"Please, InDuna Dikembe!" Olawu raised her eyes to his, ignoring the tugs from Ibawa. "I beg you! Give me an audience."

"I said be silent!" Ibawa raised his arm to strike her.

"Ibawa!" Dikembe spoke his name with an air of impatience.

Ibawa lowered his hand and turned towards Dikembe. "Yes, InDuna?"

"Do you think this little inja is a threat to me?" he asked.

Ibawa hesitated.

"You seem uncertain. If the answer is no, she is no threat, then why do you feel you must strike her? If the answer is yes, she is a threat, then how can she be here? You are my guard, Ibawa. The only way a threat can reach Dikembe is if Ibawa is dead, no?"

"InDuna?" Ibawa looked from Dikembe to Olawu.

"So, what is your answer?"

Ibawa lowered his head. "She is no threat."

Dikembe sighed. "Release her, then."

Ibawa let Olawu go, head still bowed. He raised his right forearm, and Dikembe touched it with his own. Olawu scowled and rubbed her wrists.

"We meet again, Olawu." Dikembe's gaze met hers. "Come when you are summoned." He turned abruptly, slamming his door in Olawu's face.

OLAWU PRESSED HER LIPS together. InDuna Dikembe was taunting her. But she needed him. Her family needed him.

She stared at the door as several minutes ticked by. She looked down the hall at Ibawa, who stood sentinel, his back turned to her. She had managed to sneak past the first guards with little effort, but once she was past the courtyard things had gotten tricky. She had made up a lie about going to the kitchen, then snuck away to find InDuna Dikembe's chambers. She would have gotten past Ibawa if she'd chosen to strike him, but she feared InDuna Dikembe would punish her for injuring his guard.

She continued to wait by the door. Time slowly floated away, but it didn't quiet the rage she felt inside. Had InDuna Dikembe forgotten her? He had told her to wait, but what did he mean? Would he summon her another day? Was she to wait outside until he called for her?

Olawu rubbed her neck and wrists. Both ached with the strain of the day. She had hauled the laundry of a family of seven to the river, washing their clothing in exchange for a jar of yams. Ugami had accepted her sacrifice gratefully, but the tension between them remained. Ugami could not marry before Olawu, and Olawu had no intention to marry anytime soon. If this plan did not work, Olawu's entire family would suffer. She had to endure.

A cool, evening breeze passed through an open window at the end of the hall where Ibawa stood. It felt good on her skin, which had begun to bead with a thin layer of sweat. How much time had passed? She placed her ear to InDuna Dikembe's door. She could not hear anything. Perhaps he had fallen asleep?

Olawu huffed in indignation. InDuna Dikembe may make her wait, but she did not have to wait in silence. She raised her hand to the door, poised to bang on it with all of her might, when InDuna Dikembe's voice rang out.

"Come Olawu!"

Olawu lowered her hand and opened the door. She resisted the urge to glare at InDuna Dikembe as she approached. The room lay on two levels, with a pair of steps between them. Ornate weapons made from steel and wood hung from the walls. A water basin filled with blue lotus flowers stood on one side.

Dikembe sat comfortably at a wooden table, scribbling on a map. A large, flat bed rested in the corner. Olawu stopped at the steps and lowered herself in a bow, placing her hands above her head.

"InDuna Dikembe, please hear my request." He ignored her, and Olawu took a deep breath. "Please, InDuna Dikembe, I beg you to hear my request."

"Get on with it." Dikembe spoke without looking away from his map. Olawu raised her head and took a deep breath.

"A great tragedy has befallen my family, InDuna Dikembe. My umama lay crippled at home. My sisters, Kimani and Ugami, are days away from starvation. It is forbidden for me to work to support my family, and because my ubaba, the great udokotela of Kanakam died a year ago, there is no man to protect us. I come to you, great InDuna

Dikembe, asking for you to take responsibility for my family and protect us."

"You speak as though your suffering is unique, Olawu. There are many who are days away from starvation." Dikembe lifted the map from the table and studied it closer.

"Please, InDuna Dikembe! I beg you not to turn a blind eye to us. Please remember my ubaba's kindness and repay what you owe my family."

"And what do I owe your family?" Dikembe looked up at her, a sudden scowl on his face.

Olawu looked him in the eyes. "Your life."

He chuckled and lowered the map, giving Olawu his full attention. His eyes fell to the blue lotus barrette in her hair.

"Where did you get that?" He demanded, approaching Olawu and snatching the barrette from her hair.

"It was a gift." She winced as the barrette caught in her braid. "A thank you to my ubaba from a grateful umama. One who begged him in the dead of night to have mercy on a stranger and save her son. A boy bleeding from the heart with an Oloko arrow in his chest. A boy with the birthmark of a lotus flower grafted in his neck. The same birthmark that rests on yours, because you are the boy my ubaba saved."

Dikembe lowered himself to the floor until his eyes were level with hers. "And did you think by coming here, by making demands of me, that you would save yourself?"

Olawu drew back at the anger she saw in his eyes. "InDuna Dikembe-"

"I did not come here to become the champion of widows and orphans, Olawu. Remove such thoughts from your mind."

Olawu licked her lips. "I cannot."

"You cannot what?"

"I cannot believe that you are so heartless. That you would turn your back on our family. What if my ubaba had done the same? What if he had sent your umama out into the cold with nowhere to go?"

"Then *my* ubaba would have come and razed Kanakam to the ground!" Dikembe snarled, lifting Olawu from her feet and pushing her towards the door.

"Perhaps I was a fool to come here." Olawu stood her ground. "But InDuna Dikembe, you must help us. Without your protection, my sisters and I will be condemned to the Choosing. We will be purchased for the price of a few isitshalo and forced to live as slaves!"

Dikembe loomed over Olawu, his body nearly touching hers. He lowered his face, his lips near her ear as he spoke. She could feel the heat of his breath as his words washed over her. "Do you think you have some hold over me, inja? Do not come to me with stories, making demands of me. It is I who will make demands of you." Dikembe straightened himself. His cold, dark eyes burned into hers. "Leave. And accept your fate just as every other woman in this village."

"I cannot!" Olawu cried.

Dikembe shook his head and laughed. "You are not special, Olawu. Damn your ubaba for making you believe otherwise."

Olawu's temper boiled over at his words. She knew it meant the death of her, but she did it anyway. Her hand struck his face. Hard. So hard she drew blood. Dikembe stared at her in shock. Olawu stared back at him. And then she fled. Past the door, past Ibawa, past the courtyard. She feared every step would be her last, half expecting the guards to come after her. But no one followed.

Still, Olawu ran. She didn't stop until she reached the bamboo protecting her hut. She leaned on the wall, gasping for air as her mind swirled.

Oh God, what had she done?

Chapter Thirteen

The Choosing was mere days away. Olawu woke up every morning in fear. She was afraid they would starve. She was afraid InDuna Dikembe would retaliate against her and her family, though so far, he hadn't. And she was afraid that one day men would come and take her and Ugami to the market and sell them as wives.

The Choosing was an annual tradition. Pootagi women and girls with no husband would be taken from their homes to the marketplace. Any male age twelve and older could participate in the Choosing. It was ideal for men who were too poor or too cheap to pay a hefty bride price.

For the dowry of their bride, all a man had to do was pay for an isitshalo, a plantain. Each isitshalo was marked with a number representing the buyer and laid out on the table. Buyers could barter for multiple isitshalo to increase their odds. Often there were more buyers than there were girls. Each girl would pick one at random, and the number would be called out. The buyer would come up and eat the isitshalo raw, and that would be the end of it. They were married.

The girl had no choice, no say in the matter. It was a disgusting practice. Olawu had said as much the first time she had witnessed the ceremony. But she had not thought of it again until the year Ubaba died.

Now the Choosing was constantly on her mind. It haunted her dreams and followed her around like a shadow. She hoped that keeping busy would distract her, but the reminders were everywhere. There was a buzz in Kanakam as the days drew closer. It was in idle conversations at the river. It was in the marketplace, where a large platform had already been constructed. Even the sheep were affected by the Choosing. They weren't fed the scraps of the isitshalo, since no merchants were selling them until it was time for the Choosing. Olawu hoped she wouldn't go mad before then.

DIKEMBE SHOULD HAVE been studying the maps for the dam construction, but he found himself distracted. His eyes kept wandering towards the blue lotus barrette resting on his table. He'd have to ask his mama about it the next time he was in Borimbe.

Dikembe chuckled and rubbed his jaw. Olawu had bloodied his lip. No one, man or woman, had ever done that before. No one had ever gotten close enough. It had surprised him. He should have punished her for it, but he couldn't bring himself to do it. She had borne his insults to her, but speaking ill of her ubaba had pushed her past her limit. Her ubaba meant to her what his Mama meant to him. He would not have tolerated such words, either. And for his Mama's sake, he would bear it.

Dikembe stared at the barrette again. He remembered the first time he saw it in his mama's hair. On his first trip to the market in Borimbe, Mama had given him strict instructions to stay close. But Dikembe was too excited by the many carts and merchants and soon wandered off. They'd lost track of one another, and Dikembe was lost in a sea of people. He'd gone after every dark woman with long braided hair, asking if she were his mama. None of them were. When she finally found him, he was sleeping in a heap of rotted vegetables near a sheep pen, eyes and face covered in dried snot and tears.

From that day on, she wore a blue lotus flower in her hair, so he would always recognize her. She had the barrette made not too long afterwards. The glass had glistened and sparkled in the sun like a pendant full of magic. It suited her.

Dikembe's thoughts drifted back to Olawu. The barrette had suited her, too. She looked good in blue. He'd had to force himself not to look at her when she'd entered his room. It wouldn't do for her to think he found her interesting. And yet, Dikembe found himself thinking about her daily. He sighed and rolled up the maps on top of his table. He couldn't concentrate. Hondo knocked on the door, and Dikembe called him in. They exchanged a friendly tap of forearms before Hondo gave his report.

"Yero and the others found the Oloko camp. They will strike tonight. They should have the way cleared by morning."

Dikembe nodded. "Let's ride out soon, then." Dikembe packed for a few nights' journey and he and Hondo rode towards the northeastern mountain range.

YERO WIPED HIS SWORD while Gamba and Boku continued to scout the area. By their count no one was missing, but they knew better than to make assumptions. They were InDuna Dikembe's personal guard for a reason.

There were nearly a dozen bodies strewn across the camp. Yero and Gamba had attacked initially, while Boku hid in the woods to take care of stragglers. They rummaged through the Oloko's supplies, but aside from a couple of spears, dried berries and meat, there wasn't much there.

Boku ran up to Yero, raising his forearm in greeting. Yero tapped it and sighed. "Not much here for a scouting group, Boku."

Boku scratched his thick beard and shook his head. "Doubt they were scouting for more than food, Yero. Half of them were women. Three of them children, no bigger than my boy, Jezari."

Yero turned towards Boku. "Children?"

Boku nodded and pointed. "In the woods. There."

Yero walked into the trees, slowly stepping over roots and rocks, following the path of crushed earth until he reached a small body. He bent down. In the early light of dawn, the boy's face was as soft as an angel's. Two more small frames rested not far from the first. Yero swallowed the bile rising in his throat. He clenched his jaw and stood, nostrils flaring.

Boku had done as InDuna Dikembe had commanded. No survivors. But that didn't quell Yero's anger. When Boku approached, he wanted to rip his throat out.

"Gamba gave us a signal. Someone is approaching."

Yero nodded and they hid in the trees to wait. They heard the heavy breath of horses before they saw the riders. A low whistle rang out. That was Hondo. He and InDuna Dikembe had arrived. They left their hiding places and rushed to greet one another. Gamba and Boku were in high spirits as they spoke with Hondo and InDuna Dikembe. Yero could not bring himself to join them and hung back. He spoke when spoken to, but was otherwise silent.

Hondo noticed first. "Yero? Your words speak success, but your eyes speak failure. Has something happened?"

"The way is clear!" Gamba chimed in. "There were no other Oloko in the area. Just this group here."

"Strange thing, having Oloko this far north," Boku added. "They were not prepared for an attack. We dispatched them quickly."

"We'll make camp and continue to scout the area." Dikembe stared at Yero as he spoke. "I want to be sure there are no Oloko hidden in these mountains."

"Yes Dikembe." The men nodded in agreement. Hondo and Gamba began making a fire while Dikembe and Boku began a patrol of the perimeter. Yero disappeared into the trees.

DIKEMBE AND BOKU RETURNED to camp, greeting Hondo and Gamba as they sat by the fire. Yero wasn't with them.

"Did something happen?" Dikembe asked Boku, who shook his head.

"He's been like that all morning." Boku shrugged. "But as I said, our attack was met with little resistance."

"Do you want me to look for him?" Hondo offered.

"No. Yero can handle himself. He'll return when he's ready."

They shared a meal and laughter, then took turns canvassing the surrounding areas. When they returned to camp, Hondo assigned watches for the night. By Dikembe's watch, Yero still had not returned.

"Boku?" Dikembe woke him from his sleep, and the seasoned guard immediately reached for his spear.

"InDuna?" Boku's eyes were alert in the dark. "Is there danger?"

"No. I need you to keep watch until I return." Boku nodded and stood, stretching and yawning as Dikembe headed into the forest.

Dikembe did not mind the sounds of birds and predators passing through the trees. He had a dagger at his waist and was used to the sounds of the night. His steps were soft and quiet as he listened, searching for any sound that seemed out of place. As he traveled through the trees, he heard it. The sound of rock clipping rock, as though someone were stacking them on top of each other. Dikembe followed the sounds through a field of wild millet. They led him to Yero.

Dikembe watched as Yero piled rocks in a heap on top of each other. There were two other rock piles on either side.

"Yero?" Dikembe called out to him. Yero turned and locked angry eyes with him. Dikembe walked towards him and extended his right forearm. Yero lowered his head, but did not raise his arm. "Yero!" Dikembe spoke forcefully. Yero turned away from Dikembe and continued placing the last remaining rocks on the heap.

Dikembe grabbed his arm, stopping him before he could lay the final rock. "Explain yourself!"

Yero struggled against Dikembe's grip, but only briefly. He dropped the rock and hung his head. "Forgive me, InDuna Dikembe. I am not myself."

Dikembe released his arm. "What is all this?"

Yero looked at the rock piles, as though seeing them for the first time. "I could not let them be ravaged and carted away by animals."

"Who?"

"The Oloko children." Yero shook his head, visibly at war with himself. "I hate the Oloko, Dikembe. They killed my Mama. They killed my Baba. They killed my brothers. If not for InDuna Dike, they would have killed me, but . . ." Yero did not finish.

"There were children in the camp." Dikembe spoke the words quietly. A moment passed between them and neither spoke. Dikembe looked at his friend and raised his right arm again. This time Yero responded, tapping his right arm against Dikembe's.

"Forgive me, Dikembe."

"Yero." When Yero looked up, it was with eyes full of anguish. "The war with the Oloko has taken many lives. Before it is over, it will take many more. Do not falter now."

"I will not."

Dikembe squeezed Yero's shoulder. "You did well today."

"I'll take the next watch." Yero slipped out from under Dikembe's grip and walked away. Dikembe stared at the piles again, picking up the last rock and placing it gently on top.

Chapter Fourteen

The day of the Choosing, Olawu could not breathe. Her heart pounded like an msondo drum. Sweat dripped from her body as though she were roasting in a kiln. Her stomach was in knots.

They were barely getting by with favors from neighbors. Something had to give. She saw it in her umama's face. She heard it in the quiver of Ugami's voice. They were out of options.

Still, Olawu clung to hope. InDuna Dikembe was not in Kanakam, but perhaps when he returned, he would help them. He had not taken her head for striking him. Perhaps she had struck a nerve. But suppose she hadn't? What if he truly had turned his back on them?

The Choosing would begin at midday. Olawu did her chores as usual, trying hard to suppress her growing panic. She distracted herself with words, reciting the day's tasks out loud. She muttered to herself as she washed laundry in the river.

"Strong strokes up and down on the rocks. Ten times this way. Ten times that way." So busy were her thoughts that she didn't hear the warning of the merchant class approaching.

"Get out of the way, inja!" A brawny boy of twelve shoved Olawu aside, sending her garments floating down the river.

"Ach!" Olawu went after the laundry, ignoring the belligerent howls of the young boy. Weighed down by her lengthy kaftan, Olawu was unable to move fast enough to catch every piece. A tall, dark figure in an orange and black kitenge scooped up the runaway laundry, toting it back to where Olawu stood in the river. He switched the clothes from his right hand to his left, then offered his right hand to Olawu. It would have been easier to just offer her his left hand, though it was disrespectful. His gesture was not lost on Olawu. She took his hand, and he pulled her out of the river.

"Thank you." Olawu released his hand as soon as she was out of the water. He offered her the laundry and she snatched it quickly. She looked up at him, noting his kind brown eyes and admittedly handsome face. His smile sent warmth to her cheeks.

"You're too close, Pootagi." The young boy scowled. "Get off of the bank!"

Olawu took several steps away from the river, realizing her error. The young man followed her, grabbing her basket.

"Here, let me help you with that." He didn't wait for her reply and began walking with her. She smiled, grateful for a moment's kindness.

"I haven't seen you in Kanakam before?" Olawu fiddled with her braid.

The young man shrugged. "I'm visiting my family. My name is Businge. What is yours?"

"Her name is inja!" The young boy laughed. Olawu bit back a response.

"Hold your tongue, Jacan!" Businge shouted. "Please forgive my cousin. He is terribly spoiled. I did not catch your name?"

"Olawu."

Businge smiled. "Olawu. Such a beautiful name. It suits you."

"Where are you from, Businge?"

"Borimbe. My ubaba is visiting Kanakam for a few days, but we will be leaving today. I am sad that I did not meet you sooner, Olawu. I am even sadder that I can take you no further. I must look after Jacan. An ibhubesi was spotted near Kanakam a few days ago, and I promised my auntie I would look after him."

"Oh." Olawu tried to hide her disappointment as Businge handed her basket back to her.

"Perhaps we shall meet again, Olawu?"

She nodded a goodbye and watched Businge return to the river. It wasn't long before her mind drifted back to the Choosing. By the time the sun reached the middle of the sky, there would be pandemonium in the market.

Olawu made up her mind. She simply would not go. They could manage as Pootagi for a little while longer. Even if she had to catch their food in the woods, they would find a way to survive.

OLAWU RECOGNIZED THE voice of Chief Umdaka right away as he shouted through the streets. Her hands trembled as she hung the laundry behind their hut.

"Pootagi!" Chief Umdaka shouted. "It is time for the Choosing. Come!" The men spread out, going from one hut to the next to grab the girls and women who would participate in the Choosing. When Olawu ran to the front of the house, one of the men was waiting for her.

"Come on!" He grabbed her arm, but she pulled away.

"We do not wish to participate in the Choosing." Olawu huffed. "Leave!"

"There is no man here, Pootagi. Unless you women are breaking the law, you cannot survive in such a state. Come to the Choosing. Now."

"I will not!" Olawu shook her head in defiance. "Move along."

The young man scoffed and disappeared behind the bamboo wall. He returned with Chief Umdaka.

The Chief approached in his ceremonial dress. His belly and chest lay bare, save a row of lioness teeth strung across his neck. He had on a short skirt cloth made of fur, which exposed his vulnerable bits when the wind blew just so.

"What's the problem?" The Chief eyed Olawu.

"This inja says she will not come to the Choosing, Chief Umdaka."

"Hayi! Every Pootagi must come to the Choosing."

"I will not." Olawu shook her head.

"If not you, then someone else from your family." He turned to the other man. "Open the door. Bring out her sisters."

Olawu flattened herself against the front door, blocking them. "You cannot take my sisters! Ugami cannot marry before me, and Kimani is but a child!"

"The rules are different on the day of the Choosing, inja." The Chief did not hide his disdain. "On this day any Pootagi girl can be married, regardless of age or order."

"We do not wish to be married," Olawu repeated. "We refuse."

"Very well." The Chief licked his lips and gave instructions to the other man. He left quickly, returning with a group of others. Chief Umdaka turned to them and spoke in a loud voice. "We have a Pootagi refusing to attend the Choosing. Witness this day, that this insolent child has refused to do her duty. In refusing the Choosing, she has chosen to be broken!"

Olawu's breath caught in her throat. Her eyes darted all around as three men approached her, lips curled into sneers. One of them handed Chief Umdaka a club. Olawu's eyes widened in fear as the front door swung open.

"I will go!" Ugami rushed from the house and approached Chief Umdaka.

"Ugami!" Olawu pulled at her sister's arm, but Ugami stood her ground.

"I will go to the Choosing on behalf of our family." Ugami repeated the words on trembling lips. Chief Umdaka nodded and the men took her sister away.

Olawu stood, frozen, as they disappeared behind the bamboo. Ugami was going to take her place at the Choosing. Her sister, not yet fifteen, was going to be sold. She was a child. Olawu regained her senses and ran.

"Ugami!" She called out to her sister as she chased the crowd of men and Pootagi moving to the center of the market. She finally caught up to Ugami and pulled her away. "Ugami, I cannot let you do this."

"I cannot let them break you, Olawu! Do you not realize what that means?"

Olawu nodded. If Ugami had not stepped in, Olawu would have been crippled for life, just like Umama. "You do not have to do this." Olawu stared at her sister, communicating all the love and earnestness she could. Ugami should not have to suffer for her sake. She had failed them. She would accept her responsibility. "I will go to the Choosing for our family."

"Olawu?" The fear in Ugami's eyes broke her heart.

"Do not worry about me, Ugami." She kissed her and sniffed. "I will do what I must. For our family." The men began to grab Ugami, but Olawu stopped them. "Let her be. I will go up." They shrugged and pulled Olawu forward.

"Olawu?" Ugami's eyes filled with tears as Olawu joined six other women on the platform. Baskets filled with raw, yellow plantain stood next to a large wooden table in the middle. The Chief walked to the front of the platform and addressed the growing crowd.

"People of Kanakam! It has been our tradition for generations to care for the whole of our village by providing protection to the most vulnerable, the most pitiful among us. And who is more pitiful than a Pootagi? Who least able to care for themselves than a woman? And so, we begin our tradition. Men! Look before you at the women on this platform. We have six needing home and husband. If you desire to take on this noble cause, then place your bids with the isitshalo. Increase your odds and buy many. You will receive a wooden needle with your number. When a Pootagi picks your number, bring me the needle, and lay claim to your bride by consuming the isitshalo. When you are done, so is your duty. Let the Choosing begin!"

The Chief clapped his hands, and the crowd cheered as men approached the baskets, bartering for isitshalo with guinea fowl and pottery. Olawu looked on anxiously as an older man bartered one of his sheep for dozens of isitshalo. When the final basket was emptied, the bidding ended. Chief Umdaka stepped onto the platform and addressed the crowd once more.

"Men, your bids are on the table! We will begin with the youngest, most desirable Pootagi first."

Olawu swallowed the bile in her throat as Chief Umdaka pulled a young girl, not much older than Kimani. She looked terrified as he pushed her towards the table. Her hand trembled as she passed over the isitshalo, unsure of which one to grab. It was an impossible choice. Olawu felt a deep shame for her village. This was not right.

Chapter Fifteen

Dikembe and Hondo entered the village of Kanakam at a slow trot, taking in the near-empty streets as they passed through the main road.

"Why are the streets so empty?" Dikembe mused. Hondo shrugged and continued to scout out the area, a deeply ingrained habit since their early warring days. Dikembe's mind was on other things. Mainly, the look on Yero's face when they had left the Oloko camp.

A shout rang out somewhere near the marketplace, followed by cheers. Hondo and Dikembe both looked at each other.

"The Choosing is today," Hondo recalled. "Have you ever seen one since coming to Kanakam? I've always been curious."

Dikembe sniffed and shook his head. "What interest would I have in such things? Let's go, Hondo." He dug his heel into his steed, and they sped away towards the citadel.

OLAWU'S STOMACH SOURED as a middle-aged man stepped up to the platform and plucked the isitshalo from the young girl's hand. He ate the raw plantain with such vigor that she gagged in disgust. Egged on by the gleeful cheers in the crowd, he carried the girl off in tears.

Olawu grieved for the poor girl. How could they call this right? Human beings being carted off like chattel to be used and abused by strangers was not charity. It was slavery. Olawu's chest swelled with heat at the wrongness of it all.

Another young girl was pulled to the front, but Olawu's feet carried her to the table before her mind knew what she was doing. She pushed the young girl aside and glared at Chief Umdaka. "I want to go next."

The Chief laughed and sent the other girl back in line. "Look how eager this Pootagi is to find her husband!" he shouted. "Surely she is more desirable than the rest?" At that, the men cheered and hooted. It made Olawu want to tear them to pieces. She walked to the edge of the platform, staring at a sea of brown faces. A part of her hoped to find Businge in the crowd. Another part of her felt relieved when he wasn't.

She stared at the men of her village, eyes blazing. "Pootagi or not, woman or not, we are people. It is wrong to force us to marry in order to survive. If the people of Kanakam truly wish to protect the most vulnerable, start by ending the Choosing!"

Her protestations were met with jeers and angry shouts. Olawu looked out at the crowd before her. She grew up with many of them. They had played in the river together, shared meals and laughs and stories. At one time, they had been her friends. When had that changed? Their eyes were full of such disdain. Had she truly been so blind to the wrongs of Kanakam?

The Chief pulled her back towards the table. "Time to meet your husband, Pootagi!" he shouted. Olawu's fists clenched with rage. They hadn't listened to her. Not one of them. Tears fell from her face as Chief Umdaka pushed her again. "Pick your isitshalo, Olawu."

She wiped her face. Though it pained her to do so, she grabbed the first one she saw. What choice did she have?

The Chief took the isitshalo from her hand and held it up high. "Eight!" The crowd began cheering with excitement as a young man in a red kaftan stepped forward.

Olawu's stomach churned as Batiko smirked at her.

"Olawu! I told you I would have you." She shook her head, feeling sick. "Do not look so worried. I will be gentle, tonight."

Her chest tightened. Bile rose to her throat. She didn't know what was worse. Marrying a stranger, or marrying him. What sort of life would she have with Batiko? He was spiteful and underhanded. And yet, there were moments when he'd been kind and thoughtful, too. If she gave him a chance, would he be a good husband to her?

Batiko stepped onto the platform. Before he grabbed the isitshalo, he reached for Olawu's hand. "Dear Olawu." He smiled and looked up at her. "You belong to me, now." He rubbed her face with his left hand, making it clear how little he valued her.

As Batiko handed his needle to Chief Umdaka, Olawu's gaze found Ugami's trembling form. Tears pooled down her face from eyes filled with fear.

She could not accept this. For her sister's sake, she would not.

Olawu grabbed the isitshalo from Chief Umdaka. She tore off the peels and broke it in half before stomping the soft plantain into a mushy heap on the platform. She glared into Batiko's shocked eyes and screamed with all of her essence.

"I belong to no one!"

In a flash, Chief Umdaka grabbed Olawu by the hair, throwing her from the platform with a violent thrust. Her mind shattered into a million pieces as her head hit the ground. Chief Umdaka shouted at her, spat at her heels, then shouted at the crowd. Men approached with sticks and clubs. She knew she would soon be broken. She thought of her umama, of how she'd crawled home, bleeding and bruised with her legs twisted behind her. This was not the life Olawu wanted for herself, but she would not be enslaved. Not by anyone.

Batiko approached calmly, and the men slowed their movements. He kneeled beside her, caressing her face with his palm before reaching his fingers to the back of her head. He pulled hard at the roots of her hair, forcing Olawu's face back. He leaned in close, whispering in her ear.

"You still do not know your place, do you, inja?"

"Let me go!" Olawu spoke the words through clenched teeth. To her surprise, Batiko did just that. His eyes grew round as a scream rang out. More shouts followed, and the marketplace dissolved into mayhem. Olawu heard a growl before she saw it.

Ibhubesi.

DIKEMBE AND HONDO TURNED as they heard the screams. They did not sound like the riotous shouts they'd heard just moments before. These screams were laced with terror. An alarm rang out. Two short blasts of a horn, followed by a third that was loud and long.

Hondo stared at Dikembe. "What is that?"

"There's a lion in the village." Dikembe frowned and kicked his horse, galloping back towards the marketplace. Hondo turned his horse and followed.

OLAWU RUSHED TOWARDS Ugami as villagers scattered through the marketplace. Sheep and fowl were abandoned, carts overturned, and little ones left to fend for themselves. Olawu turned her face away when the ibhubesi caught hold of a young lamb left behind by its owner.

She turned towards her sister, who stood frozen in place, eyes wide as she stared at the giant cat.

"Ugami, we must get home!" Olawu shouted at her, grabbing her hand. Ugami stared as Olawu tugged at her, leery of the ravenous predator. But the ibhubesi had already moved on from the lamb, the half-eaten carcass left to spoil in the sun. Where had it gone?

Ugami froze, pulling Olawu back and nearly sending them both to the ground.

"Ugami, we mustn't stop!" Olawu's tone held an edge as she pulled her sister forward. Ugami held fast, planting her feet as her nails dug into Olawu's wrists. "Ugami!"

Her sister pointed ahead of them, and Olawu's voice drifted away. She spotted the ibhubesi, joined by a second, much larger one. Both stalked the marketplace with a lopsided gait, slashing at anyone who got too close. A few men of Kanakam rushed into the marketplace with spears, but retreated hastily when they saw that there were two.

The ibhubesi stood in the middle of the market. The first had a mouth white with heavy foam. After a moment, they separated. The smaller one ran towards the center of the village. Olawu saw its target. A small boy, no older than two or three, stood alone and vulnerable as he cried in the road. Olawu rushed towards him, oblivious to Ugami's shouts to return. This ibhubesi was acting strangely. From her distance she could hear its labored breathing. If it had a sickness . . .

Olawu stared at the young child, then at the ibhubesi. She would not make it in time. Olawu slowed to search for a weapon. She grabbed a brick from the ground, prepared to haul it at the large cat, but paused as Dikembe's dark tunic came into view. He intersected the ibhubesi, slashing its side and sending it howling as it fled. His guard Hondo followed the beast on his horse, trailed by a small band of villagers armed with spears and clubs. Olawu shivered. Just moments earlier, they would have used their clubs on her.

Dikembe kneeled in front of the child, wiping his tears with a tenderness she hadn't known he possessed. The moment ended quickly as the second ibhubesi attacked, catching Dikembe off guard as he blocked the child from its claws. Olawu remembered the brick in her hand and hauled it at the ibhubesi. The brick connected, and the beast turned its yellow eyes on her. She shouted and screamed and clapped, distracting it as Dikembe took the boy to safety.

The ibhubesi roared and ran towards her. Olawu continued to taunt the lion as she darted away, zigzagging through the market as it gave chase. This ibhubesi did not have the same sickly look as the first, and its breathing was strong and powerful.

Olawu cursed as the lion pounced, missing her by inches as she turned a corner and ran down an alleyway. Her kitenge caught on a laundry line and she tripped, crashing into a cart. Olawu's mind teetered for only a moment before instinct took over. She grabbed a piece of broken wood and pushed herself into a narrow space between two huts.

She slammed the wood hard against the cat's face as it pounced, pushing herself further back as she fended off its assault. The lion snarled and slashed at her, shredding the tops of her feet to ribbons. Olawu screamed in pain as another swipe of its paws cut at her knees. She beat at it with the makeshift club, each blow getting weaker as the ibhubesi's counter attacks grew stronger. The beast howled with a terrible shriek before all went silent around her.

Chapter Sixteen

Dikembe pulled his sword from the ibhubesi's side and pushed its still form away from Olawu. She lay unconscious, her bloodied form wedged in a narrow space between two huts.

"Foolish girl." He muttered the words as he gingerly placed his hands beneath her. She could have run to safety as the others had. Instead she had distracted the beast and put herself in danger. Dikembe clenched his jaw as he walked back towards the marketplace, Olawu in his arms.

She had begged him for help. He had dismissed her without a thought. And still, she had saved his life. Guilt pricked at him, but he shoved it down. When Dikembe reached his horse, he looked down at Olawu's bloody feet. What if she could not walk again?

"InDuna Dikembe!" He turned around as a man in red rushed over. "You are carrying my bride." Dikembe looked down at him with narrowed eyes. Where had he been while Olawu was in danger? No doubt cowering behind a row of bamboo until it was safe. Dikembe did not bother to hide his contempt, and ignored him.

Batiko scowled as Dikembe placed Olawu on his horse. "InDuna, you must not interfere. Olawu is mine by right. InDuna!" Batiko raised his fist but Hondo quickly intercepted with a blade to Batiko's throat.

"Do you dare to strike InDuna Dikembe?" Hondo's eyes blazed.

Batiko withered and carefully shook his head. "I only wish to claim what is mine."

Dikembe whirled around, his imposing frame forcing Batiko to shrink further. "In Borimbe, if a woman is abandoned by her husband, then she can be claimed by another. Olawu is no longer yours."

"But-"

"Olawu is no longer yours!" Batiko's scowl deepened, but he remained silent. Dikembe looked again at Olawu. She was losing too much blood. "Hondo will repay your bride price. It is more than you deserve." Hondo lowered his blade with a grunt before tossing a bag of coins at Batiko's feet. Dikembe mounted quickly, careful to shield Olawu's head and feet as he rode to the citadel.

As soon as he was in the courtyard, Dikembe began barking orders. One of the guards offered to carry Olawu, eliciting a growl and a sharp reprimand. He alone would touch her.

Dikembe carried her to his room and lay her on the bed, shouting for servants to bring him water, basins, ointment, bandages. He rejected every offer to take over, cleaning and wrapping her wounds himself. He'd seen enough battle to at least do that much.

The mighty Olawu, the girl with fire in her fingertips, looked so small and frail laying on his bed. Seeing her this way made his heart ache. Dikembe lowered his head to his hands. He would make this right. From now on, Olawu was his to care for.

Chapter Seventeen

Olawu woke to a throbbing ache in her feet. She cried out, and two strong hands held her close.

"Olawu? Are you in pain?" The sound of a male voice startled her, and she leaned back against the wall. She wasn't at home. The bed she lay on bore sheets she did not own. The face beside her belonged to InDuna Dikembe. He lay next to her, his bare chest exposed in the moonlight. Olawu shook her head, disoriented, and Dikembe moved to the end of the bed, where her feet were heavily wrapped. Blood seeped through the bandages.

Dikembe walked to another part of the room, returning with water, fresh bandages, and a bottle of something Olawu didn't recognize. He carefully unwrapped the old bandages, placing them into a basin as he exposed her bloodied feet.

Olawu looked away, clenching her teeth as he poured the bottle of liquid over her wounds. Tears fell from her eyes and she gasped in pain, unable to hold in her cries. Dikembe worked quickly, washing and rewrapping her feet before returning to her side.

"Try to rest, Olawu." He spoke softly to her, leaning her back down onto the bed. Olawu began to protest, but was too tired to put up much of a fight. She lay back and drifted off to sleep.

OLAWU OPENED HER EYES and her pulse quickened. Dikembe's face was close to hers, his hand resting on her shoulder. If she reached out, she could trace the outline of the scar on his chest.

She moved back to put some space between them, but the pain in her feet stopped her, and she cried out. Dikembe's eyes flashed open and he quickly sat up.

"Olawu? Are you in pain?"

Her face warmed at his tenderness. This was the second time he had asked her such a question. It touched her. "It's fine," she lied. Memories of the Choosing rushed in. Of Batiko's smirk. The Chief's angry scowl as he threw her to the ground. The ibhubesi.

What happened to Ugami? She needed to get home. She needed to check on her umama and her sisters. "Thank you, InDuna, for your kindness. I will return home now."

She made to leave, but Dikembe grabbed her arm and pulled her back. "Do not be foolish, Olawu. Your feet are not healed. You cannot walk on them, yet."

"It's fine, I'll-"

"Lay back down on the bed."

"I'll rest here for a while, then I must return home."

"Do not think of such things. Lay here and get well." Dikembe got up and left the room. It felt much bigger without him in it. Olawu winced at the intense throbbing in her feet. It felt as though a thousand tiny needles were sticking into her at once. Dikembe was right. She could not walk. Not yet.

A few minutes later, he returned with a bowl of steaming soup. He sat on a stool near the bed and carefully lifted Olawu towards the side closest to him, despite her protests.

He offered her a spoonful. "Eat."

She tried to grab the spoon, but he swatted her hand away. "I can feed myself, InDuna Dikembe. My hands are fine."

"Don't be so stubborn, Olawu. You will eat by my hands." He put the spoon by her lips and she parted them, accepting the warm, sweet broth with vigor. She hadn't had anything so tasty in months. All too soon the bowl was empty, and Olawu had another problem to deal with.

"Um, InDuna Dikembe?" She lowered her eyes.

"Yes, Olawu?"

"May I use your waste pot over there? If you'll leave, it will only take me a moment."

Dikembe's reply was to lift her out of bed and set her on the pot himself. It was only then that Olawu realized she was no longer wearing her kaftan. She was wrapped in a thin, cream-colored kanga that barely covered her bottom. Her cheeks burned as Dikembe waited for her to finish. He did not seem bothered at all. It infuriated her. His offer to wash her sent her over the edge.

"InDuna Dikembe, do you mean to humiliate me while I am in your care? Please, allow me to bathe myself!"

"You are injured, Olawu. I will not allow you to injure yourself further." He lay her back on the bed and proceeded to wash her from head to toe. He was careful to keep her most vulnerable areas covered, and didn't linger, but it still sent heat to Olawu's cheeks. His touches may as well have been flames against her skin. Did he not have any women in the citadel to assist her?

He helped her into a fresh kanga, this one blue but just as short, before covering her with a soft blanket.

"Rest now." He sat in the stool, watching her. Olawu meant to stay awake, but it wasn't long before sleep overtook her.

DIKEMBE'S EYES STUDIED the rhythms of Olawu's breathing as she slept. She looked so vulnerable. The bleeding was under control, but he still worried that she would not be able to walk. He clenched his fists, remembering the man dressed in red, claiming to be her husband. Why had he abandoned her? Were the men of Kanakam all cowards?

Dikembe froze as Olawu groaned in pain. He knelt in front of her, stroking her hair as she shifted beneath the sheets. She pretended in front of him, but Dikembe knew she was in great pain.

"Stubborn woman," he whispered as he returned to the space beside her. He was not like the men of Kanakam. He would never abandon her. He would stay by her side and protect her. She belonged to him now.

Chapter Eighteen

"How does that feel?" Dikembe asked as he gently rubbed the tops of Olawu's feet with his fingers.

"Tender, but only a little," Olawu confessed. InDuna Dikembe had been good to her. He fed her, he bathed her, he dressed her wounds, he massaged her legs. Though being so close to him made her uncomfortable, she was grateful for his help. It had been over a week since the Choosing, and the wounds were healing. The ones on the outside, at least.

"InDuna Dikembe? I must return to my family. I've been gone so long they must be worried. And I'm worried about them."

"Do not think of such things." Dikembe dismissed her with a wave.

"But, InDuna Dikembe, my family-"

"Are taken care of, Olawu. Set your mind at ease." The sincerity in his eyes made Olawu's spirits lift.

"Thank you, InDuna, for your kindness."

"What kindness is that?"

"Helping me, and taking responsibility for my family."

"I'm taking care of what belongs to me. That is not kindness, Olawu."

"Belongs to you?" Olawu's brows descended in confusion. What did he mean by that? A knock at the door disrupted her thoughts.

"InDuna Dikembe? It is Hondo."

"Come in." Dikembe continued to gently massage Olawu's legs. Hondo gestured him forward, and he rose to another corner of the room, though Olawu could still hear them. "What is it?"

"I just received word from InDuna Dike. He wishes us to return to Borimbe."

Dikembe nodded. "You go on ahead. I will follow in a few days."

"The letter sounded urgent, Dikembe. I do not think he wishes to wait for you to," he looked at Olawu, "finish your business here."

"Do not concern yourself with matters that do not concern you." Dikembe spoke the words with an edge. "Go ahead and meet with him. I'll follow in a few days."

Hondo seemed like he might protest, but thought better of it. "Yes, InDuna." He tapped his forearm against Dikembe's and left.

Dikembe stared at her a long while before finally approaching. "Olawu? We're going to try something today." She nodded as Dikembe placed her legs over the side of the bed. "Try to stand, okay?"

She put weight on her feet and immediately felt pain. She blew out a slow breath.

"Does it hurt?" he asked. She nodded. "Can you bear it?"

Olawu waited a moment for the sharp throbs to subside. She nodded again. "I think so."

"We're going to take a few steps now, okay?" Dikembe held her carefully as she placed one foot, then the other, in front of her, then turned her around to sit back on the bed. Just those few steps had been exhausting, but the discomfort she felt paled in comparison to the first few days. She could bear it.

"I think if I walk often, I will get my bearings in a few days."

"Good. We are leaving in three. My baba needs me in Borimbe."

She nodded. "I wish you a safe journey, InDuna Dikembe. It will be good to be home again. I miss my umama and my sisters."

"What is this talk of home?" Dikembe chided. "I told you to put such things out of your mind. You are coming with me."

Olawu shook her head. "You need not worry about me further. It is enough that you are taking responsibility for my family."

"Even so, you will come with me, Olawu."

She stared at him, confused. "Did your ubaba summon me as well?"

Dikembe laughed. "No. Why would he?"

"Then I do not understand. InDuna Dikembe, why would I come with you to Borimbe?"

"Because I want you to. Because you belong by my side, Olawu."

"I do not wish to go." Olawu frowned as a slow terror crept up her spine.

"You will go."

"InDuna Dikembe, you are taking things too far. It is not right for me to be here in your room, much less traveling outside the village with you."

"What isn't right about it? You belong to me. I shall take you where I please."

Dikembe's words stung as though he'd struck her. "I do not belong to anyone. Why would you say such a thing?"

Dikembe sat beside her on the bed. He held her chin in his hand and pulled her face close to his. "Olawu, of this thing you must be very clear. You are mine." He kissed her gently on the lips before releasing her. "Rest now."

Olawu's nostrils flared in anger as she watched Dikembe leave, the sweetness of his kiss tainted by his words and the bitter taste they left behind.

Part Two

Borimbe

Chapter Nineteen

I t didn't take Olawu long to decide she hated traveling by horse. Though Dikembe had her wrapped securely in his arms, the journey to Borimbe was hard on her. Each clop of hoof to ground hit as hard as a rock. They traveled from sunrise to sunset. Olawu feared traveling alone would be dangerous, but Dikembe did not share her worry.

This was her first trip away from Kanakam, but Olawu could not enjoy it. She spent most of her time trying not to vomit on Dikembe's horse, and she cried often. Dikembe helped her mount and dismount, and he massaged her feet whenever they rested, but it made no difference. She was miserable.

By the time they reached Borimbe, she'd had enough. But past the gates, they traveled through a maze of mortar homes that climbed up and up until they reached a colossal fortress built on a high cliff. The courtyard buzzed with activity as Dikembe dismounted. A female servant immediately began fussing over him, taking his riding tunic while others began tending to the horse.

Dikembe reached for Olawu and she fainted. He pulled her close to him, speaking her name softly.

"Olawu? Are you in pain?" She moaned, and he kissed her forehead before bringing her inside. He dismissed all offerings to carry her, taking her through the halls until they reached his rooms. His female servant followed closely behind him, rushing forward to open the door and clearing the way to the bed. Dikembe placed

Olawu on the bed and sat beside her. His servant began washing his feet.

"Naomi." Dikembe said her name without looking. "Tend to Olawu while I am away."

"Yes, InDuna."

Dikembe leaned down towards Olawu, his mouth barely an inch from hers. "Olawu?" he whispered her name, caressing her face as he pulled back a flyaway strand of hair. "I'm sorry the journey was so rough on you. I would stay and care for you myself, but my baba is waiting. Naomi will take care of you. I trust her."

Olawu's eyes flicked down towards Naomi, then back up at Dikembe. "I want to go home."

Dikembe shook his head. "Your home is with me, Olawu."

"Have you taken me as your slave, then?"

Dikembe laughed. "No, Olawu. You are my wife."

Olawu swallowed. InDuna Dikembe had not taken care of her and her family for her ubaba's sake, nor for the sake of kindness. He meant to possess her. His regard for her was no different than Batiko's or any of the men of Kanakam. The safety she had felt in his care quickly vanished, replaced by a growing rage.

"I did not give my consent!"

"Even so, you are my wife."

Olawu looked at Dikembe's lips, so close to hers, then back to his eyes. "Wife, slave, what is the difference if I have no say?"

Dikembe sighed and kissed her forehead. As he stood, so did Naomi, helping him into a fresh, dark brown tunic. "I will return soon."

She watched him leave, trembling with fury as she twisted the sheets in her fists. How far would he take things? What sort of man was he? Olawu stared nervously at Naomi. She watched the young girl as she poured fresh water into a basin and brought it over with cloths. Naomi began wiping Olawu's face and hands. Her touches were gentle, but quick. She'd done this hundreds of times, no doubt.

"Naomi?" Olawu spoke her name with unsteady lips.

"Yes, Mama InDuna?"

"May I have some water?"

"Of course." Naomi set down the cloth and dipped a cup into a large basin of fresh water. She helped Olawu sit up on the bed and handed her the cup.

Olawu sipped the water as she took in her surroundings. The room was three times larger than the room in the citadel, and the furnishings would have put kings to shame. The bed could have fit her entire family, including her ubaba. It was covered in gold embroidered linens, and the bed was framed by four long posts.

Rugs and tapestries danced throughout the room, featuring elephants and leopards. The windows had painted glass panes, and there were basins and jars everywhere. The one closest to her bed smelled of spices. She guessed cinnamon or clove. Olawu finished her water and Naomi took her cup.

"Would you like more water, Mama InDuna?" Naomi asked. Olawu shook her head, watching Naomi as she resumed her tasks.

"Naomi?"

"Yes, Mama InDuna?"

"How long have you been with InDuna Dikembe?"

Naomi paused in thought. "Many years, Mama InDuna. At least twelve."

Olawu raised her eyebrows. "You must have been very young. I've never heard your dialect before. Are you from Borimbe?"

Naomi's eyes flickered up to Olawu, suddenly fearful. "N-no, Mama InDuna."

"Where are you from?" Naomi looked uncomfortable. Olawu sat up as Naomi began washing her arms. "Naomi? You do not have to be afraid of me. And you do not have to speak to me if you do not want to. I was just curious."

Naomi nodded. "Forgive my hesitation, Mama InDuna. I am from the Oloko tribe. My village was destroyed when I was four or five, and I was given to InDuna Dikembe."

Olawu's eyes widened in surprise and she leaned forward. "You are Oloko? Do you remember your village?"

Naomi nodded. "I remember having a doll made of cloth with string for hair. I remember my mama and my baba. I remember the men who took them away that night." Naomi shook her head and continued washing Olawu.

"Do you not hate them?" The bitterness in her own voice surprised her.

Naomi shook her head. "No, Mama InDuna! I am loyal to the Dikebe tribe. I would never hate InDuna Dikembe."

"But they killed your family, Naomi." Olawu shook her head. "If I were you, I would hate them."

"I do not!" Naomi insisted. "Please do not say such things, Mama InDuna."

"Do not worry, Naomi. I am like you."

"What do you mean, Mama InDuna?"

Olawu looked at the door, her anger giving way to hurt. "I am a slave." Naomi still looked confused. "I am not here of my own free will."

"I'm sorry, Mama InDuna."

"You can call me Olawu."

"Very well, Mama Olawu."

Olawu sighed. "Naomi, you say you were given to InDuna Dikembe?"

"Yes, Mama InDuna." Naomi caught herself. "Mama Olawu."

"For what purpose?"

"Whatever purpose he requests, Mama Olawu."

"I see. How old was InDuna Dikembe when you first met him?"

"InDuna Dikembe? Perhaps he was nine? Not much older than me."

Olawu absorbed the information. She wasn't entirely sure how to word her next question. She was even more concerned with the answer.

"Naomi?" Olawu began.

"Yes, Mama Olawu?"

"InDuna Dikembe? Has he ever forced himself on you?"

"It would be impossible to force his will, Mama Olawu, for his will is my will."

Olawu bit her lip. This was going to be tricky. "But has he ever treated you in an unpleasant way?"

"I am his servant. It is my duty to obey him."

"You are a person, Naomi." Olawu could not hide her frustration. "You have a soul. You were made in the image of God, the same as InDuna Dikembe. You were born with a will of your own. Do these things not matter to the Oloko? Or do they just not matter to you?"

Naomi faltered, unsure of how to respond. "Have I displeased you in some way, Mama Olawu?"

Olawu softened her tone. She hadn't meant to yell at the poor girl. But it gave her another idea. "No, Naomi, you haven't. But InDuna Dikembe, have you ever displeased him?"

"He has not expressed displeasure in me."

"Has he ever yelled at you?"

"No, Mama Olawu."

"Has he ever hit you?"

"No, Mama Olawu."

That was something. She pushed forward. "Has he ever taken interest in you? As a woman, I mean?"

Naomi's eyes lit up in understanding. "You mean, am I his mistress?" Naomi actually laughed at that. Olawu's cheeks burned with heat. Naomi noticed Olawu's discomfort and immediately stopped laughing. "Forgive me, Mama Olawu. You do not have to worry about InDuna Dikembe. If he has given you his heart, it belongs to you alone."

"It's not his heart I'm worried about," Olawu blurted thoughtlessly. Naomi cleared her throat and finished cleaning Olawu before helping her into a fresh kaftan. It was a soft, green and white fabric that felt cool against her skin. Naomi braided Olawu's hair, stroking it gently with her fingers.

"Your hair is beautiful," Naomi crooned as she applied oils to it. "It is not as long as Mama InDuna Dhakiya's, but it is a similar texture."

"Dikembe's umama? What is she like?"

Naomi smiled. "She is very kind and beautiful. If it were not for Mama InDuna Dhakiya, I would not have been treated so kindly. Because of her, my life was spared, and I was given to InDuna Dikembe. You will like her, Mama Olawu."

Olawu nodded. She had liked her the first time they met.

"YOU SUMMONED ME, INDUNA Dike?" Dikembe bowed before his baba with both arms crossed above his head.

InDuna Dike tapped his arms, and Dikembe rose. "An Oloko tribe destroyed another Dikebe village four days ago."

Dikembe frowned. "Where?"

"Chigami. There were few survivors."

Dikembe scowled. The Oloko were becoming bolder. They usually did not wander far from their eastern valleys, but of late, their raids were spreading closer and closer to Borimbe.

"I want construction on the dam to begin as soon as possible, Dikembe. Have you gone over the plans I sent you from Basange?"

"Yes, InDuna. I intend to speak with him while I'm here in Borimbe."

"Good. His son will likely remain in Kanakam to oversee construction once it begins. Be sure to speak with him as well."

"Of course, InDuna. Is there anything else? Hondo said your letter seemed urgent."

"And yet I did not see you until four days later." His baba gave him a chastising glare. "War is coming, Dikembe. We must be prepared for it. Once the dam is complete, the valley will dry up, and the Oloko will have no choice but to bring the fight to us. When that happens, we must strike them hard."

Dikembe nodded. "I will not fail you, InDuna. Do you wish me to stay in Kanakam?"

He shook his head. "Kanakam is under control. We'll keep men posted at the citadel, but I'm confident Basange and his son can handle things from here. I want you in Borimbe, training men for war."

Dikembe nodded. "As you wish, InDuna." He lowered his head and raised his forearm. InDuna Dike smiled and raised his in return.

"Be sure to speak to Mama InDuna tonight."

"I'll head to her rooms now." Dikembe nodded and left. He was anxious to speak to his mama. Thoughts of Olawu all but consumed him, and he needed her counsel. He walked through the long halls until he reached her door, knocking four times and then pausing between the fifth to signal that it was him. She opened her doors wide, but her smile was even wider.

"My son!" she exclaimed. Dikembe gathered her in his arms. His frustrations melted away as she rubbed his back. "Come in, Dikembe. We have much to discuss. Have you spoken to your baba already?"

"Yes, Mama. I always speak to him first so I can spend the rest of my time with you."

"Oh, but you won't be doing that any longer, will you, Dikembe?" She gave him a sly look. He returned it with a puzzled one. "Have a seat."

He obeyed and sat while she fed him cakes and told him stories about everything that had happened in Borimbe while he was away in Kanakam. He listened politely, not wanting to interrupt, though he cared very little for the disputes between the baker and the butcher. His mama gave him another funny look before offering him something to drink.

"Are you bored, Dikembe?"

He blinked. "No, Mama. It's just-"

"You have something to tell me." She grinned. "I already know, Dikembe. From the moment I saw you enter the courtyard, I knew something was different."

"You saw me?"

"From that window right over there." She pointed to a window in her room. "She must be very special. Is she more beautiful than your Mama?"

"She?"

"Oh, I almost forgot." She grabbed a small box from a table and handed it to him. Inside was a jade ring with a jaguar carved on the top. "I had it made as soon as I heard the news."

"News?" Dikembe gave his mama another puzzled look.

"Oh, don't look so surprised, Dikembe. I am your mama, after all. Try not to think any less of Hondo if you intended to keep it a secret. I had three days to pry it out of him."

"Oh." Dikembe began to follow. "You know about Olawu?"

"Is that her name? Oh, that's lovely, Dikembe! I won't keep you any longer from her, and I won't ask you any more questions. Be sure to give her the ring tonight. She should know what she means to you if you intend to keep her."

"What exactly did Hondo tell you?"

His mama smiled. "Everything, of course."

Dikembe smiled back. He'd played this game before with her. "You don't know anything, do you?"

"I know that she's special enough to keep your baba waiting." She smirked. "Go to her now. We can talk more when I return."

Dikembe frowned. "Return? Where are you going?"

"I leave for Ingala in the morning. My bibi is unwell. I shall return after her funeral."

"Oh." Dikembe kissed her. "I wish you a safe journey, Mama."

"Mhm." She waved him away, and Dikembe left her room, anxious to get back to Olawu.

Chapter Twenty

O lawu didn't think she'd ever get used to waking up next to Dikembe. He had a commanding presence, even while he slept, and it unnerved her. She desperately missed her sister. Sleeping beside Ugami had never made her feel like throwing up. But that was exactly how she felt this morning, and nearly every morning when she opened her eyes and saw his dark face close to hers. Her stomach twisted into knots, and she became acutely aware of how close every inch of him was to every inch of her.

Olawu pushed herself away from him and into a sitting position, waiting for her heart to beat at a normal pace. She needed to get away from him. She slowly swung her legs to the other side of the bed, lowering her feet to the ground. Before she could stand, his hand was around her wrist.

"Olawu?" he spoke sleepily. "Where are you going?"

Olawu took a deep breath to calm her thumping heart. Why couldn't he just sleep?

"I need to relieve myself," she lied. "Please don't get up. I can do it myself."

Dikembe sat up and pulled her back towards him. His forearm rested casually around her belly as he rested his head on her shoulder.

"My Olawu," he spoke softly. "I wish to do everything with you, but you do not share the same sentiment. Very well. Today I shall leave you to yourself. If you wish to walk the halls and courtyard without me shadowing your every move, you may do so. You can even go to the market if you'd like. I have but three rules."

Olawu cleared her throat and tried to ignore the searing heat she felt where his fingertips touched her skin. "What rules are those, InDuna?"

"First, you must not leave Borimbe. Get the thought out of your mind."

"But my family-"

"I am your family, Olawu."

"But what will my umama do without me? My sisters Ugami and Kimani? They have no man to protect them."

Dikembe sighed before continuing. "Second, you must take Naomi with you wherever you go. She knows this fortress well and can guide you through Borimbe."

"But you haven't answered my questions about my family." Olawu's frustrations grew. Dikembe drew back, and she wondered if she had angered him. He returned just as quickly, placing a small box in her lap.

"Third and final rule. You must wear this ring. And promise to never take it off." Olawu opened the box. A jade ring with a jaguar carving lay inside.

Dikembe had completely disregarded her. Left up to him, she would never return home. Olawu would have to figure out a way on her own. But first, she would need to gain his trust. She placed the ring on her finger and turned towards him.

"Am I allowed to have rules of my own?" she asked, a challenge in her eyes.

Dikembe rubbed his chin in thought. "Alright, Olawu. You may have one rule."

"Do not come to my room unless I summon you."

Dikembe frowned and shook his head. "This is not a good rule, Olawu."

"Then I do not agree to yours." Olawu began removing the ring. Dikembe stopped her, placing his hand over hers.

"Olawu. If you do not wish to see me in your bed, I can accept that. But entering your room freely is a necessary thing."

"Why is it necessary?"

"What if you are sick or unconscious and unable to call to me for help?"

"Send in Naomi!"

"What if she is also unconscious?"

"Then send *anybody* else!" Olawu saw that her last remark stung. She'd gone too far. "InDuna Dikembe. I cannot bear to have you here. I am not used to any man but my ubaba. I cannot bear the thought that you may come to me at any moment, no matter how I feel. I cannot bear it."

Dikembe clenched his jaw and nodded. "I can make no promises, Olawu. But I will try to respect your wishes. And I promise not to enter your bed unless you ask." Dikembe kissed her softly on the cheek and rose.

"Naomi?" he called softly. Naomi stood from where she lay at the foot of the bed. "From now on you will attend to Olawu. Where she goes, you must also go."

"Yes, InDuna."

Dikembe took a long look at Olawu before leaving the room. Olawu let out a sigh of relief before collapsing onto the bed.

Chapter Twenty One

Olawu had never known a place like Borimbe. The colors and sights and smells drew her in the moment she stepped outside the fortress. The market boasted wares far grander than Kanakam's. Merchants sold exotic spices and fabrics in colors Olawu did not know existed. The buildings were made of brick and stone. Many of them towered above her, though none were as grand as the fortress. The massive walls of stone surrounding Borimbe were a credit to the skill of the Dikebe.

Kanakam's fortifications were pitiful by comparison. The walls of Kanakam, made of bamboo shoots tied together, barely kept out wild dogs and other small predators. Borimbe's walls would thwart a small army.

Naomi proved an excellent guide, navigating through alleyways and side roads to take Olawu wherever she desired. They spent most of the morning walking through the market. Olawu was shocked to see both men and women selling items. She was even more shocked when Naomi asked if she wished to buy anything.

"Mama Olawu, would you like to purchase this fabric?" Naomi asked as Olawu's fingers caressed the deep purple satin.

"I was just thinking it would make a lovely kitenge for my sister, Kimani."

Naomi nodded and pulled out a pouch filled with gold. "I'd like to buy this fabric." She looked at Olawu. "Would four yards do, Mama Olawu?"

Olawu's eyes widened, and she yanked the pouch from her. "What are you doing, Naomi?" She turned towards the merchant. "We are not trying to buy anything!"

The merchant gave her a strange look. "Is the price too high? I can give you for less." Olawu calmed the pounding in her chest as she looked from the merchant's confused eyes to Naomi's.

Naomi reached for the pouch. "Mama Olawu, are you alright?"

Olawu released it, feeling foolish. "I don't want the fabric," she whispered. Naomi nodded and waved the merchant away.

"But wait!" The merchant pushed the fabric back towards Naomi. "I give you a good price. Extra fabric, too!"

Naomi ignored him and guided Olawu to a small building with tables and stools arranged outside. She pulled out a stool for Olawu to sit.

"Are you sure you are alright, Mama Olawu?" Naomi looked genuinely worried.

Olawu shook her head in bewilderment. "They let you buy and sell here in Borimbe?"

"Yes, Mama Olawu. Um. That is what the marketplace is for." Olawu stared at Naomi, and the girl withered. "I do not mean to speak out of turn, Mama Olawu. I am just confused."

"I am the one who is confused, Naomi." Olawu watched in wonder as a man in a light brown kaftan served them tea. He asked her politely if she wanted milk or sugar with it. She asked for both. The combination was delightful.

Naomi tried to hide her smile as she watched Olawu sip the tea. "Do you like it, Mama Olawu?"

"It's wonderful, Naomi!" Olawu grinned as she took another sip. "I've never had tea with sugar before, and only a few times with milk."

"Olawu?"

Both women turned at the sound of her name. Olawu's eyes lit up as she recognized the man approaching.

"Businge!" She stood to greet him. He looked better than she remembered in a grey and blue kaftan draped with a long black tunic. His smile sent warmth straight to her heart, as well as her cheeks.

"I hoped I would see you again, Olawu, but I never expected to find you here. May I treat you to a meal? The best roasted fowl in Borimbe is just steps away."

Olawu nodded in excitement and took Businge's outstretched hand. Naomi followed behind them, eyes darting from one to the other. Naomi's apprehensive face may have bothered her another day. But with Businge so close, her thoughts were only of him.

"How are you enjoying Borimbe so far?" Businge asked as he walked with her through the streets.

"I love it!" Olawu admitted. "It is very different from Kanakam. I cannot believe I saw a female merchant. Is that common, Businge?"

"Not common, but not forbidden. Anyone can become a merchant so long as they can pay their tribute. In Borimbe, women are free to buy and sell just as the men are."

"Are they also free to work in other places?" Olawu asked.

Businge nodded. "Women may work and learn a trade, so yes, it is very different from Kanakam. I was very surprised to learn of some of the customs of your village. It is not a place I would like to live if I were a woman. But I am glad to find you in Borimbe. I hope you decide to stay."

Olawu smiled at his words, and Businge stopped in front of a building with several windows. A heavenly smell wafted from inside. Her grin widened as she breathed it in. Businge pulled out a stool for her and sat on the opposite end. Naomi stood near a wall, out of sight. A short woman wearing a brown kaftan approached them.

"Two half birds please." Businge's voice was light and friendly. The woman smiled and left. Olawu watched the exchange with interest. What sort of place was Borimbe?

"It smells so good!" Her mouth watered as a steaming bowl of roasted meat was placed on a different table.

"If I am not working with my ubaba, I am here. I cannot get enough of this place. I hope you love it as much as I do."

"What kind of work do you do with your ubaba?" Olawu asked.

"My ubaba is a craftsman, the best among all the Dikebe tribes. I've apprenticed with him for the last five years. Finishing the citadel's tower in Kanakam was my first independent project. My ubaba made the plans for the citadel and things were going well, but then he had to return to Borimbe and left another man in charge.

"He was lazy and very sloppy. The tower was nearly destroyed, because he did not do the work properly. My ubaba sent me to finish the job, and you saw how it looked. Olawu? Are you alright?"

Olawu had grown still at Businge's words. That accident had brought Businge to Kanakam. But it had also taken her ubaba away.

Businge crinkled his brow and placed his hand on her forehead. "Are you unwell, Olawu?"

She shook her head and stood. "I'm sorry, Businge. I think I need to leave."

"Yes, you should rest." Businge called out to the kitchen. "Bring the fowl to go, Jogo!" He steadied Olawu with one arm and carried a small basket of food in the other. "Do you know where you're going?" he asked.

Olawu shook her head. "Naomi knows the way. Do you have any brothers or sisters, Businge?"

"I had a younger brother, but he died shortly after birth. Do you?"

"Two younger sisters, Ugami and Kimani. Ugami is very sweet and sensible, but also very shy. Kimani is full of mischief, but gives the best hugs. I miss them and my umama." They passed Borimbe's eastern gate and Olawu stopped. "Businge?"

"Yes Olawu?"

"Can a woman become an udokotela in Borimbe?"

Businge scratched his chin. "To be an udokotela in Borimbe, you must first apprentice for an udokotela. They would not accept a woman, I think. But it is not a forbidden thing."

"Hmm," Olawu murmured. "Businge?"

"Yes?"

"In Kanakam, women are not allowed to leave the village without a man. Is that true in Borimbe?"

Businge nodded. "That is also true of Borimbe. But it is not safe for a woman to travel alone. There are many dangers. Are you already thinking of leaving, Olawu?"

She laughed, but when she turned towards Businge, he had a different look in his eyes.

"Olawu, may I ask you a question?"

Olawu cleared her throat and nodded. "Yes?"

He set down the basket and turned towards her, gently taking her hands in his. "Olawu?" He froze as his eyes landed on the jade ring on her finger. He stared at it a long time before his gaze returned to her face. "What brings you to Borimbe?"

Olawu opened her mouth to reply, but no words came out.

Businge lowered his head. "This ring. It means that you are with InDuna Dikembe?"

Olawu could not speak. She shook her head, but Businge released her hands.

"I misunderstood, Olawu. Forgive me."

"Businge." Olawu spoke his name softly. Businge picked up the basket and placed it in her hands. For a brief moment his fingers touched hers. Olawu wished the touch would never end, but it did.

"I wish you well, Olawu. I will return to Kanakam in a few days with my ubaba. Is there a message I can give to your family?"

Olawu nodded, blinking back tears. "Yes. Tell them I'm alright and that I hope to see them soon. My family's hut is the first on the main road, closest to the river."

Businge nodded. "I will give them the message. Take care, Olawu."

Olawu swallowed a sob. Watching Businge leave felt like watching the sun set for the last time before the rainy season.

Chapter Twenty Two

"Naomi, what is this?" Olawu slowed her steps as they passed by a curtain of beads stretched across the front of an arched entry. She had asked Naomi to take her to the marketplace again. Now that she understood the way buying and selling worked in Borimbe, she wished to try it for herself.

Naomi looked where Olawu pointed and smiled. "The healer takes her patients there."

"*Her* patients?" Olawu raised her eyebrows and Naomi nodded. There was a female healer in Borimbe?

"Yes, Mama Olawu. She is the only traditional healer in Borimbe."

"What does she do?"

Naomi bowed her head. "I could not say for sure. Would you like to speak with her yourself?"

Olawu's intrigue heightened at the thought. "Yes. Can I just go in?"

"I will go in ahead of you." Naomi disappeared behind the beads, and Olawu caught the faint scent of jasmine. She returned a few moments later with a smile on her lips. "Sangoma will see you now."

Olawu crossed over the threshold and into a small room. Herbs and oils filled the shelves on each wall. The smell of jasmine was strongest, coupled with sage and lemongrass. Olawu stared at the contents on one shelf. Pots of rooibos root, bitter melon extracts, and periwinkle filled one row. Her ubaba had kept the same herbs in his healing hut.

"Mama Olawu? This way."

Naomi guided her to a separate room where a short, but elegant woman sat on a rug laid out on the floor. Her dark hair, braided into a crown, was streaked with white. Her deep purple kitenge complemented the purple and gold bands on her wrists and the flecks of purple in her eyes. She smiled at Olawu, bowing with her arms extended above her head.

"Mama Olawu, it is my honor!"

Olawu held the woman's hands and gently lifted her to her feet. "Please do not bow to me." She frowned. "I am just as you are. Naomi says you are a healer, Sangoma?"

Sangoma nodded and patted Olawu on the cheek. "What is it you wish to have cured, Mama Olawu?"

"I do not need a cure, but I do have questions. Is it true that you are the only healer in Borimbe?"

The woman again nodded. "There are two udokotelas in Borimbe, but I am the only healer of the old ways."

"How did you come to be the healer here?" Olawu asked.

"Before the Dikebe came here, Borimbe was a small village. Healing is in my blood, as it was in my mama's, and her mama's, on to four generations."

"What is it you heal, Sangoma?"

"Matters of the body, the mind, the spirit. And the heart." Sangoma's gaze was perceptive as she took Olawu by the hand. "I am not like the udokotelas. I do not possess their modern skill and knowledge. But I do possess the wisdom of six generations. Is there something else you wish to know, Mama Olawu?"

"The people of Borimbe? They accept you, though you are a woman?"

Sangoma shook her head. "Rejecting my wisdom would be rejecting Borimbe's own rich heritage. That would be foolish. But there are fools in Borimbe."

Olawu nodded. "Is there another who will inherit your knowledge, Sangoma?"

"No. I have no daughters. I have but one son, and he is perhaps the greatest fool in Borimbe."

"I have seen your pots, Sangoma. They are filled with the very things my own ubaba would use. He was an udokotela in my village. You must be very wise."

Sangoma chuckled. "My son is an udokotela as well. He would not agree with you or your ubaba. He has learned much from the eastern foreigners who visit Borimbe. He has no use for my remedies, so he chose another fool to learn from."

"Could you not become the third udokotela of Borimbe if you wished, Sangoma?"

Sangoma clucked as she moved towards the front entry. "I will leave such things to my son. Besides, there has never been a woman udokotela in Borimbe or anywhere."

"But if you wished to be, could you?" Olawu found herself holding her breath as she waited for Sangoma's answer.

"The only way to become an udokotela in Borimbe is to apprentice with an udokotela. And neither of those men would ever take a woman as an apprentice."

Olawu's heart sank at Sangoma's words. Businge had said as much. "Is there no other way, Sangoma?"

The woman lifted her eyes in thought. "If InDuna Dike acknowledged someone as an udokotela, then that may be enough." Sangoma laughed. "But it is more likely for a woman to be an apprentice than to be acknowledged by the InDuna."

Olawu bowed her head, disappointed. "Thank you for your help, Sangoma."

"Just a moment, Mama Olawu." Sangoma grabbed her by the hand. "You said your ubaba was an udokotela? Do you have some skill in healing as well?"

"My ubaba taught me everything he knew." Olawu said the words proudly.

Sangoma nodded and squeezed her hand. "Then perhaps you should speak to InDuna Dikembe? Surely he will help you if you wish to become an udokotela?"

Would he? Olawu did not think so. Even if he agreed to help her, there was no guarantee he would keep his word. Somehow, she would find a way to follow in her ubaba's footsteps. With or without Dikembe's help.

Chapter Twenty Three

Dikembe was agitated. Olawu had not summoned him to her room, and it had been weeks already. She left early in the morning with Naomi and often did not return until late at night. He had plenty to keep him busy, InDuna Dike made sure of that, but it didn't stop him from thinking about her. He missed waking up to her in the morning, running his fingers along her beautiful, dark skin. Getting lost in those deep, brown eyes.

He needed her. But she seemed to be doing just fine without him.

Dikembe paced his room over and over, at war with himself. He had promised Olawu that he would not enter her room without permission. No. He had made no promises there. He said he would try. And so what if he broke his promise? They were his rooms, anyway. She would not like it, but it was time for Olawu to know her place. She was his wife. She needed to start behaving like it. He would not force her. But he would make his expectations clear.

Dikembe clapped his hands together. He had a plan. Olawu would not refuse him tonight. He called for a servant. He would need help making the preparations. When Olawu returned with Naomi, he would be waiting for her.

OLAWU WALKED DOWN THE hall with Naomi, nibbling on a piece of meat. She had not realized that Businge's guilty pleasure would become her own, but every time they visited the market, she found herself in front of the shop, ordering roasted fowl.

"Naomi, won't you try some?" Olawu offered her a piece, but Naomi shook her head.

"Mama Olawu, it is for you to enjoy. It brings me joy just watching you. Food makes you very happy."

"Mm, it does!" Olawu laughed as she bit into another leg. "But Naomi, I don't think I've ever seen you eat, and you spend all day with me. I'm worried that you'll waste away."

Naomi shook her head as she opened the door to her room. "Mama Olawu, please don't worry about me. I do not eat much, nor do I eat often. It has been this way my whole life."

Olawu entered the room and froze. Her basket fell to the floor, and Naomi rushed to pick it up.

"Mama Olawu, are you alright?" Naomi's voice trailed off as she looked from Olawu to Dikembe. She placed the basket to the side and bowed. "InDuna."

"Naomi, leave." Dikembe ordered.

"Naomi, stay."

Naomi looked from Dikembe to Olawu and wrung her hands. "InDuna? Mama InDuna?"

"Must you trouble Naomi?" Dikembe asked. "She can stay if you wish, but I thought you would prefer the privacy."

"What are you doing here?" Olawu scowled. "You promised!"

"I said I would try, Olawu. I did not promise."

"You promised not to come to my bed, and yet you're sitting on it!"

Dikembe stared at the bed and shrugged. "Come sit with me, Olawu. I have prepared something for us."

"I'm not going anywhere near you."

Dikembe held up a tray of sweets and fruits. "I should not have to go to such lengths, but very well. Come, Olawu. Eat with me."

Olawu didn't move. "Can I not entice you with food?" Dikembe sighed and lowered the tray. "Fine. If you will not come to me, then I will come to you."

He walked over to Olawu. His tall, muscular frame towered over her. He knelt down until their eyes were level, but Olawu turned her face away.

"Look at me, Olawu," he whispered. "Can you not see how much I want you?" Dikembe turned her face towards him, rubbing his thumb across her cheek.

"Can you not see how much I despise you?" she hissed. Dikembe straightened himself and scowled.

"You are my wife, Olawu. You cannot expect to hold me at bay forever."

"And you cannot expect me to believe what you say if you cannot keep your word!"

"I said I'd try. I tried. I need you, Olawu. I need my wife." Dikembe pressed his lips against hers, but Olawu pushed him back.

"And what makes me your wife, Dikembe? Did you eat my isitshalo? Did you pay my family a bride price? Did you ask for my hand?"

"Olawu."

"I did not ask for this. I did not ask for you. Men like you are all the same. You take and you take and you take, never once asking, never once waiting for permission. I know what I am worth. I know who I am. My ubaba taught me long ago what love looks like, and I will accept nothing less."

"Damn your ubaba, and damn you, Olawu!" Dikembe grabbed her forcefully. "You say men like me are all the same? Is that what you really think? Should I prove you right? Should I just take what I want, here and now?"

Olawu glared at him. "You are no better than Batiko! Take what you will, but know that you will never have me."

OLAWU'S WORDS STRUCK hard, and Dikembe blinked. He stared at her fiery eyes, took in the way she trembled beneath his grip. Her frown deepened, as did her hatred for him. This was not what he had hoped for.

He loosened his hold, and pushed her away. "Damn you." Dikembe stormed out, slamming the door behind him.

Chapter Twenty Four

Olawu stared at the massive beast in front of her, and for a moment, she hesitated. Naomi had shown her where the horses were kept, and she'd even ventured to ride one once or twice, with help. But this was something entirely different. She was going to mount this monstrosity and trust it to take her home.

She could not stay. She wanted to be free of Dikembe. She had tried avoiding him, but after tonight she realized that avoiding him was not enough. He did not see her as a person. He saw her as his property. It was only a matter of time before he forced himself on her. She'd rather die under the hooves of the brown mare than be forced into slavery.

She led the mare from the stable and into the open air before trying to mount her. After a few bruising failures she finally succeeded, but the feel of the horse moving underneath her made her uneasy. She traveled at a slow trot until she reached the eastern gate.

She led the horse past the men guarding the gate, pretending to head in the opposite direction. They glanced her way before returning back to a game of stones. Olawu kept close to the gate, but out of sight, waiting for other travelers to enter or leave. Once the gates opened, she would bolt past the guards and towards the river. From there she would travel upstream until she reached Kanakam.

Her wait was short. A traveling merchant approached the gates. The guards questioned him for a few minutes before letting him pass. As soon as the gates were opened, Olawu shot out into the night, holding on for dear life as the chocolate mare sped away from

Borimbe. The guards shouted angrily behind her. Comping hooves quickly followed as the guards gave chase.

Olawu's stomach twisted and she kicked the mare's hide, willing her to go faster. The mare obliged, and Olawu tightened her thighs around its back to keep from being flung into the dirt. Another shout rang out, much closer.

She turned to get a glimpse of the guards, but it proved a fatal mistake. She lost her bearings, and her hold on the reins, and went flying through the air. She landed in a heap on the ground as the mare continued to gallop away.

Olawu knew something was broken. Judging by the snap, it was most likely a carrot. Despite the pain, Olawu laughed at the memory of her and her ubaba practicing with vegetables in the healing hut. The vibration of approaching horses sent a shiver up her spine, and the memory faded. The horses snorted and stomped beside her as the men jumped to the ground.

The guards drove their feet into her back and sides, but she was too dazed to lift an arm in defense. She thought the beating would never end, until a kick to the head sent her world spinning.

"YOU'RE IN A MOOD, DIKEMBE."

Dhakiya sat beside her son, whose body was strewn across her bed with his head towards the ceiling. Worry lines marked his face as he stared at nothing. She stroked his cheek and kissed his forehead.

"Why are you here, my son?"

"Where else do I have to go?" He pouted. "You are the only one who truly loves me, Mama."

"Fighting with Olawu already, I see?"

"She does not fight fair."

"Don't pout, Dikembe."

Dikembe sat up and stared at her. "I don't understand, Mama. I thought I did as she wanted. But she seems only to hate me for it."

Dhakiya sighed. "I suppose you won't be asking me about my trip back home, then?"

Dikembe groaned. "I forgot. How was your trip? Your bibi, did she?"

"Pass away? Yes. Just moments before I arrived. Time is such a precious thing. We do not know how much of it we have."

"Mama? The barrette you wear in your hair? The one with the lotus flower? Do you still have it?"

"Yes. I wear it very often. Why do you ask?"

"Is it the only one you have?"

"Do you not like it?"

He shook his head. "In Kanakam, there was a girl who had one just like it. She said you gave it to her."

Dhakiya nodded. "Ah yes! The udokotela who helped me in Kanakam has helped us once before. Do you not remember?" Dikembe shook his head. "I suppose not. You were so badly hurt. We had been traveling towards Ingala to visit my family when the Oloko attacked us. Your baba was not with us, but his guards were. They sent us to travel up the river while they fought off the Oloko. We managed to get away, but they found us within a day's time. You were struck in the chest with an arrow. I carried you in my arms and ran to the closest light I saw. I ran into the village. I begged at every hut, but no one would help. Then I knocked on the udokotela's door. His wife did not want us to go in, but he helped us anyway. He had two other daughters. I remember his oldest daughter watching over you, as though she were your guardian angel. Before we left for home, I gave her my barrette."

Dhakiya sighed. "I meant to properly thank the udokotela in Kanakam, but I never got the chance. I felt so terrible when I found out he died. Do you know how his family is doing? I would like to offer our assistance to them. Kanakam is unkind to its women."

Dikembe groaned as he lay his head back again. "I thought perhaps she made it up."

"Who are you talking about, Dikembe?"

"Olawu. She is the daughter of the udokotela, Mama. She came to me asking for help. She told me that you gave her the barrette, but I did not believe her and refused." Dikembe looked up at his mama. "She saved my life in Kanakam."

"The ibhubesi?" Her eyes warmed in understanding and Dikembe nodded.

"She was wounded because of me, and left vulnerable, so I took her as my wife, and I brought her here. But she cannot stand the sight of me."

"Oh, Dikembe." Dhakiya sighed.

"What was I to do? She asked me to take responsibility for her family. I've made her part of mine. What more does she want from me?"

"What did you fight about tonight?" Dikembe did not answer. "Dikembe?"

He sat up and kissed her. "It's getting late. You should rest, Mama."

"Dikembe, what did you do?"

"Mama, the ways of a man and his wife should stay between-"

"Dikembe. What did you do to that poor girl?" Dikembe faltered, and Dhakiya narrowed her eyes. "Never mind. Take me to her."

"She is probably asleep, Mama."

"If she is asleep, I will not wake her, but you will take me to her now."

Dikembe nodded in obedience and escorted her to Olawu's room. When they opened the door, her bed was empty. Dikembe walked around slowly, scanning the room. Naomi wasn't in her spot near the foot of the bed, either.

"Is this the room she stays in?" she asked. Dikembe nodded. "Would she have gone to another room?"

"Possibly. She did not like my being here."

"Where is Naomi?"

Naomi entered the room just as Dhakiya spoke her name. Her eyes widened in surprise at the sight of both Dhakiya and Dikembe.

"Mama InDuna! InDuna Dikembe!" She bowed deeply despite the bowl of soup in her hand.

"Naomi, where is Olawu?" Dikembe asked, his words laced with agitation.

"Mama Olawu was here when I left." She frowned. "She was asleep, and so I went to the kitchen for supper."

"How long were you in the kitchen?" Dikembe asked.

"Well, I . . . um." Naomi's eyes brimmed with tears. "Please forgive me, InDuna! I thought Mama Olawu was asleep, and so I stayed a bit longer in the kitchen than I normally would."

"Doing what?" Dikembe growled. "Were you consorting with the rats, Naomi? Your job is to attend Mama Olawu at all times, how hard can that be?"

"Forgive me, InDuna!" Naomi begged. "My weakness has angered you."

"Your weakness?" Dikembe began, but Dhakiya stopped him.

"Leave the poor child alone, Dikembe."

He scowled and grew quiet, pacing the room. Mid-stride, he stopped and sat on the bed. He stared at a tray laid out on the table beside it, and frowned.

Dhakiya watched him with a worried expression. Something had definitely happened.

DIKEMBE DIDN'T KNOW where Olawu was. It gnawed at his insides. How could he keep her safe this way?

He sat on her bed and stared at the tray of uneaten sweets beside it. He'd had them specially made for her. She hadn't touched a single one. Dikembe leaned in closer. The jade ring he'd given her rested in the center.

"No." He breathed out the word. She wouldn't dare. Would she?

Chapter Twenty Five

Businge yawned as he and his baba plodded down the main road towards Borimbe.

"We're nearly home." His baba chuckled. "You'll see your bed soon enough."

Businge grunted and shook himself. "How long do you think it will take to have the plans approved by the InDuna?"

"Not long," his baba replied. "All the framework for the dam is done. Once men from the other Dikebe tribes are sent to dig the trenches, we'll begin construction. You've done well in Kanakam, Businge."

"Thank you, Baba."

"Quiet night," Basange mused. "Perhaps we should sing a song to keep us awake?"

Businge laughed at that. "I do not think men with voices like ours should sing, Baba. We may offend the angels if we try."

"More likely the horses." His baba laughed and Businge joined him, but both quieted at the sound of an approaching rider.

"Baba, do you hear someone coming?"

He nodded and looked down the main road. The outline of a dark brown horse galloped towards them. The charger was unmanned.

"That can't be good." Businge frowned. "Looks like a rider lost his horse." Businge whistled at the mare and ran his horse alongside it. The mare slowed, and Businge grabbed the reins.

"Why don't you ride on ahead, Businge? See if the rider needs help. I'll bring the horse."

Businge handed the reins to his baba and sent his horse into a gallop towards Borimbe. He slowed when he caught sight of two other horses. Seeing two men stomping and beating a third, he sped up again.

Businge cried out a warning as he approached. "Hayi!" He jumped off of his horse and began pushing the men away.

"What are you doing, eh?" One of the men scowled. "Mind your own business!"

"Show some restraint!" Businge pushed him again. "How many times must you kick a man before you are satisfied, eh?"

The second man spat. "As many times as we wish when it is a woman."

Businge looked down at the small, slender frame and his mouth went dry. He did not have to remove her hand from her face to know it was Olawu. She moaned in pain as he cradled her in his arms and lifted her from the ground.

"Would you be so cruel if this woman were your mama? Your sister? Hm?" Businge chastised them. "Are you animals? Look at her. Look at what you've done! Do you know who this is?"

"Inja!"

Businge glared at the man until he withered. "She is InDuna Dikembe's wife." The men glanced at each other, suddenly nervous. Businge began walking towards Borimbe, Olawu in his arms. She seemed too frail to place on his horse.

"Hayi! Master?" One of the guards placed a hand on his shoulder. "We did not know who she was. She came flying out of the gates on the horse, and we went after her. We did not know who she was. We just did what we were supposed to do."

"Yes." The other guard chimed in. "Master, tell InDuna Dikembe that we did nothing wrong."

"Please Master," the other added. "Do not worry okay? We will bring your horse to the gate. Please forget our faces."

Businge ignored them as he continued towards Borimbe. The guards followed behind him and continued their pleas for leniency. He was glad to be rid of them once he passed through the gate. Businge studied Olawu's face, which had begun to swell near her eye. His heart threatened to sever in two at the sight.

"Poor Olawu," he whispered. "What were you doing out here? Has InDuna Dikembe mistreated you in some way?"

Olawu did not answer. Businge pulled her in closer.

"I do not know what to do. If InDuna Dikembe has caused you harm, then I would take you from him. My mama and my baba and I would help you and keep you safe from him."

Olawu moaned again, and Businge rested her head against his shoulder.

"But what if you were not running from him? If I brought you home, there would be misunderstanding between you and InDuna Dikembe. I would not wish to cause you greater distress." He stopped. "If I go down this road to the right, I will be home. Would you be at home with me?"

Her only reply was a shuddering breath.

Businge looked up towards the fortress. "If I take this road going straight, I will bring you to InDuna Dikembe. Tell me what you wish, Olawu. I will do as you say."

Businge placed his head on top of hers, taking in the faint smell of coconut mixed with soil. He scowled and clucked his tongue.

"I blame that spoiled brat, Jacan! If it weren't for him, I could have taken you home with me from Kanakam. If you were willing. Even now, InDuna Dikembe be damned. He's spent his life hauling spears. I've spent mine hauling stones. I'm sure I would win in a fight, though he has an army. But I would fight for you, and win, if that's what you wanted?"

Silence answered him. He sighed and lowered his head before continuing on towards the fortress.

DIKEMBE RUSHED DOWN the hall towards the stables, ignoring questions from his mama. He didn't bother with his riding gear. There wasn't time. Olawu was foolish enough to leave Borimbe. He needed to get to her before someone else did. He noticed right away that the dark mare was missing. There was no way Olawu could handle a horse that size and speed.

Dikembe mounted his black horse and headed out through the courtyard. Naomi waited for him there with a cloak, but he rode past her. Halfway through the entrance, he stopped, spotting Olawu draped in the arms of another man. He leapt from his horse and ran towards them.

"Olawu?"

Fear and regret tugged at his insides. She was hurt. Badly. Her left arm hung at an odd angle. Blood and dirt covered the rest of her. He didn't like the way her head rested against that bastard's shoulder. He wanted to tear Olawu from his arms, and nearly did, but Businge pulled back.

"Give her to me." Dikembe heard the desperation in his voice.

Businge locked eyes with him. They'd met many times before on friendly terms, but in his eyes Dikembe saw a challenge. "Is she safe with you, InDuna?"

The question sparked his ire, and Dikembe took another step forward. What business was it of his?

Olawu's eyes fluttered open and she cried out in pain.

"Olawu?" Both men spoke her name at the same time.

Olawu lifted her head towards Businge, and her face lit up. "Businge?"

"It's alright, Olawu." Businge smiled at her before returning his attention to Dikembe. "InDuna? Is she safe with you?"

Dikembe swallowed the curses in his throat and nodded. Businge began transferring Olawu into his arms, but she yelped when Dikembe touched her.

"What is it?" Dikembe asked.

"It's broken."

"I can carry her inside." It took all the willpower Dikembe possessed to agree. He did not want to cause her further injury. He led the way and Businge brought her into her room, laying her gently onto her bed.

When Businge stood to leave, Olawu grabbed his hand. "Please don't go."

Businge placed his hand over hers and whispered something to her. It hurt to watch their exchange. Olawu offered Businge a warm smile before releasing his hand.

Dikembe stopped him on the way out. "What did you whisper to her?"

Businge sighed. "I told her not to worry, and that her sister Ugami sends her love from Kanakam."

Dikembe looked from Olawu to Businge. "What happened?"

"Let's talk outside, InDuna."

They stepped out of the room, stopping just outside the door, and Dikembe crossed his arms. "Now tell me what happened?"

Businge stared at him. "Something or someone made Olawu leave Borimbe tonight. I do not know if it was you, or if it was something else, but I will say this. If Olawu comes to harm again, then you are to blame."

"Mind your words, Businge." Dikembe growled.

"You are her husband, InDuna. Protect her." Businge's eyes communicated more than Dikembe wished to see.

"Stay away from my wife."

Businge bowed his head. "As you wish, InDuna."

Dikembe watched him leave, sensing that Businge would do the exact opposite.

Chapter Twenty Six

Olawu thought she would go mad. She'd spent several weeks in bed, staring at nothing but the same ceiling and walls with only Naomi as her companion. Dikembe had kept his distance, much to Olawu's relief. They'd brought in an udokotela to help her, but he was inexperienced. She had to talk him through setting her bone properly.

She knew resting her arm was critical to proper healing. But resting her arm also meant she was stuck here. She had no plans to run again, at least not yet. Still, she wished she could visit the market with Naomi. She missed Businge, too. If she were honest, she hoped to run into him again, but he and his ubaba were likely working in Kanakam by now, anyway.

A knock sounded at her door, and Olawu grew still. "Who is it?"

"It's Dikembe. I've brought the udokotela."

Olawu's stomach twisted at the sound of his voice. She had not seen Dikembe in days. But he was only bringing the udokotela to her room. That was okay, right?

"Come in," she said. Dikembe entered with the same udokotela who had treated her before. He stood near the door as the udokotela examined her. Naomi stayed near the foot of the bed, waiting for instructions.

"How are you feeling, Olawu?" the udokotela asked.

"I am much better. I think we can remove the wrappings now."

"Let's have a look then." The udokotela pressed her forearm in several places, asking if she had swelling or pain. She didn't. He cut away her wrappings, which felt like heaven to her. She flexed her fingers and rotated her arm. The bone had healed nicely, as far as she could tell. The udokotela agreed.

"She is good as new!" The udokotela bowed to Dikembe.

"Thank you." Dikembe guided the udokotela to the door, but didn't follow him out. He looked at her, and she shrank back, suddenly feeling exposed. She pulled the covers up until they reached her neck.

Dikembe's eyes grew stern as he spoke. "Olawu."

She licked her lips and retreated further into her covers.

Dikembe sighed. "I am glad to see you recovered. But leaving Borimbe was a dangerous thing to do. If you insist on doing such foolish things, you should at least know how to properly defend yourself. I will give you a week to strengthen your arm. Then we will begin."

"Begin what?" Olawu asked.

"Your training. Naomi cannot protect you, and I cannot always be with you. You must learn proper defense."

Dikembe left swiftly after that, leaving Olawu to her thoughts.

OLAWU HELD THE SPEAR in her right hand and swung it around. She and Dikembe stood in one of the training rooms in the fortress. This one had a wide open space with weapons laid out on each side.

Dikembe had told her to select her weapon of choice. She had immediately chosen the spear. It looked very dangerous, and she liked the way it felt in her hand.

"Are you ready?" Dikembe asked. He himself was unarmed. Olawu wasn't sure what he planned to do with no weapon, but she wouldn't ask questions. She had stabbed him with a spear in her dreams many times. Why waste an opportunity?

"I'm ready!" Olawu stood with the spear pointed towards Dikembe. He began to approach her and she charged him. She pulled the spear back, then thrust it forward.

Dikembe deflected the spear with his hand, sending it flying across the room. Olawu's arm jerked to the side with it, and her hand burned where the wood chafed her skin. Dikembe continued his approach and Olawu stepped back.

He stopped an inch from her face and grabbed her hands. "Hold your weapon firmly, Olawu. I should not be able to knock it from your grasp so easily."

Olawu scowled and pulled her hands from his. She grabbed the fallen spear and positioned it in front of her again. "I'm ready."

Dikembe sighed and approached her. Olawu thrust forward again with the spear. This time Dikembe grabbed it and pulled her forward. Olawu stumbled into his chest, and he pushed her down. Her spear was in Dikembe's hands now.

He turned it towards her, the point inches from her chest. "You must study your opponent, Olawu. Do not expect me to act in the same way each time. Again!"

He returned her spear and helped her up. She took it and held it out in front of her.

Dikembe studied her a moment. "Wait, Olawu." He adjusted her stance, instructing her to widen the space between her feet and shift the placement of her hands. "You must be balanced with a spear, and flow with the natural movements of your body. You see?"

Olawu had to admit, she handled the spear much better. Dikembe was a good teacher. They practiced all afternoon, until they both glistened with sweat. Olawu found herself disappointed by how slow her movements were. She never struck Dikembe even once.

"That's enough for today." Dikembe took her spear. "We will continue tomorrow, and every day until you are as fit as any Dikebe warrior."

"Then will you have me join your army?" Olawu quipped.

Dikembe shook his head. "Women are not allowed to fight." His demeanor changed and his voice grew stiff. "I'll have food brought to your room. I'm sure you're hungry. Until tomorrow."

He left abruptly, leaving a panting Olawu standing by herself.

Chapter Twenty Seven

"Olawu, focus!" Dikembe growled as he pulled her forward. Olawu shifted and grabbed his arm, twisting it behind his back. He jerked forward and bent down, sending her over his back and to the ground, but Olawu quickly recovered and rolled away. She swept her leg out and underneath Dikembe's feet, but he flipped backwards before she ever touched him.

Olawu ran forward, excited for an opening, but Dikembe's foot connected with her jaw, sending her sprawling backwards. She fell to the ground, winded by the blow. Dikembe stood over her, concern etched in his face.

"Olawu? Are you alright? You're bleeding." She nodded and wiped the blood from her mouth. Dikembe offered her his hand and she took it, pulling him down and flipping him over. He landed hard on his back and Olawu laughed.

"You must never trust your opponent!" she teased.

Dikembe chuckled before rolling on top of her. "And you must take every opportunity you're given. Instead of laughing on the ground, you should have laughed on your feet."

Olawu tried to pull free from the weight of his body, but he held her fast. Their eyes met. Olawu's breathing changed as Dikembe's face hovered over hers. She saw the longing in his gaze. For a moment, she felt it, too. And then, the moment passed.

Dikembe grunted. "That's enough for today."

Olawu opened her mouth to reply, but he was gone before she could get the words out. They'd sparred together for months now, moving on from the spear once Olawu perfected her technique. She had considerable skill in the staff, bow, and even a curved sword. Every day, she looked forward to training. It took her mind off of her pain.

She missed her sisters and umama. She missed swimming in the Kanak river, and molding ugali into silly shapes before eating it with Kimani, and shooing the cattle on the hills outside their village. More than anything, she missed using her hands to heal, like Ubaba.

The people of Kanakam had rejected her the moment her ubaba died, but Borimbe was a poor replacement. Aside from her trips with Naomi, Olawu knew very little of Borimbe, and even less about its people. If her own village had not accepted her, what hope did she have of becoming an udokotela here? Sangoma's roots in Borimbe were deep, and still many rejected her or dismissed her gifts as a healer. Would they accept Olawu as anything more than Dikembe's wife?

Olawu sighed as she left the training grounds. Perhaps a talk with Sangoma would lift her spirits. The healer had a knack for soothing her with words that no medicine could ever match. Sickness of the soul and mind needed healing just as much as the body, and some things could not be fixed with bitter melon extract. What she lacked in surgical skill, Sangoma made up for in intuition and wisdom. Perhaps she could steer Olawu down the right path.

Olawu found Naomi, and they traveled down the streets of Borimbe until they arrived at the familiar curtain of beads. Olawu entered with Naomi behind her, calling out to the woman.

"Sangoma? Are you here?" Olawu heard voices in the back room and stopped to wait. She was surprised to see the familiar face of the udokotela.

"Mama, I will return with what you asked for. Please do not worry." The udokotela raised his eyebrows in surprise. "Mama

Olawu? What are you doing here?" His eyes traveled to her left arm, and worry shadowed his face.

"All is well," Olawu reassured him. "I came to see Sangoma for advice. She is your umama?"

He nodded awkwardly before making a hasty retreat. Olawu walked into the back room and greeted Sangoma with a smile.

"How are you today, Mama Olawu?" Sangoma asked. "Did you see my son on the way in?" Olawu nodded and grinned. Sangoma's face was bright with elation. "Foolish boy. Perhaps he is a little less foolish now that he has encountered you, Mama Olawu."

"Me?" Olawu crinkled her brow in confusion.

"He visits me often now, asking me for advice and herbal remedies. He told me he met InDuna Dikembe's wife and was ashamed at his own ignorance. He learned more from you in a few minutes than he's ever learned from that crusty old udokotela, eh? Perhaps there is hope for him yet. But I suppose every frog is a gazelle in the eyes of its mama."

Olawu laughed. "I am glad he is treating you well, Sangoma."

Sangoma smiled and extended her arm towards a mat. "Sit, Mama Olawu. Tell me what ails you today?"

Olawu's tears fell before her words could leave her mouth. "I miss my umama and my sisters, Sangoma."

"Oh child." Sangoma wiped Olawu's tears with her thumb. "When did you last see your family?"

"More than a year has passed."

"And the Dikebe are preparing for war. There is not much time for travel when conflict draws near. Here." Sangoma poured her a cup of steaming tea. Olawu sniffed the fragrance of rooibos root and smiled before sipping it. "What of the other thing, Mama Olawu? Have you spoken to InDuna Dikembe of your desire to become an udokotela?"

Olawu shook her head. "No. We have only just begun to . . ." Olawu hesitated, unsure of how to describe her relationship with Dikembe.

"To what? What were you going to say?"

"We have not seen eye to eye on many things. But we have been spending more time together lately."

"Do you think he will not agree to help you?"

"I do not know."

"If you want to go fast, go alone. If you want to go far, go together." Olawu smiled at the familiar proverb as Sangoma reached for her hand. "Try your best, Olawu. If you want something, you must fight for it, eh?"

Olawu nodded. Though her hatred of him had dulled, she still did not trust Dikembe. The last time she had asked him for something, he had broken his promise. But Sangoma was right. If she wished to be an udokotela, she would have to fight for it.

DIKEMBE POURED THE cool water from the basin over his head, drenching his dreads in the afternoon sun. His body felt as though it were on fire. He scooped up another bowl of water, pouring it onto his neck and letting it run down his bare chest. Olawu would be his undoing if he weren't careful.

"You okay Dikembe?" Hondo asked as he watched Dikembe pour another bowl of water over his head. "I did not think our practice drills were so challenging."

"It's nothing, Hondo." Dikembe splashed water in his face and rubbed his eyes.

"The men are waiting in the courtyard, InDuna." Hondo raised his forearm, and Dikembe tapped it.

"I'll be along shortly."

Dikembe dried in the sun before pulling his kaftan over his chest. Having Olawu so close had ignited the very feelings he'd been trying to bury. Had he imagined it, or did she feel the same? He wasn't sure. But he could not bear her rejection a second time. He would keep his distance until she said otherwise.

He joined his men in the courtyard. They had drilled with Hondo all morning and Dikembe in the afternoon. All of Borimbe buzzed with energy. War was coming. The Oloko had attacked another village, this one less than a day's journey from Borimbe. InDuna Dike had already summoned the Chiefs from all the Dikebe tribes. They would soon be heading into the valleys to seek out the Oloko and force them to withdraw to the eastern mountains.

Dikembe addressed his men, who stood with staffs and spears. "The Oloko have grown more bold in their attacks. You are Borimbe's defense. You will guard her with your lives."

"Yes, InDuna!" they replied.

"You will not cower, you will not falter, you will not draw back. You are the mighty warriors of the Dikebe tribe!"

"Yes, InDuna!" they shouted.

"You have trained well today. Go to your homes tonight. Eat with your families, sleep in your beds. And be ready. When InDuna Dike commands it, be ready."

"Yes, InDuna!"

Hondo signaled their dismissal and the men dispersed. He stood by Dikembe, watching him with a careful eye.

"Is there something bothering you, InDuna?"

"Olawu." Dikembe sighed.

"Have you not worked things out with her yet?" Hondo seemed surprised. "I thought you were doing alright?"

Dikembe shook his head. "She has never once asked for me, Hondo. She's been in Borimbe a year." He ran his hands through his hair.

"Perhaps you should show her that you wish to be summoned?" Hondo suggested.

"I tried that Hondo. It did not work."

"You?" Hondo laughed. "The great InDuna Dikembe tried something and failed? How many times did you try? Was it ten times she rejected you? Twenty?"

Dikembe hesitated before he spoke. "Once."

Hondo laughed. "Just one time, Dikembe? And you have given up? Olawu is a smart girl. You are hopeless."

"Hondo!"

Hondo gave Dikembe a serious look. "If you want something, you must fight for it. Is that not what your baba taught us long ago? Is that not what we're teaching our men even now? How can you act this way?"

Dikembe shook his head. "It is not the same thing."

"War is war." Hondo sniffed. "Whether it is for land, or for love, it is a fight that cannot be won in one try. I'm disappointed in you, Dikembe."

"So, what should I do?" Dikembe asked. "Hondo, I do not think she wants my affection. I do not wish to trouble her."

Hondo thought for a moment. "Well, you could give her a gift?"

"A gift?"

"Yes! Women love pretty things. Get her something nice from the market."

"I don't know," Dikembe hemmed.

"If you are afraid, I will go with you. That way, we can be sure it is something nice. Aich, you are truly hopeless, Dikembe."

"Alright." Dikembe nodded. "After I train with Olawu tomorrow, we will go to the market."

Chapter Twenty Eight

Olawu couldn't concentrate as she sparred with Dikembe. Her talk with Sangoma had left her tossing and turning all night. She needed to speak with Dikembe, but her stomach filled with a thousand tsetse flies whenever she saw him. Never had she felt more nervous.

She wasn't following through with her punches, and Dikembe tripped her several times. Her movements were sluggish, and so were her reactions. He dodged another swing and flipped her over. Olawu lay on her back, too flustered to rise.

"Dikembe!" She finally conceded. "I cannot fight with you today."

He sat beside her on the ground.

Olawu took deep, slow breaths to calm her rapidly beating heart. Dikembe looked down at her, face pensive. *Be brave, Olawu. Now is your chance.* "Dikembe, if I wished to become an udokotela, would you help me?"

His eyes seemed to relax, and he nodded. "If that is what you wish."

That was not the answer she expected. "You would help me?"

"It would not be easy. There has never been a woman udokotela in all of the Dikebe tribes, but if that is what you wish, I will help you."

Olawu's heart stirred at his words.

"Olawu?" He spoke her name quietly. "Today will be our last training session."

She sat up. "Why?"

"War is coming. I must focus my energy on training my men. Hondo has divided the work with me so I can train with you, but now it is time to do my duty. And." He looked at her. "You are as capable as any Dikebe. When you are focused, that is."

Olawu smiled sheepishly. "I did not sleep well last night." She stared at the floor to keep from gazing into Dikembe's eyes. "I will miss our training together."

Dikembe nodded and stood, helping Olawu to her feet. He looked as though he might say something to her, but changed his mind.

She risked looking up into his face as she stood. He looked back at her, his dark eyes searching. She tilted her chin up, and he placed his hands on her shoulders. Her pulse quickened at his touch, and she swallowed, but she didn't move away. Dikembe lowered his head, and she closed her eyes.

"InDuna!" Hondo's booming voice echoed down the hall, shattering the reverence of the moment. Dikembe released her and stepped away.

Hondo walked into the room and extended his forearm to Dikembe. Cheeks burning, Olawu left the room as quickly as her legs would carry her.

DIKEMBE GLARED AT HONDO, tapping his forearm more forcefully than necessary, but Hondo didn't seem to notice.

"Are you ready, InDuna?" Hondo looked over him. "It does not look like you did much work today. You are not even sweating."

"Your timing, Hondo," Dikembe muttered and walked out of the training room. Hondo shrugged and followed him.

OLAWU

OLAWU STARED AT THE sky, oblivious to Naomi's questions as they walked through the market streets. It was cloudy, and the breeze flowing through the buildings brought all the sweet and savory smells of Borimbe's tastiest treats to her nose.

She remembered laying on her back with her ubaba, staring up at the clouds on days like this. They used to imagine what it would be like to live in the sky, hopping from cloud to cloud, soaring with the birds. Then he would lift her high into the air, turning her to and fro as she held out her arms.

Her heart had felt lighter than air in those moments. She had felt something similar with Dikembe this morning. When he had lowered himself to kiss her, her heart had lifted. She didn't think it was possible to feel this way with him. But after all these months of training, something had changed. She could become an udokotela here and make her home in Borimbe. And perhaps, she could make her home with Dikembe.

"Mama Olawu?" Naomi was finally able to cut through Olawu's thoughts.

"Yes, Naomi?"

"Would you like me to fetch you something to eat? You haven't eaten since this morning."

"I'm not really hungry." Olawu smiled. "Naomi?"

"Yes, Mama Olawu?"

"Do you think Dikembe would share a meal in my room if I asked?"

Naomi looked shocked for a moment. "You wish to invite InDuna Dikembe to your room?"

"Yes. I think so. Do you not think he would come?"

Naomi chuckled. "Mama Olawu, he would let nothing stop him."

"Naomi!" Olawu laughed. "You're very funny."

Naomi stifled a grin. "What would you like to serve InDuna?"

"Something simple." Olawu shrugged. "Let's go to my favorite spot and pick up some roasted fowl." Naomi nodded in agreement, and they weaved through the streets until their noses met with the savory scent of roasted meats. Olawu was pleasantly surprised to find Businge sitting in one of the stools.

"Olawu!" He greeted her, standing to his feet.

"Businge!" She rushed over to him, greeting him with a hug. Businge smiled at the warm greeting and offered her a stool.

"I was hoping I would see you here today." He grinned. "Would you like to share a meal with me?"

"I'm only here to order food to go, Businge. How long have you been in Borimbe?"

"Two days. I leave tomorrow to return to Kanakam. I've come here every day, hoping to see you in the market. I've missed you, Olawu."

She smiled. "I missed you too, Businge. Is there any news from my family?"

"Yes! They are all doing well. I have a package for you from Ugami."

"Where is it? Did you bring it?" Olawu's eyes traveled over Businge, searching.

"I'll give it to you in just a moment. But Olawu?" Businge took her hands in his. "I must ask you something?"

His expression changed, and Olawu's breath caught in her throat. "Yes?" Businge's calloused hands felt warm and comforting against her palms. They reminded her of her ubaba.

"When I left you in Borimbe last, you were badly hurt. I hated to leave you, but I hoped InDuna Dikembe would care for you. Please tell me honestly. Were you running from him that night?"

Olawu looked down at Businge's hands. The question had caught her off guard. She was not sure how to reply. "Businge, I . . ."

"It's okay, Olawu. I think I already know the answer, but I wished to hear it from you. If you are afraid of InDuna Dikembe, I can protect you."

"I'm not afraid of Dikembe." Olawu shook her head.

Businge nodded as he continued to rub her fingers. "Why do you no longer wear his ring?"

Olawu's cheeks flushed. "Oh. I lost it."

"I see." Businge looked up at her, and their eyes met. "Olawu? If you wish to remain with InDuna Dikembe, I will not interfere." He squeezed her hands and pulled her closer. "But if you cannot bear it, I am here. You are not alone in Borimbe."

"Businge, that is kind of you to say-" Olawu began.

"Please do not misunderstand me." Businge's eyes grew soft. "I would do anything for you. Even if you do not feel the same way, know that I am your friend. If you come to me, I will not turn you away. And I would not ask for anything you cannot give. If you wished to stay with me in Borimbe, or return to Kanakam, or even go to some other place, I am here for you. Always."

Olawu's eyes glistened with tears at Businge's sincerity. "Thank you, Businge. You have always been so kind to me."

"I wish the world were kind to you. I regret that I cannot make it so. I have one final question, Olawu, if you can bear it?"

"Yes?"

"Do you love Dikembe?"

Olawu shook her head as tears fell from her eyes. "I don't know, Businge."

"Then there is hope for me." He smiled and stood. "I should head back. But first, as promised, this is for you." Businge removed a parcel from the travel bag strapped across his shoulder and handed it to her. "If you wish to reply, I will wait for you at the eastern gate tomorrow morning." Businge took her hand and kissed it. "Be well, Olawu."

DIKEMBE SMILED AT THE tiny carved box in his hand. Hondo had helped him pick out the golden barrette inside, but the box had been his idea. It was orange and red with a bridge carved on the top. He hoped it would be the first step in building a bridge between he and Olawu.

"InDuna Dikembe, it will take me a little time for the barrette. Would you like to wait?" The merchant gave him an apologetic look. Dikembe was finally getting the broken blue lotus barrette fixed so he could return it to Olawu. He had hoped it would be ready by day's end.

He looked to Hondo, and his friend shrugged. "I will do the evening training, InDuna."

Dikembe nodded his thanks and tapped Hondo's forearm, then set the box down in front of the jewel maker. "Wrap them all together when it's done. I'll be back later."

The jewel maker nodded and continued his work. Dikembe idly roamed the marketplace, thinking about Olawu. She spent a lot of time with Naomi in the market. Buying and selling still seemed like such a novel thing to her. He was glad she enjoyed it so much.

"Buy a flower for your love?" A merchant shoved a purple lily in front of him. Dikembe shook his head and was waving the merchant away when he caught sight of Naomi. She sat near a small shop with her head leaned against the wall. If she was at the market, that meant Olawu was here, too.

Dikembe returned to the flower merchant. "I'll take the flowers."

He bought as many as he could carry and began searching for Olawu. He spotted her at a table near the shop, sitting next to Businge. It irritated him to see her with him, but when Businge held her hands in his, Dikembe froze.

He watched their exchange, stunned by the intimate way Businge leaned in towards her. Olawu did not pull away from him. Not once. Not even when he kissed her hand.

Dikembe's mouth went dry, and he crumpled the flowers in his fist. He remembered the way Businge had carried Olawu home. The way she had rested her head on his shoulder. How she'd clung to him, begging him not to leave her. Dikembe let the flowers fall to the ground and walked away.

He needed to clear his head. He needed to think. He needed to wrap his hands around Businge's throat. It had taken months for Olawu to open up to him just a small amount. It seemed whatever they'd shared this morning was already forgotten.

Chapter Twenty Nine

Olawu tried on another kaftan before settling on her original choice. It seemed silly, fussing so much over what she wore, but if she was going to make an effort, she may as well put everything into it. Her original choice was a royal blue kaftan with golden embroidery along the collar and hem. Naomi had braided her hair and decorated it with gold clasps. Olawu considered adding a blue lotus flower to the crown of her head, but thought it would be too much. Tonight would be a small step.

She looked at the silver platter on the bed, filled with fresh fruit and roasted meats from the market. A jar of jollof rice sat in the center, rounding out the meal. Naomi entered the room and Olawu's breath caught in her throat.

"Is he coming?" Olawu asked, her stomach in knots.

"Yes, Mama Olawu. He's on his way now."

"Thank you, Naomi." Olawu smiled and began fiddling with the placement of the food on the platter. She hoped Dikembe would enjoy it as much as she did. A brief knock at the door sent her heart into a flurry.

Naomi smiled and opened the door, bowing to Dikembe as he entered. Olawu smiled shyly as he walked in. He looked around the room, seeming agitated as he moved from the window to the foot of the bed.

"Hello, InDuna Dikembe." Olawu greeted him, bowing with her knees to the ground and her hands above her head.

"Olawu."

There was something different in his voice. It made her even more nervous as she stood. "Thank you for coming, InDuna. Please sit."

Naomi offered Dikembe a stool placed by the table in the room. Dikembe sat, and Olawu joined him. Naomi brought the tray and placed it in the center of the table before taking her place at the foot of the bed.

"I hope you'll like it, InDuna. The roasted fowl is from my favorite place at the market, and I made the rice myself."

"Why am I here, Olawu?"

Dikembe's intense gaze landed on her, and Olawu's courage dissipated. "I wanted to tell you something, InDuna Dikembe. Something unexpected has happened."

Dikembe cut her off. "I've already figured it out."

"You have?"

"Yes. Though some may call it cruel."

Olawu frowned. His tone was angry and hostile. "Are you alright, InDuna?"

"You've never invited me into your room. Not once, Olawu. And now here you are, dressed in blue and gold, attempting to placate me with smooth words and a sweet face. Pretending to be innocent."

"Innocent in what, InDuna?" She gave him a puzzled look.

"I saw you with Businge today." Dikembe's eyes were accusing as he glared at her. "I saw how you clung to each other."

"Dikembe, you misunderstand-" Olawu began.

"Do I? Then clear up the misunderstanding for me, Olawu. What was it that Businge told you?"

Olawu's cheeks burned with heat, and she found herself at a loss for words.

"Your hesitation is all the proof I need. If you do not want me in your bed, fine. I can bear it. But I will not allow you to run to someone else's."

"Dikembe!" Olawu's voice returned.

"From the very beginning I made one thing clear to you, Olawu. You belong to me."

Olawu's temper ignited and she stood. "Have I not made *myself* clear, Dikembe? I belong to no one!"

Dikembe stood and swept his hand across the table, sending the platter and all its contents flying. "You seem to have forgotten your place, Olawu. So I shall remind you. I hope you enjoyed your visit to the market today for it will be your last. There will be no more visits with Businge or anyone else. You will remain within the walls of this fortress. If you wish to leave your room, I will know about it. I will know your every move. If you fail to obey me in this-"

"Then what?" Olawu scoffed. "You will beat me? Break me? Do what you will, Dikembe. I will not be confined by you! If you wish to punish me, I will gladly bear it!"

Dikembe growled. "Not you. Naomi."

Olawu's eyes widened in shock and she looked towards Naomi. The girl's eyes flashed with fear as she looked from Olawu to Dikembe.

"You wouldn't." Olawu couldn't keep the tremble from her voice.

"Let me be clear, Olawu. If you step foot outside of this fortress, Naomi will be punished for it."

"How could you do such a thing?" Olawu cried. "Naomi has been nothing but loyal to you!"

"Then control yourself. If you do as I say, no harm will come to her."

"Isilo esikhulu!" Olawu screamed. "Get out!" She tossed a piece of meat at him, followed by another piece of food and whatever else her hands found.

How could he be so cruel?

DIKEMBE LEFT THE ROOM in a storm, calling for two of his guards. "Gebo! Yurin!"

The two men emerged from the shadows. Gebo's eyes traveled to the door, then back to Dikembe.

"You will watch this door night and day. When Mama Olawu leaves, and when she returns, you will report it to me."

"Should we stop her, InDuna?" Gebo asked.

"No." Dikembe frowned as Olawu's curses came through the door. "For now, just watch."

"Yes, InDuna."

Dikembe took one last look at the door and walked away.

Chapter Thirty

"Mama Olawu?" Naomi placed her hand on Olawu's shoulder, and she looked up. Naomi's stricken face belied the calm in her voice. "Mama Olawu, please rest?"

Olawu nodded, and Naomi guided her to her bed and removed the clasps from her hair. "He would not do it, would he Naomi?" Olawu asked. "If I left the fortress, he would not really hurt you, would he?"

Naomi shook her head. "I've never seen InDuna Dikembe this upset before, Mama Olawu. Would you disobey him?"

Olawu saw the fear in Naomi's eyes. She wanted to comfort her, but Olawu could not lie. "I cannot be a slave to him, Naomi. I do not wish to see you hurt, but I cannot promise I will obey him."

Naomi nodded and kissed Olawu on the cheek. "Rest now, Mama Olawu. I will clean up this mess."

Olawu closed her eyes, listening to Naomi's soft sounds as she tiptoed through the room and eventually out to the kitchen. She took in a deep breath, hoping sleep would take her in its arms, but it eluded her. She stared out in the darkness, heart torn in two.

How had things gone so wrong? It started as a misunderstanding, but Dikembe acted as he always did. He still thought of her as his property.

Olawu sat up, remembering the letter from Ugami. "Naomi?" She called out into the dark, but Naomi had not returned from the kitchen yet. Olawu found a candle and lit it, then opened the parcel Businge had brought for her. Her breath caught as she removed the cream-colored tunic her ubaba used to wear when he worked at the healing hut. She found a letter from her sister nestled in the center.

Olawu cradled the tunic in her arms. It still smelled faintly of Ubaba. She put it on, wishing that the arms of the tunic still held her ubaba. It landed close to her ankles. It had barely reached Ubaba's knees. Olawu stifled a sob and opened Ugami's letter:

Sister

I hope you are well in Borimbe. Umama is doing fine. She has some pain, especially on rainy days, but is otherwise in good spirits. Kimani grows more beautiful every day. I wonder how you managed to do so much work without collapsing. I can barely haul the laundry to the river.

I miss you so much, Olawu. Businge has been very kind to us. He visits with us every day when he is here in Kanakam. He is so handsome, too! He promised if I wrote to you, he would bring you my letter when he returned to Borimbe. You know I cannot give a letter to anyone in Kanakam. I am so glad Ubaba taught us to read and write. I hope you are able to write me back.

Do not worry about us. We miss you, but we are well cared for. Since the Choosing, InDuna Dikembe has kept a guard posted by our hut. He is very nice, and he helps me take the laundry to the river. I really do not know how you did it, Olawu.

Batiko came by a few times, but the guard chased him away.

Every week, food is delivered from the citadel. I ask them often about you, but they never tell me anything. All we knew before Businge arrived was that you were in InDuna

Dikembe's care. I did not even know you were not in Kanakam.

Tell me all about Borimbe? And InDuna Dikembe? Is he kind to you? He must be. I already know he is handsome.

Umama sends her love, and Ubaba's tunic. She thought it would bring you comfort. Be well, Olawu.

Love, Ugami

Please, please write me back, Sister!

Olawu could not hold her cries in. She missed her family more than words could express. But for Ugami's sake, she would try.

She began writing a reply, remembering that Businge promised to wait for her by the gate in the morning. She sealed her letter with a kiss and set it on the table beside her. Naomi still had not returned from the kitchen.

Olawu decided to go find her, thinking it would be better for Naomi to go to Businge. That way Olawu wouldn't put her in danger. She put on her sandals and left her room, but was startled by the presence of the two guards standing outside her door.

"What are you doing here?" Olawu narrowed her eyes at them. The guards looked at each other, but said nothing. "Did InDuna Dikembe send you?"

"Yes, Mama Olawu." One of the guards nodded. "Please, do not mind us. Go on your way." Olawu headed towards the kitchen, stealing wary glances behind her to see if the guards followed. They didn't.

Olawu continued down the dark hall, wondering what kept Naomi. She was likely eating. Olawu had discovered that Naomi ate most of her meals at night, if she ate at all.

Whispered voices rose from the kitchen and Olawu paused. She recognized Naomi's voice and tiptoed forward.

"Yero, we can't!"

"Naomi, I love you. Please do not be afraid."

Olawu peeked her head into the kitchen. Naomi stood near one of the stoves, arms locked around the neck of a guard. His hands rested on her waist as he bent down to kiss her. Olawu's mouth rounded, and she pulled her head back and out of sight.

She tiptoed back to her room, glaring at the guards when she passed them. As she sat on her bed, she thought of Naomi and her lover, wondering how long the two had been meeting in secret. She looked at the letter for her sister and sighed. She would wait for Naomi to return and then ask her to take the letter to Businge.

That's what she intended to do. But when Olawu opened her eyes again it was morning. She sat up in a rush as the early dawn peeked through her window.

"Naomi?" Olawu called for the girl, but she didn't answer. She rounded the bed, but Naomi was not in her usual spot. She wasn't anywhere in the room at all. Naomi would not have spent the whole night with the guard, would she?

Olawu looked out at the window. How long would Businge wait for her?

If she took one of the horses, she could sneak out quickly and return before morning drills began. So long as she wasn't caught, no harm would come to Naomi.

Olawu swallowed a lump in her throat as she thought of Ugami's words. Dikembe really had taken care of her family. She couldn't believe he would actually hurt Naomi. Perhaps he had only spoken the words in anger.

There was no telling when Businge would return to Borimbe. Olawu made her decision. She would sneak out, quickly and quietly, then hurry back. She still wore Ubaba's tunic, but there was no time to change. She left her room, letter safely tucked in the pocket of the tunic, and walked towards the training room.

Once the guards were out of range, she hurried outside and took the long way around to the stables. She glared at the chocolate mare, passing it over for the small, brown and white that suited her far better.

She pulled herself up and trotted out, waiting for the morning guards to clear the courtyard before making her escape. She didn't know if they knew to look for her, but she couldn't take any chances.

Chapter Thirty One

Dikembe walked the halls of the fortress in a foul mood, plagued by his last encounter with Olawu. Things could not have gone worse between them.

At the sight of Hondo's smiling face, Dikembe nearly turned the other way.

"InDuna!" Hondo shouted and raised his arm in greeting. "How did things go? Well, yes?"

Dikembe scowled and tapped his arm. "Hondo, you know nothing of women at all."

"What happened?" Hondo frowned. "Did she not like your gift?"

Dikembe opened his mouth to speak, but one of the fortress guards rushed forward.

"InDuna? Come quick! It's Yero!"

Hondo and Dikembe both took off running towards the courtyard. InDuna Dike stood with his arms crossed in the center. Two figures crouched before him, huddled against each other. Dikembe recognized their faces.

"Yero?" Dikembe looked from Yero's bloodied face to Naomi's.

"He was caught at the southern gate deserting." The guard spat at Yero's feet.

"InDuna Dike! Please, I can explain." Yero's words were silenced by a kick to the face. Dikembe reached for Naomi, but she flinched at his touch.

"Forgive me, InDuna Dikembe!" she cried. "Please don't blame Yero. It was my fault. He was only trying to protect me."

"Protect you from what?" Dikembe asked.

The sound of approaching hooves sent his eyes towards the entrance. Olawu met his gaze, and she halted her approach. Dikembe flexed his jaw. It had not even been a day, and she'd already disobeyed him.

Olawu's gaze shifted to Naomi, then grew wide. She continued forward, her gaze fierce as she dismounted and came straight for him.

"Is this the kind of man you are?" she asked. "How could you do this?"

Dikembe grabbed Olawu's hand before it reached his face. "Hondo, take Mama Olawu to her room." Hondo nodded and pulled a screaming Olawu away.

InDuna Dike spat. "You know how I feel about deserters, Dikembe. But he's your guard, so I'll leave it to you."

His father left, and Dikembe raised his head to the sky. Olawu misunderstood, but it did not matter. He let out a flustered breath and glared at Yero. "You faltered."

Yero spat blood from his mouth. "I fell in love, InDuna."

Dikembe's laugh was bitter. "The Oloko are bearing down on us. Every day they threaten Borimbe. We should be training our men to fight, not killing them for making stupid mistakes." Dikembe took a sword from one of the guards and pointed it at Yero's neck.

"Do what you must, InDuna. I could not leave her to you."

"Fool!" Dikembe raised the sword above his head. As he brought it down, Naomi screamed, shielding Yero's body with hers. Dikembe stilled his sword.

"Please spare him, InDuna!" Naomi cried. "He would not have left if it weren't for me. I told him I was afraid of you. I should not have said such things. It's my fault. Please!"

Dikembe tossed the sword. "Is this what you think of me, Naomi? Yero? Do you all think me a monster? You who have known me since I was a boy? You truly have no faith in me?"

"Please!" Naomi cried.

Dikembe clenched his jaw and hauled Yero to his feet. "Go. Take your horse and Naomi and leave Borimbe. Do not show your face to me again. If you return to Borimbe, I will not hesitate to kill you."

Yero nodded and lifted his forearm. Dikembe cast a glance towards Naomi, then walked away.

HONDO WAS NOT SURE what to do with Olawu. She was much stronger than he remembered, and she fought like a devil. It took all of his strength, plus the two guards outside her door to subdue her.

"Mama Olawu, I do not wish to hurt you." He pleaded with her for the hundredth time. "Please, do not try to leave."

"Do not try to stop me!" Olawu punched Hondo in the jaw and attacked Gebo. He held her at bay with his arms, but she head-butted him, bloodying his nose. "Where is Dikembe?"

"Mama Olawu, please!" Hondo pulled her off of Gebo with Yurin's help.

"Let me go!" Olawu screamed as the men pulled her back and forced her into a stool.

"My nose!" Gebo moaned as he tried to stop the blood. He stood up straighter as Dikembe entered the room. "InDuna!"

All eyes turned to Dikembe as he made his way towards Olawu.

"Isilo esikhulu! Monster!" Olawu rose to strike him, but Dikembe caught her arm in the air. He pulled her towards him and kissed her hard. Olawu tried to push him, but he kept a strong hold on her. She wrenched her face away, snarling and screaming at him.

"Say what you will of me, Olawu. I know you hate me. You think me a monster. So why should I not act as one?"

Olawu screamed as Dikembe forced her face towards him, kissing her again.

"InDuna!" Hondo cried in protest, then grabbed Dikembe by his shoulder, pulling him away from her. "What are you doing?"

"Taking what's mine!" Dikembe snarled.

He grabbed Olawu and tossed her onto the bed, but again Hondo pulled him away, turning him around. "This isn't like you, Dikembe. Is this about Yero?"

Olawu stood, the rage on her face matching the scowl on Dikembe's. "What have you done with Naomi?"

"Consider her dead!"

Olawu raised a hand to her mouth. "What did you do to her?" She struck his back with her fists, and Dikembe turned, grabbing her wrists. Their breath came in pants as they glared at one another. "Let me go!" Olawu demanded through clenched teeth.

"Not until I'm satisfied." He kissed her a third time.

"InDuna!" Hondo tried to pull him away, but Dikembe would not release his hold on her.

"Dikembe!"

Dikembe released Olawu as the stern voice of Mama Dhakiya filled the room. He turned to her, a question on his face. "Mama? Why are you here?"

"I came for Olawu. I saw her taken from the courtyard. What have you done, Dikembe?"

All the air left the room at Mama Dhakiya's words. Hondo looked from Dikembe to Olawu. Something had gone horribly wrong.

DIKEMBE LOWERED HIS head, deflated by the horror on his mama's face. Did she believe him to be a monster, too?

He looked back at Olawu, who glared at him with red, swollen eyes. He recognized her anger, her hatred. But in the heat of her gaze, he saw something else. Fear.

Dikembe took a step towards her, but she flinched and backed away. His eyes traveled to her wrists, purpled with bruising. Guilt swirled in his chest, forcing him out of the room with his eyes to the ground. He could not lift his head for the shame.

Chapter Thirty Two

Hondo silently watched as Borimbe's finest warriors finished their drills. Dikembe stood beside him, giving instructions as the men fought in pairs.

"Watch your stance, Olo! Use your back leg to absorb the force of the blow, Egawa! Strike harder, Mubaba!"

Hondo cut in after a few more minutes. Dikembe would work them to the ground at this rate. "That's enough for today."

The men bowed before replacing their weapons and heading out. Hondo turned to Dikembe. "Are we going to talk about what happened this morning, InDuna?"

Dikembe shook his head.

Hondo waited a moment. "Dikembe?"

"I lost my temper."

"You lost control of yourself." Hondo sighed and shook his head. "What about Yero and Naomi?"

"I sent them away."

Hondo grunted. "InDuna Dike will not like that. Damn Yero and his heart. And with Naomi, of all people. Is that why you were angry? Because he took Naomi away?"

Dikembe shook his head. "It was my fault, Hondo. Yero, Naomi, all of it. I lost my temper with Olawu, and I threatened Naomi to get back at her. Naomi told Yero, and he took her away to keep her from harm."

Hondo shook his head. "What a mess. I take it Olawu does not know?"

"She thinks I beat Naomi to punish her for leaving. She knows nothing of Yero."

Hondo sighed. "Yero knew the consequences of his actions. Why did you not kill him? Because you felt responsible?"

"I would have. But Naomi came between us."

"Ach! Could you not beat him, instead? Yero is our best tracker."

"You know he cannot return to us, Hondo."

Hondo nodded sadly. "What will you do about Olawu?"

Dikembe lowered his head. "I will let her go."

"Go where?"

"Back to Kanakam if she wishes. Or perhaps she can remain here as an udokotela. She is already more skilled than the ones in Borimbe."

Hondo grew quiet as he studied Dikembe. He scratched his beard. "InDuna, would it not be better to speak to her? Work out your misunderstandings?"

"She's in love with someone else, Hondo. I no longer wish to stand in her way. I've lost the right to."

"Ach! No wonder you have gotten nowhere with Olawu. You're so pigheaded!"

"Pigheaded?"

"Even if she loves another man, do you think it is right to hide from her? Be brave, Dikembe. Let her tell you where her heart lies."

"It does not lie with me."

"You are hopeless, InDuna." Hondo shook his head and exhaled. The hairs on the back of his neck stood on end, and he grabbed his spear.

"What is it, Hondo?"

He pointed to the trees beyond the courtyard. A tall, lanky figure approached, limping towards the entrance. Hondo squinted and lowered his spear. "I do not believe it! It is Yero."

Dikembe clenched his jaw and unsheathed his sword. He approached Yero with a scowl as he raised his sword to his neck.

"Did I not make myself clear?" Dikembe growled.

Yero blinked. "You did."

"Give me one good reason why I should not gut you where you stand?"

Yero looked up at Dikembe. "Because you are my brother."

"That will not save your life, Yero."

"I did not come here for myself, InDuna. I came here for you."

Dikembe lowered his sword and stared.

"You are my brother in arms, InDuna. My friend. I know what it means, showing my face again. But I could not leave things between us as they are."

"What about Naomi?" Dikembe asked.

"We are in agreement. InDuna, you have never given us reason to believe you would harm us. But I never thought I could leave your side until I fell in love. And now I know that I would do anything for her. I thought it would be the same between you and Olawu. Because I faltered, I assumed you would, too." Yero dropped to his knees and bowed before Dikembe with both his forearms raised. "Forgive me, InDuna."

Dikembe glared at him. "Do you think you can win me over with words, Yero?"

"Either kill me or accept me as your brother, InDuna. I will accept nothing else."

"Bastard!" Dikembe spat. "You have no idea the trouble you caused today." Dikembe sighed. "Hondo? You'll get your wish. Yero, get up!"

Yero lifted his eyes.

"You wish to be my brother? You'll have to fight for it."

Hondo grinned as Dikembe stormed towards the training grounds. "Come, Yero!" He pushed Yero forward, laughing as he followed behind them.

OLAWU SNIFFED AND SMOOTHED out her ubaba's tunic, trying hard to calm her rapidly beating heart, and failing. A knock at her door sent it straight to the ceiling. Her hands trembled as she searched the room for a weapon. The doors opened, and Olawu whirled around.

"Mama Olawu?"

Olawu set down the clay pot in her hands and rushed towards Naomi. She looked haggard and miserable in her bloodied, tattered kitenge. "Naomi!"

She took her gently by the hand and led her towards the bed. Naomi resisted when Olawu tried to make her sit. Instead, Naomi fell prostrate to the ground and laid her head on Olawu's feet.

"Please forgive me, Mama Olawu. I did not mean to cause so much trouble."

Olawu shook her head and joined Naomi on the floor. "No, Naomi. This isn't your fault. InDuna Dikembe is to blame, not you!"

"No! Please do not blame him. It is my fault. I should not have run away with Yero."

"You ran away?"

Naomi nodded. "I did not know they would mark Yero a deserter if he left Borimbe with me. When they found us, they beat us and dragged us back here. I'm so sorry, Mama Olawu. It was selfish of me to leave."

"You weren't beaten by InDuna Dikembe?"

"No. I should never have told Yero what InDuna Dikembe said."

Bile rose in Olawu's throat. "What happened to you in the courtyard?"

"InDuna Dikembe spared Yero and let us go, but we could not leave things as they were. We had to make things right. I'm so sorry, Mama Olawu."

Naomi cried at her feet and Olawu stroked her hair. "It's alright, Naomi." As Naomi wept on the floor, Olawu let her own tears fall.

Chapter Thirty Three

D ikembe paced in front of his warriors, inspecting their armor as he passed by. "Tonight, the Chiefs of all the surrounding Dikebe tribes will be dining at the fortress here in Borimbe. Their safety lies in your hands."

"Yes, InDuna!"

Dikembe stared long and hard at one man, lifting a line of straw from his shoulder. "Do not falter tonight."

Yero nodded. "I will not fail, InDuna."

Dikembe nodded and Hondo dismissed them.

"I see Yero has accepted his demotion graciously," Hondo mused.

Dikembe sighed. "Perhaps, in time, he can return to us. But the men know he is a deserter. He has to be punished to discourage other such acts."

"To be sure." Hondo nodded. "How's your shoulder?"

"It's fine." Dikembe scowled. Even beaten half to death, Yero had put up a good fight. He'd been sore for days afterward.

"The jewel maker from the market brought the box and the barrettes we purchased. It seems you forgot them at his shop. I left them in your room."

Dikembe ignored Hondo's exaggerated sigh.

"Have you spoken to Olawu?"

"Have you nothing better to do than to stick your nose into my problems?"

"You are my life, InDuna. I cannot be satisfied until you are." Hondo bowed in jest, but Dikembe again ignored him.

"Keep your wits about you tonight. If the Oloko were going to strike Borimbe, tonight would be the night to do it."

THE ENTIRE FORTRESS was on high alert. The kitchen hummed with activity, and a large number of guards patrolled the halls. Dikembe and his personal guard would be the only ones allowed in the banquet hall, aside from the Chiefs themselves, their personal attendants, and the kitchen workers.

Dikembe kept to one end of the dining hall, close to his baba, while Hondo guarded the other. Dikembe noticed that the Chief of Kanakam was not present. It seemed the rumors that Chief Umdaka lay on his deathbed were true. His son Zulu would take his place, but he was not present either.

"InDuna Dike!" Chief Ugogi of Simabwe greeted them. His earrings swung freely from his low-lying lobes. "Simabwe is ready and willing to take on the Oloko. We can pledge thirty men to take the fight to the plains."

"Thirty?" Chief Kimala of Oraji scoffed. "Oraji is half the size of Simabwe and we plan to pledge one hundred men!"

"Should we really be discussing war so close to masika?" Chief Oaxaco of Shimbu shook his head. Long, red tribal tattoos marked his skin from his head to his bare chest. "The rainy season is nearly upon us, and the eastern plains are prone to flooding and mudslides. InDuna Dike, I do not think it would be wise to take on the Oloko at this time."

"So what do you propose we do? Wait for them to slaughter us in our sleep?" Chief Kimala banged his fist on the table. "We must drive them out of their lands and push them so far east they fall into the sea!"

Chief Pusaka of Chigami chimed in. "The Oloko all but wiped out my village. My baba, Chief Pugata, was slaughtered in his sleep. I say we strike the Oloko now before they attack another village!"

Chief Zigula of Ingala took that moment to speak up. "What of the plans you spoke of, InDuna Dike? You said you had a solution for driving out the Oloko?"

"Yes." InDuna Dike nodded. "We've established Kanakam as a crucial village for maintaining control over the water supply to the valleys. My son Dikembe can speak more on this matter. Dikembe?"

Dikembe pulled his attention away from the young girl pouring water into cups. He did not recognize her as one of the regular kitchen servants. He motioned for Hondo to keep an eye on her as he addressed the other chiefs.

"As you all know, the Kanak River flows from the Kanagari mountain ranges all the way through the eastern and western valleys, supplying water to both the Dikebe and the Oloko. With the help of our best craftsmen, we have devised a way to reroute the Kanak river so that it flows only towards the western tribes."

"How will you do that?" Chief Zigula asked, stroking his long beard.

"We're building a dam at the base of the Kanagari mountain range, which rests just North of Kanakam. We're also burying conduits and aqueducts that will lead water to reservoirs throughout the Dikebe tribes."

"You can do that?" Chief Oaxaco looked incredulous. "How ingenious!"

"How soon will construction be complete?" Chief Ugogi asked.

"The dam should be completed in another four or five months. Once it's done, we will be able to limit the water supply of the Kanak river, and with the conduits in place we can fill the reservoirs one by one. It will take some time to build reservoirs in every village."

"Yes." InDuna Dike cut in. "We will need to prioritize who will get their reservoirs first. And we will need men to assist with construction and digging, in addition to warriors. I am grateful for your continued support." InDuna Dike made eye contact with each of the chiefs, communicating his expectations.

"InDuna!" Hondo called out to Dikembe just as the young servant girl pulled a dagger from her kaftan. Dikembe guarded his baba with his body, preventing her from stabbing InDuna Dike in the chest. The dagger sliced into Dikembe's shoulder, but Hondo appeared at Dikembe's side in moments, breaking the girl's wrist and forcing her to release the dagger.

The girl howled in pain, but that did not stop her from cursing InDuna Dike and all the tribes of Dikebe before Hondo silenced her with a blade.

"Baba, are you alright?" Dikembe asked.

InDuna Dike grunted and stood. He glared at the body on the ground and spat. "Damn the Oloko. Sending in a woman to do a man's job. How did she get past the gates of Borimbe? We'll need to search for others. She could not have entered without help."

Dikembe began to speak, but paused as a searing pain shot through his shoulder. He gripped the table and groaned. "We'll send scouts to." He shook his head, unable to get the words out. His mind grew sluggish, and he lost his grip on the table.

"InDuna?" Hondo reached out to him as he stumbled. "Get an udokotela. Now!"

Hondo helped him to the ground, examining his arm. The wound was not very deep, but the blood dripping from his shoulder looked thick and dark. Hondo looked up at InDuna Dike. "I think Dikembe has been poisoned."

"Poison?" Chief Kimala stood, eyes wide. "Do not drink the water that girl served. It is poisoned!" All the chiefs threw out their drinks.

Hondo frowned. "I think it was the dagger."

"Just as well, better safe than sorry," Kimala grumbled.

Hondo pressed at Dikembe's wound to staunch the blood. Dikembe's heart raced in his chest, and he found it difficult to breathe.

Hondo cursed as more dark blood pooled between his fingers. "The udokotela will take too long. Gebo! Fetch Olawu. Tell her InDuna Dikembe has been poisoned." Gebo rushed out of the banquet hall.

Dikembe shook his head, but Hondo squared his jaw and scowled. "Do not be pigheaded, InDuna. Just promise to hold on, eh?"

OLAWU RACED THROUGH the stone corridors until she reached the banquet hall. She entered a room filled with men, many with bewildered expressions at the sight of her. She ignored their stares and searched the room until she found him. Dikembe.

She rushed forward, joining Hondo and Dikembe on the ground to get a better look at his wound. "I need a sterilized blade and fresh water." Hondo ordered a servant to fetch them, and she looked at him. "How long has he been like this?"

"A few minutes, no more than ten."

"The poison is moving quickly. We need to slow it down, but his heart is beating too fast."

"Olawu?" Dikembe spoke her name weakly.

"Shh, don't speak, InDuna." The requested blade arrived, and Olawu drove it deep into Dikembe's skin, just below the stab wound.

"What are you doing?" Hondo asked in alarm.

"Draining his blood. Help me turn him on his side." Dikembe gasped for air as Olawu and Hondo turned him. Blood dripped from Olawu's incision, but Dikembe's breathing grew more erratic.

"Is it working?" Hondo asked.

Dikembe began to seize, and Olawu shook her head. "This won't work." She placed her mouth over Dikembe's wound and began to suction the poisoned blood out. She spat into a bowl and drew out more until Dikembe's muscles relaxed.

When his heart rate slowed and his breathing returned to normal, Olawu stopped. The udokotela arrived and, with the guards' help, carried him to his room.

"Do you keep leeches in Borimbe?" Olawu asked as she rinsed her mouth.

"Yes." The udokotela gave a slow nod as he stared at her blood-streaked face.

"He will need to be treated with leeches until all of the poison is removed from his system. Can you manage it?"

The udokotela nodded a second time, but Olawu didn't like the way he trembled. "Just bring me the leeches, and I'll take care of their application."

"I will watch you." He looked relieved as he spoke. "Leeches are a very new technique to me."

Olawu glanced at the men surrounding her. They all stared, mouths agape. She wiped her mouth on her sleeve and bowed to InDuna Dike before leaving the hall.

HONDO WATCHED THE FORTRESS guards lift Dikembe from the floor and onto a cot to be taken to his room. Were he not charged with protecting the Chiefs, he would have joined them. The Chiefs' silence soon gave way to grumbles and angry shouts.

"That settles it!" Chief Kimala exclaimed. "We should strike the Oloko hard. Punish them for daring to attack the InDuna himself!"

A clamoring of agreement sounded throughout the hall and InDuna Dike nodded, clenching the arm of his chair. "Ready your men. We will mobilize across the valley and drive out the Oloko tribes. They'll pay for what they've done."

Chapter Thirty Four

Dikembe opened his eyes and groaned. His chest boiled with heat with each breath. He shifted in an attempt to sit up, but a wave of nausea kept him down. His limbs were heavy and sluggish, his mouth dry. He turned his head. A foolish move. Pain bit into his neck and wouldn't let go.

He searched the room as far as his eyes would travel. Someone had to be nearby. A servant or guard to help him. Light seeped in from an open window. It danced along the long, dark hair of a beautiful Kanakam woman. Dikembe blinked in surprise. Olawu rested against the side of his bed, her head cradled in the crook of her arm.

"Olawu?" he croaked. She lifted her head and placed her hand on his sweat-soaked forehead.

"You no longer have a fever. That's good. How do you feel, InDuna? Are you in pain?" Dikembe groaned in reply, and Olawu took his hand in hers. "Bear it for a few more days. The leeches will remove the poison from your system, and soon, you can try to move around a little."

"How long have I been here?" he asked.

Olawu shushed him and pressed a bowl to his lips. "Sip this slowly." Dikembe obeyed. His dry throat burned a little less with each sip, and Olawu set the bowl aside when he'd taken enough to satisfy her. "You've been in and out for three days now."

He absorbed the information, soaking in her presence with it. Fresh shame bloomed with the fire in his chest. He lifted his head, enduring the pain so he could look at her properly. He could not yet meet her eyes. He settled on her face, instead. "Olawu?"

InDuna Dike entered Dikembe's room and Olawu lowered herself to the floor.

"Dikembe, we have important matters to discuss." InDuna Dike waved his hand in dismissal and Olawu stood to leave. "The Dikebe tribes are mobilizing and will meet in the eastern village of Kisuma in a week's time. From there we will travel to the eastern valleys where the Oloko live and make them pay for what they've done to us. I need you to lead with me, son. Will you be ready?"

"InDuna Dike." Olawu bowed herself to the ground. "Please forgive my interruption, but InDuna Dikembe is in no condition to leave. The poison has not yet left his blood stream, and he is too weak."

"Olawu." Dikembe cut her off, sensing his baba's irritation. He sat up slowly, swallowing bile as his head began to swim. "I will be ready, InDuna Dike."

"Dikembe, you cannot!" Olawu stood in protest. "You cannot even walk. How will you wield a weapon?"

"You should teach her better manners, Dikembe."

Dikembe swallowed and closed his eyes. "Olawu. Leave us."

OLAWU PRESSED HER LIPS together as she stormed out. She waited for InDuna Dike in the hall. When he finally left Dikembe's room, Olawu bowed again, knees to the floor.

He stopped in front of her and waited.

"Forgive me for speaking out of turn, InDuna Dike." She hesitated. She knew, as a woman, it was not considered her place. But Ubaba had always put his patients first, and Dikembe's body was too weak. He needed more time. "InDuna Dikembe is not yet recovered. I fear his health will suffer if he is pushed too soon."

"I see that you care for my son." InDuna Dike spoke softly. "But you do not understand the Dikebe. He will fight." He looked down at her. "Make sure that he is ready."

"He needs more time!" she cried.

"Your talents have commended you for the task. I am confident you will live up to my expectations. And if you succeed, you will have my blessing as an udokotela."

Olawu raised her brows in surprise.

"Do not look so shocked. Dikembe has spoken to me of your desire to become an udokotela in Borimbe. This is your chance to prove yourself."

"I fear you overestimate me, InDuna Dike." Olawu lowered her head.

"Olawu, Dikebe men are very simple. Our bodies recover quickly when our hearts are happy. You have everything you need already. Take care of my son, and when we return from the valley, I will establish you as an udokotela."

"Yes, InDuna Dike."

"Take my advice to heart, Olawu. Make him happy. And mind your tongue."

Olawu dipped her head, then returned to Dikembe, who slept soundly on his bed. She placed her hand on his. "Your ubaba says you will recover quickly if you are happy, Dikembe. I will take his words to heart and try not to trouble you." Her hand lingered a moment more, then she left him to sleep.

DIKEMBE OPENED HIS eyes as the door closed, already missing the warmth of Olawu's hand on his. "Forgive me, Olawu," he whispered. "It seems I am the one always troubling you."

Chapter Thirty Five

Dikembe circled the courtyard, observing as Hondo ran drills with the Dikebe warriors. Olawu walked beside him, eyes alert as she hovered over him. If he made the slightest whimper, she'd pester him with questions. So, he held in his groanings and tried to bear the pain in his chest.

The Dikebe would leave in two days. Over eight hundred warriors from twelve tribes would join InDuna Dike in the village of Kisuma. Dikembe and his baba would lead them deep into the eastern valley to seek out the Oloko tribes. With such large numbers, they were certain to succeed. But Dikembe needed to be strong.

"Your legs seem weak," Olawu noted as he stumbled over a rock.

"I am fine, Olawu. I was not paying attention."

"Then pay attention. If you become lost in thought during battle, you will certainly die."

"I am not in battle now."

"No?"

Dikembe stopped and looked at her. "What is it?"

"Why do you fight me, Dikembe?"

"You tell me to rest, I rest. You tell me to walk, I walk. You tell me to eat, I eat! I do everything you ask, Olawu."

"That is not what I mean."

Dikembe sighed. "What is it that you want?"

"I want you to be happy. I have tried music and reading, given you all of your favorite foods. I bring you gifts and sing you songs. I even brought all of your guards to play games with you, Dikembe.

You smile and you thank me, but you are still unhappy. What else can I do?"

Dikembe shook his head. "Nothing. Please do not trouble yourself."

"You are not healing fast enough, Dikembe. You will not endure the journey to Kisuma on such weak legs."

"I told you, Olawu, I'm fi-" Dikembe's legs buckled as Olawu swept her feet beneath him. He landed hard on his back, and Olawu pinned his arms with her knees.

"I have never bested you, Dikembe. Never! And yet you are here on the ground, as helpless as a child. If you do not improve, you will die in the valley." Olawu's eyes glistened with unshed tears.

Dikembe groaned as he shifted under her weight, but he could not move her. How could she not know that having her this close was torture for him? "Olawu, get off of me!"

"Tell me what would make you happy?"

"Olawu!" Dikembe growled.

"Tell me!"

Dikembe swore as he met her gaze. Her brown eyes twinkled in the mid-afternoon sun, and his heart ached with longing. He wanted to get lost in her eyes, drown in the river of her touch. But how could he? She did not love him. She did not want him. And he did not deserve her.

"Tell me, InDuna? What would make you happy?"

Dikembe needed to put space between them. But her eyes were searching his, demanding he answer her. Perhaps the truth would frighten her, and she would keep away.

Dikembe sighed. "It would make your InDuna happy if Olawu were by his side always."

"Oh."

The simple word escaped her lips. He wanted to kiss her softly, deeply, desperately. If there weren't so much between them, he may have tried. But he had forced their last kiss upon her, shattering what little trust they'd had. Never again.

Olawu freed his arms and stood, offering him her hand. Dikembe took it, both relishing and hating the warmth and desire that sparked between their fingertips.

"You should rest, InDuna." Olawu mumbled the words and rushed off.

Dikembe watched her leave with a growing sadness. It seemed he had scared her away, after all. He spat on the ground, but the bitter taste in his mouth remained.

OLAWU STARED AT THE reflective glass in front of her. She ran her hand through the long, dark curls she'd spent her whole life cultivating. But it would not serve her cause to keep it. A stray tear escaped, and she wiped it away.

Whether she agreed or not, Dikembe would soon be off to war. But he still needed treatment, and infection would set in without proper care. There would be another udokotela on the battlefield, but it gave her no peace. He was the oldest udokotela in Borimbe, and, according to Sangoma's son, the most arrogant in all of the Dikebe tribes.

The udokotela aside, the thought of Dikembe leaving her, and possibly never returning, left her with an unexplainable ache. She did not know their future. A part of her hoped, but she shoved it down. InDuna Dike had tasked her with caring for his son. To do that, she would remain at his side.

She put on her ubaba's tunic and practiced a few words. "Hello. I am your udokotela. No, lower, Olawu." She took a deep breath and tried again. "I am the new udokotela. I am at your service. Ach, that sounds even worse." She cleared her throat and tried a third time, channeling some of the voices she heard at the market. "InDuna Dikembe! Listen to your udokotela. Hm, that's better."

She continued to practice until she was satisfied with the sound of her voice. "Now for the hard part." Olawu removed her ubaba's tunic and grabbed a sharp knife she'd taken from the kitchen. She stared at her hair one final time before she began to cut.

Thick tresses fell to the floor around her feet. She tried not to cry, but could not help it. When she finished removing the long pieces, she grabbed another blade. This one she ran slowly across her scalp, front to back, until all the hair disappeared.

Her task completed, she wiped away her tears and put her ubaba's tunic on once more. She stared at her reflection and smiled. "Hello! Call me Ola."

Chapter Thirty Six

Dikembe did not enjoy Businge's presence, and he let it show. He looked over the set of maps Businge had brought him without offering even the slightest courtesy. He offered no raised arm; only thinly veiled hostility. "How is construction in Kanakam?"

"The dam is nearly finished. My baba will continue to oversee the work in Kanakam in my absence."

Dikembe looked up at Businge. "Your absence?"

Businge nodded. "My baba is too old to fight. I will take his place and join you tomorrow."

Dikembe scowled. "My baba is as old as yours, and he will be leading the charge."

"Your baba is a seasoned warrior. Mine is not. I've seen my share of battles, and I'm not afraid to fight. Baba is a craftsman at heart. Please accept me, InDuna Dikembe."

Dikembe swallowed a retort and nodded. He did not like Businge, but he was right. Though they had never fought side by side, Businge had experience. "Once the dam is complete, will you be able to obstruct the water here?" Dikembe pointed to where the Kanak river split into the eastern valleys.

"Not directly. We will build a smaller dam to restrict the water flow to the east and allow the Kanak river to flow naturally, but with a lower water level. This will ensure that the Dikebe tribes will still have access to the river while the reservoirs are being built."

"Good work, Businge. InDuna Dike will be pleased to hear of it."

Businge nodded and cleared his throat. "Are you recovered, InDuna?"

Dikembe bristled. "I am well enough. Why do you ask?"

"I did not expect to find you in your bed at this late hour. Will you be able to make the journey to Kisuma?"

Dikembe scowled and opened his mouth to reply, but a knock at his door interrupted him. "Come in!" He continued to glare at Businge.

"InDuna Dikembe! I have been sent to examine you. I am your new udokotela."

Dikembe glanced at the udokotela. "Where is the other one?"

"He could not make it, and I am much better, anyway. I will give you your treatment today."

He shrugged and folded the maps, handing them back to Businge. "Very well. Businge, you may go."

Businge turned to leave but hesitated on the way out. "Olawu?"

Dikembe looked first at the door, then at Businge, who stared stupidly at the udokotela. He glanced at the cream-colored tunic, broad shoulders, and bald head atop a round face, stopping at the eyes.

Dikembe sat up in shock. "Olawu!"

"Call me Ola." Olawu extended her hand to Businge. "Could I not fool you, Businge?"

"Your hair!" Businge placed his hand on the smooth skin atop Olawu's head. "You cut it?"

Olawu turned to Dikembe, whose mouth gaped. "Are you ready for your leech treatment InDuna?"

"Olawu, what . . . happened to you?" Dikembe asked.

"You must learn to call me Ola, InDuna Dikembe. We must keep my identity a secret if I am to sneak off to war with you."

"You . . . what?" Businge turned angry eyes at Dikembe. "You are bringing Olawu with you? Do you not know how dangerous that is?"

"Do not be ridiculous, Businge! Women are not allowed in Dikebe armies. InDuna Dikembe needs to continue his treatment." Olawu turned towards Dikembe. "I, udokotela Ola, will stay by your side, InDuna, and see to it you return in good health."

Dikembe's heart stirred at her words. She had not run away from him, after all. She meant to stay by his side. It bothered him that Businge had recognized her first, but he was touched by her efforts, nonetheless.

"You did this for me?" he asked.

She nodded. "I sewed pads into my kaftan, you see? And I have many yards of wrapping around my chest. All to make InDuna Dikembe happy. Are you happy now, InDuna?"

Dikembe was happy. He was *very* happy.

"Olawu." Businge sighed. "Please give InDuna Dikembe and I a moment?"

Olawu wagged her finger at Businge. "Call me Ola."

"Ola. Please?" She nodded and stepped outside Dikembe's door.

"InDuna, you cannot let her do this."

Dikembe was inclined to agree, but he did not wish to agree with Businge. "Do you not have faith in her, Businge?"

"This is war! It is dangerous and dark and no place for Olawu. Would you really have her put herself in danger for you?"

"You and I both know that there is no stopping her once she sets her mind on something. Besides, I will take care of her."

Businge scoffed. "How will you manage it in your weakened state? You cannot guarantee her safety. It is your job to protect her, and taking her to the heart of the Oloko valley is the opposite of that!"

"Such passion, Businge, is better placed on the battlefield. I do not care to hear it when you are discussing my wife." Dikembe stood, squaring off with him. They glared at one another, communicating without words. "You are right, Businge. It is my job to protect

Olawu. But if I tell her not to come, she will try to sneak away. Being on her own is far more dangerous than having her by my side, surrounded by an army of Dikebe warriors. And neither I nor Olawu needs your permission. If you truly wish to keep her safe, then keep your eyes sharp, and be careful with your words."

Businge dipped his head. "I would never put Olawu's life in danger. I know the penalty if she is found out. You will do what you feel is best, but know this. If you fail to protect her, I will not hesitate to do the job for you. I will not hold myself back. I would give my life before I let anything happen to her. I only hope you are willing to do the same."

"You've made yourself heard, Businge. Leave."

BUSINGE SHOOK HIS HEAD and left Dikembe's room. When he met with Olawu outside the door, he stopped.

"Is he ready now?" she asked.

He nodded. It seemed much had changed since they last spoke. He lowered his head, resigned. "You must really love him." He whispered the words, then walked away.

Chapter Thirty Seven

On the day the Dikebe tribes were to meet across the river, Dikembe woke in the highest of spirits. Anticipation buzzed in the air, and with every greeting, with every raised forearm, he saw his excitement mirrored.

He met Hondo in the training room, eyes sharp and smile wide. Hondo strapped Dikembe into his armor, and they tested out their spears.

"It's been too long." Dikembe stretched his arms, breaking in the aged leather with each rotation.

"It will feel like a second skin by the time we reach the eastern valleys."

Dikembe signaled that he was ready, and the two men sparred. Hondo struck first with a swift blow, but as he warmed up, Dikembe began to feel like himself again. The past two days with Olawu had been good. She sparred with him some, but mostly she helped him to stretch and gave him his treatments. True to her word, Olawu stayed close to him, even if he did not need her. It gave him hope.

"You move slowly, Dikembe!" Hondo laughed as he tagged Dikembe's shoulder.

"I'm just warming up, Hondo." Dikembe smirked and swung his staff, knocking Hondo from his feet. Hondo laughed again from the ground.

"You are in a much better mood these last few days. Are you so eager to fight the Oloko? Or is something else bringing you strength?"

Dikembe did not answer, but he did not deny the truth of Hondo's words. He offered Hondo a hand, and he took it.

"Ah, it must be Olawu. I have not seen her of late. Did you finally speak to her? Did she confess her undying love for her InDuna?"

"Fool." Dikembe scoffed.

Hondo grinned from ear to ear. "InDuna!" He slapped him on the back. "I am happy for you. And yet, I am a little sad. How will you manage so many months without her?"

"I will imagine her by my side." Dikembe grinned.

"We leave soon, Dikembe. Should I rally the warriors?"

"Yes, Hondo. I will be along in a moment."

"Saying your goodbyes? Take your time, but do not be too late. InDuna Dike may leave without you."

Dikembe watched Hondo leave, then headed to his room. He found Olawu attempting to put her armor on by herself. He watched from the door as she pulled the leather straps with her teeth.

"Those straps aren't meant for eating, udokotela." Dikembe teased.

"Ach! InDuna Dikembe, I do not think these straps fit me well."

"Not even I can place my armor on alone, Ola. Here, let me help you."

Olawu nodded, and Dikembe began tightening the straps of her armor around her shoulders and waist. It felt good to be this way with her.

OLAWU PUSHED AT THE sides of her chest as Dikembe tightened her armor. It was her first time wearing it, and she'd had to rewrap her torso several times to get the armor to lay properly. "It feels very tight."

"It is meant to feel tight, udokotela. Loose armor cannot protect your vital organs half as well. Turn around."

Olawu turned to face Dikembe, and he continued to tighten the straps around the front of her arms and across her chest. He stared for a moment at the front of her armor.

"Olawu?"

Dikembe looked at her, and she met his gaze. "Call me Ola."

"Can you breathe, Ola?"

His voice rumbled like a soft storm. His eyes were as cloudy as the sky. Olawu's chest grew tight, and she squirmed beneath his gaze. No, she could not breathe. She dared not breathe.

"This must be uncomfortable for you." Dikembe frowned. "If you cannot breathe in your armor, will you tell me?"

Olawu nodded. "Yes, InDuna."

"Good. We will be mobilizing soon. Pack your things and meet me in the courtyard."

Her eyes followed him as he retreated from the room. Only when the door closed behind him did she permit herself to breathe.

THE JOURNEY TO KISUMA took half a day. Olawu rode behind Dikembe and his personal guards. Altogether there were eight of them. Hondo took his place beside Dikembe, and the rest paired off. Gebo and Boku, Ibawa and Gamba, and Olawu beside Yurin. InDuna Dike rode ahead of them with his guards, and the rest of the men moved on foot. From this moment forward, Olawu would be surrounded by nothing but men. Women were not even allowed as cooks in military installments.

Olawu observed the hungry expressions on the faces of the Dikebe. They reminded her of the faces of the men of Kanakam on the day of the Choosing. Why were they so eager to break things? She did not fully understand the conflict between the Dikebe and the Oloko, only that it had stretched on for generations.

When all of the tribes arrived in Kisuma, InDuna Dike stood on a wall in the courtyard to address them. He raised his spear high and gave a great shout.

"Great Chiefs and warriors of the Dikebe tribes. We stand here today united as one to defend our land and nation!" The Dikebe raised their weapons in response, hooting and chanting. InDuna Dike continued on, fueled by their enthusiasm.

"For too long the Oloko have resisted the might of the Dikebe and sought to undermine our way of life. Their transgressions began long ago when the Great InDuna Dikebe sought to unite the people of the valley. His son Chief Kebe, my own baba, tried to make peace with the Oloko, and they rewarded his efforts by murdering his sons and daughters, my brothers and sisters!" At that the warriors grew angry, cursing the Oloko and spitting on the ground.

"They attacked my wife and child on the road to Ingala, piercing my son's heart with an arrow! They burned down the village of Chigami, they've terrorized the western Dikebe tribes, and just a fortnight ago, the Oloko tried to kill me. They poisoned my son, but you see that they failed.

"The Oloko do not understand how strong the Dikebe are. Look upon my son! See how well he rides. They thought they brought death to the Dikebe, but we will show them that we are stronger. We are mightier. We will not falter. The Oloko have slaughtered us by the dozens, but we will gut them by the hundreds!"

A deafening roar rose before InDuna Dike, and he raised his fist in response.

"Join together with me. Chief Oaxaco of Shimbu! Chief Kimala of Oraji! Chief Ugogi of Simabwe! Chief Pusaka of Chigami! Chief Zigula of Ingala! Chief Zulu of Kanakam!"

InDuna Dike continued, calling out all twelve tribes by name. The shouts grew to a fever pitch as each warrior cheered his chief and tribe. InDuna Dike's mouth whitened with foam as he roared along with the Dikebe warriors.

"Stand together with me, and we will end the Oloko once and for all!"

The warriors chanted "Dikebe!" until the ground of Kisuma shook with the sound. They stomped on their feet and clanged their weapons. Olawu shook her head, bewildered by their bloodlust. The men were soon divided into sections, and the official march began. They continued to chant and sing as they strode into the valley.

Chapter Thirty Eight

"**G**et them out of here!" Olawu shrieked as she blocked a blow from an Oloko warrior. Her staff chafed against her raw skin as an udokotela pulled a wounded Dikebe warrior from the muddy ground. The Oloko were retreating, but they were taking out as many Dikebe as they could on the way. Olawu pushed her staff forward, knocking one Oloko warrior to the ground. She pounded him in his chest, immobilizing him, before joining the udokotela in hauling wounded men away.

InDuna Dike's guard blew a horn signaling their pursuit. Hundreds of Dikebe warriors shouted and began to give chase to the Oloko. Olawu and the udokotela hung back, along with a few other warriors with minor wounds, and began carting men back to the Dikebe camp.

Olawu readied the infirmary tent, which already overflowed with men from the previous night's battle. There weren't enough bandages, so they'd resorted to using leaves and weaved grass for wounds.

Masika had begun. The heavy rains muddied the valley and tripped men and horses. It also made it nearly impossible to keep what little supplies they had dry and usable. The war was messy, it was overwhelming, and it seemed it would never end. Every day of battle meant more wounded, more dead.

This was the closest Olawu had ever been to battle. Dikembe had made her promise to hang back until the second horn – the signal that meant they could grab the wounded. They'd been fighting with the Oloko for months now. They won most battles, but lost some, too. Nothing could have prepared Olawu for the level of carnage left behind.

Olawu examined the arm of the wounded Dikebe warrior in front of her. He still had a section of spear sticking out from the wound. He barely flinched when she removed it, and only grunted a little when she applied ointment and wrapped it.

"Rest here," she instructed.

The Dikebe warrior shook his head. "I can be of help, udokotela."

Olawu directed him towards the other udokotela. "Help him bring in the others."

He nodded and began hauling men into the tent, careful not to use his injured arm. Olawu continued wrapping, setting, and stitching wounds until her fingers grew numb. There was so much to do, and so few to help.

Hours later, Olawu stood outside the infirmary tent and looked up at the night sky. The stars were bright and beautiful. She wondered if Ugami and Kimani were outside in Kanakam looking at those same stars. She missed her umama and hoped she was doing well. Only the InDuna and Chiefs received news from the villages, and only if it were urgent.

"Udokotela!"

Olawu looked out in the distance at an approaching rider. She recognized Hondo on his black and white horse. He carried a limp body with him.

"Udokotela!" he shouted again. "It's InDuna Dike!"

Olawu ran towards him as he maneuvered the InDuna from the horse. "What happened, Hondo?"

"InDuna Dike and his guard went after the Oloko, but they were ambushed." Several other horses approached and the riders dismounted, Dikembe among them. They gathered around InDuna

Dike and brought him into the infirmary. He bled from his mouth and torso, his abdomen torn.

"Bring him here!' Olawu made space on a worktable. The other udokotela entered the infirmary. He took one look at InDuna Dike and shook his head.

"InDuna Dikembe." The udokotela spoke gravely. "InDuna Dike cannot survive with such an injury. You should say your goodbyes."

Dikembe clenched his jaw and nodded. He stood near his ubaba and bent his head low.

"Dikembe," InDuna Dike rasped.

"Baba?" Dikembe held his hand, his face tense.

Olawu glared at the udokotela, then placed a hand on Dikembe. "Step aside, InDuna, so I can properly examine him."

Dikembe's eyes met hers. "Do you think you can save him?"

"No one can save him." The udokotela scoffed. "He's been torn in half!" Dikembe winced and the udokotela cleared his throat. "Forgive me, InDuna, but it is a hopeless situation."

"No situation is hopeless." Olawu turned to Dikembe. "InDuna Dike has a torn abdominal wall. It is a difficult surgery, but not impossible. I saw my ubaba do it, and I know how it is done."

"It can't be done." The udokotela scowled. "Your baba is conscious now, InDuna. If he dies while this udokotela is trying to save him you may lose your one chance to say goodbye."

"Have you ever done it before?" Dikembe asked.

"No," Olawu admitted. "Not on a person. But if nothing is done soon, InDuna Dike will die." Her eyes locked with his. She believed she could do it, but would he trust her? "I could not save my ubaba, InDuna. Please give me a chance to save yours."

Dikembe stared at her a moment, then nodded his consent. "Do whatever Ola tells you, no matter what it is." His hand squeezed Olawu's shoulder, and he whispered a desperate plea. "Please save my baba."

Olawu began working quickly. She prayed that she would be successful. There was no guarantee that she could save InDuna Dike, but if it was possible, she had to try.

She gave the udokotela instructions to staunch the blood from his abdomen while she gathered supplies. It would be a long night.

DIKEMBE SAT OUTSIDE his tent with his head in his hands. Night bled into morning, with no word on InDuna Dike. The pain from his battle wounds was nothing compared to the pain in his heart.

Their relationship was one of quiet understanding, communicated more through actions than words. Sparring, hunting, traveling together, engaging in battle side by side. He'd learned so much from him. Had so much to learn from him still.

Dikembe sniffed and wiped the tears from his face. How long would it be before he knew? Had he made the right choice? If InDuna Dike were to die tonight, how would he tell Mama InDuna?

A gentle hand squeezed his shoulder. "InDuna Dikembe?"

Dikembe stood and stared at Olawu, steeling himself for her news. She looked so tired and sad. "Is he?" He couldn't bring himself to say the words.

"He's resting. It is too early to say for sure, but I believe he will recover."

Dikembe's eyes flooded with tears. "Can I see him?"

Olawu nodded, and he followed her to the infirmary. His baba lay on the table, the tear at his belly completely closed. His chest rose and fell with a steady rhythm. Dikembe placed his baba's hand in his and wept.

Chapter Thirty Nine

Olawu left the infirmary tent and headed to a nearby pond to wash the blood from her hands and face. The cool, refreshing water rallied her tired body and comforted her aching limbs. She wished she could remove her armor and wash everywhere, but, for many reasons, she could not do so.

"Olawu?"

She looked up and found Dikembe standing on the bank. He sat down beside her, but the movements were stiff, his breathing stilted. Olawu placed a gentle hand on his chest. "Are you in pain?" she asked.

He nodded, and she began removing his armor to examine his wounds. Most of them weren't very deep, but one of them had sliced into the scar on his shoulder, reopening it.

"This needs to be wrapped to prevent infection." She frowned and clucked. "I'll get you a bandage."

Dikembe grabbed her hand and shook his head. "It can wait."

She returned to her spot beside him, but found it hard to breathe. It was just the armor, wasn't it?

"Olawu?"

"Yes, InDuna?"

"Thank you." He pulled her into an embrace. "Thank you for saving my baba."

Olawu wrapped her arms around him, stroking his head as he wept against her shoulder. "Thank you for believing in me," she whispered in his ear. Dikembe looked up, his nose grazing her neck as he released her.

"I'm sorry for all the ways I've wronged you and hurt you. Please forgive me."

His gaze grew intense, and Olawu's pulse quickened as he moved closer to her. Just before their noses touched, he blinked and withdrew. It seemed the moment between them had passed.

But she didn't want it to.

"Dikembe?" She placed her hand on his cheek, and his eyes searched hers. She smiled as she leaned into him, pressing her lips against his. His eyes widened in surprise, then closed as he returned her kiss. He leaned forward and grabbed her shoulders, pulling her into him, deepening their kiss. She sighed, and suddenly Dikembe pulled away.

He shook his head in apology. "Someone could see us. It is morning."

Olawu nodded in agreement, though her cheeks burned. Of course.

Dikembe grabbed his armor and helped her up. "I'll need to speak with the Chiefs this morning. I will come to visit my baba later."

She nodded again, but faltered as they walked.

"Olawu? Are you alright?" Dikembe didn't move. He watched her with worried eyes, then placed his hands on her shoulders. "You must be exhausted. Go sleep in my tent."

"I am alright, InDuna."

Despite her protests, Dikembe led her to his tent. He helped her remove her armor, then guided her to the bamboo mat on the floor. Sleep took her immediately.

BUSINGE RUBBED HIS eyes as he led his squad towards the pond. After the grueling battle the night before, they were all anxious to wash away the grime and gore.

One of them groaned. "I cannot wait to get into the water."

"Aich, my armor is cutting into my skin. Yobibi, you made it too tight!"

"It is because you are getting fat, Gosemi."

Businge chuckled at their banter. He was just as anxious as anyone to get into the water. When he spotted the pond, he froze, then turned around, pushing the men back. "Yobibi, Gosemi, Dikali! What was the state of your tents this morning?"

"Our tents?" Yobibi scratched his head. "What do you mean, Businge?"

"You are not supposed to leave your tents without rolling up your mats and cleaning your weapons. Get back to your tents, now!"

Gosemi groaned. "But you told us to do it when we got back from the pond."

"Are you talking back?" Businge pushed him again. "When I say jump, you jump. When I say go, you go. When I say roll up your mats and clean your weapons, that means you do it. Now!" Businge barked at them and they jumped in unison, returning to camp.

Businge sighed and rubbed his eyes as he lagged behind. He turned away any man who tried to access the pond until he spotted Olawu and Dikembe making their way back to camp.

"Dikembe should not be so careless." Businge grumbled to himself. He returned to his part of camp, tapping the forearms of the men in his section. They stared at him with eager faces. He nodded his permission, and they ran to the pond.

Businge spent a few moments alone, face pensive. He stared after his men, longing to wash off the night. He looked in another direction, where Dikembe's tent stood. He made up his mind and headed there. When Dikembe left his tent, Businge was there to greet him.

"InDuna Dikembe!"

Dikembe did not hide his irritation. "What is it, Businge?"

"You put Olawu in danger with your carelessness." Businge's face was stone, but his eyes blazed with heat.

"What is it you are going on about now?" Dikembe pushed him aside and headed towards the Chiefs' tent.

"I'm talking about you kissing Ola near the pond this morning." Businge grabbed him by the arm, whirling him around. "You cannot promise to protect her and then put her in harm's way."

Dikembe pulled his arm away with a growl. "Mind your words, Businge. I am in no mood for you today."

"You will be the death of her!" Businge snarled. "If she is harmed because of you, I swear before God, I will-"

"You will what?" Dikembe leveled his eyes at him. "Give me a reason to remove your head from your body. Any reason will do."

Businge clenched his fists, but softened his words as he spoke. "Please, InDuna. Be more careful."

"Get out of my sight."

Businge nodded and walked away, but he'd seen the guilt on Dikembe's face. His words had hit their mark.

Chapter Forty

Olawu opened her eyes to a sun already high in the sky. She rallied quickly and returned to the infirmary. InDuna Dike was still stable and resting. She checked on the other men in the infirmary, cleaning and rewrapping wounds, and stifling her sobs when she could not find a pulse. When the other udokotela entered the tent, she gave him an update, then left in search of suitable replacements for their dwindling supplies.

When she finally returned to Dikembe's tent, the moon stood high in an inky black sky. She lay her head on the mat and fell asleep, but all too soon Dikembe shook her awake.

"Olawu?" He whispered in the dark.

"Hm?" She opened her sleepy eyes and smiled at him.

"Tomorrow we are moving out. There is an Oloko village several miles north of here. It is suspected that the Oloko chief resides there. We are going to attack from the west and end this war once and for all. Please take care of my baba for me." Dikembe paused and winced. His hand rose to his chest, but he quickly lowered it.

Olawu frowned. "Does your wound still hurt, Dikembe?"

"Only a little."

Olawu sat up and lit a candle. She knew it was a lie. "Take off your kaftan." Her tone left no room for argument, and Dikembe obeyed. "The wound is open. I must clean and bandage it before infection sets in." She stood to leave the tent, but Dikembe held her fast.

"Stay, Olawu? Please?"

She looked into his eyes and found herself transfixed. She sat beside him, and he drew her into himself.

"We'll be leaving at first light to make it there by nightfall. I don't want to waste the time I have with you."

"But you'll be back, won't you?" Her eyes searched his, questioning.

"I will always come back for you, Olawu. Promise that you will always wait for me?"

Olawu nodded as she snuggled against his chest.

DIKEMBE OPENED HIS eyes to a stabbing pain in his chest. Olawu's top half pinned him to the mat. He slid out from under her, trying hard not to gasp from the pain. He did not wish to wake her. It was nearly dawn, and they would move out soon.

Another wave of pain shot through his chest. Dikembe grunted and squeezed his eyes shut. When he opened them again, Olawu's eyes were on him.

"What is it, Dikembe? Are you in pain? Let me take care of your wound." She left the tent and headed for the infirmary.

Dikembe pulled on his kaftan and made his way to Hondo's tent. "Hondo, are you up?"

Hondo switched the bread in his right hand to his left to tap Dikembe's forearm as he ate. "How can I be of service?"

"I need help with my armor. Have our men mobilized yet?"

Hondo began strapping on Dikembe's armor. "They stand ready near the Chiefs' tent."

"Alright. Let's head out."

OLAWU CHECKED ON INDUNA Dike when she entered the infirmary. He was awake and alert, but also in pain. She dressed his wounds and gave him water before gathering supplies for Dikembe. Chief Kimala entered the tent and greeted InDuna Dike.

"When do they leave?" she heard InDuna Dike ask.

"They should be moving out as we speak," Chief Kimala replied. "Rest well, my friend. We shall send the Oloko running tonight."

Olawu frowned and left the infirmary, feeling uneasy. She ran to Dikembe's tent, but he wasn't there. Neither was his armor. Olawu ran to the front of the camp. Most of the troops were already gone. She caught sight of Businge and his squad and ran up to him.

"Businge!" She called him over. "Have you seen InDuna Dikembe?"

"He rides at the front of the camp, Ola." Businge pointed. "They left some time ago. My squad will follow soon, but we are reserves."

"I see. Can you help me with something?"

Businge followed Olawu back to Dikembe's tent, and she handed him her armor.

"Can you help me to strap it on?"

Businge nodded and cleared his throat. He carefully tightened the leather straps around her torso, but his hands slowed as he neared her chest. "Olawu," he began. "Ugami told me what happened on the day of the Choosing."

She looked up at Businge, noting the change in his voice.

"I do not fully understand why you are with Dikembe, and I can't help but wonder. If I had known; if I had been there, would things be different now? Would you be by my side instead of his?"

"Businge." Olawu placed her hand on his cheek. "I will never forget your kindness to me and to my family."

A low rumbling sounded outside, followed by the heavy pattering of rain. Droplets of water poured into the tent, splashing on top of them. It would be another miserable day in the valley.

Businge chuckled and pulled Olawu into an embrace, then kissed her gently on her forehead. "Be well, Olawu. If all goes as planned, we shall return in three days' time. There are two hundred men staying behind to keep you and the others safe, but keep a sharp eye out."

Olawu nodded, tapping her fingers against her lips as Businge left the tent. If he and Dikembe thought she would stay here at camp and twiddle her thumbs, they were greatly mistaken. Dikembe was not in any condition to fight without help, and Olawu hadn't crossed the valley to leave him by himself.

She checked once more on InDuna Dike, leaving instructions with the udokotela for his care, then headed towards the rear of the camp where they kept her horse. She mounted the brown and white after filling her supply bag and securing her staff, then trotted off to join the Dikebe army.

She trailed behind the reserves for the better part of the day, riding alongside the rear guards and the lower chiefs. Dikembe would be furious when he saw her, so she planned to show herself when they were too far to turn back.

The rain soaked through her armor and kaftan and made visibility difficult. It wasn't long before the ground beneath them became thick and slippery. More than a few horses stumbled in the muddy terrain.

Lightning streaked across the afternoon sky, startling her horse. She shushed the mare and kept a steady hand on her reins. When the light disappeared from the sky, Olawu advanced towards the front of the ranks. She spotted Dikembe, surrounded by his guard, and approached.

Chapter Forty One

Dikembe plodded along on his horse in agony. His armor felt more like flames than leather. The rain soaked every inch of him, and his clothes stuck to his skin, further irritating his wound. He needed to focus on the battle ahead, but his thoughts kept drifting back to Olawu. The kiss they shared by the pond had been unexpected.

His heart swelled at the memory, but he needed to return from this battle in one piece. If he did not focus, he would falter. If he faltered, he might never see Olawu again. Dikembe steeled his nerves against the pain and set his eyes forward. They would arrive at the outskirts of the Oloko village soon and make ready for their attack. Once the Oloko were defeated, Dikembe could focus his attention on Olawu. On her beautiful eyes and soft, sweet lips.

"Are you in pain, InDuna?"

Dikembe smiled. He could not shake his thoughts of her. Couldn't help but imagine her soft voice, near enough to . . . Dikembe turned his head and his eyes grew wide. "Olaw-"

"I must tend to your wounds, InDuna." Olawu cut him off. "If we do not clean them properly, infection will set in."

Dikembe frowned at her. "What are you doing here? You should be at camp."

"I am your udokotela, InDuna. I must see to it that you are in good health and spirits."

"But my baba?"

"Is in good hands. I left the udokotela there with very clear instructions. Do not worry about InDuna Dike."

"This is no place for you, Ola. The Oloko are many in this village, and the battle will not be easily won. I cannot fight effectively if I am worried about your safety."

"I can handle myself, InDuna. I had a good teacher."

Dikembe opened his mouth to protest, but no words came out. What could he say? She should turn back. He knew that. But they were too far away to turn around, and he could not send her off alone. Judging by the smile on her face, Dikembe suspected she had planned it that way. She was full of unexpected surprises.

Despite the pain in his chest, he laughed. "You are stubborn, Ola."

"I prefer diligent, InDuna."

Dikembe cleared his throat and turned his eyes towards the horizon. He wanted to kiss her, but kissing an udokotela in front of his guards and all of the tribes of Dikebe would not be wise. He needed to focus. The men traveling behind him relied on his leadership in battle. With his baba back at camp, they would look to him.

Two scouts returned to Dikembe, reporting that the Oloko village was close. Dikembe nodded to Hondo, who gave the signal to halt.

"Instruct the chiefs, Hondo. No fires. No one leaves formation. On my signal we advance." Hondo clicked his tongue and his horse carried him off towards the chiefs. Dikembe dismounted and Olawu did the same, stretching her limbs.

She watched Dikembe as he gingerly rotated his shoulder, then grabbed her supply bag. "InDuna, I must tend to your wound."

"There is no time for that, udokotela."

"If you do not make time, you will not be able to use your arm at all. It has been too long already."

The sky flashed again, and a storm of hail crashed down on them. Shields and armor went up to block the tiny balls of ice, and hands held fast to reins to keep the horses from bolting. As quickly as the storm began, it stopped, and the rain returned.

"I hate this valley!" Boku grumbled as he kicked a hailstone. "Only the Oloko could live in such a place."

"Keep a sharp eye, Boku," Dikembe warned. "Now is not the time to falter."

Boku nodded and pulled a piece of bread from his supply bag. The men would have to eat quickly, if they were able to eat at all. Many chose not to, though they had walked all day without stopping. They fed off the energy of battle.

"InDuna, your shoulder." Olawu placed her hand on Dikembe's arm and pulled him towards her. A shockwave of heat coursed through her hand, traveling down to his belly. She removed his armor, not an easy task in the rain, and helped him remove his kaftan.

Dried blood mixed with fresh soiled a section of his kaftan. Olawu tossed it over his horse and examined the wound. A scarlet ring surrounded it.

Olawu tsked and grabbed a bottle from her bag. "InDuna, please forgive me," she whispered.

Dikembe's eyes narrowed, then grew wide as Olawu poured the bottle over his wound. He clenched his teeth and grunted. Just when he thought it was over, Olawu began to squeeze his wound. Blood and pus oozed out, and Dikembe's head grew dizzy with pain. He grabbed her by the arm.

"Ola, no more." His breath came in pants as he pleaded with her. She gave him a pitying look, but continued her torture. Her fingers felt like fire against his skin. Dikembe pulled her hand away, unable to bear the pain.

"I'm sorry, InDuna. The infection has to be removed. It travels like poison in your blood stream, and though it moves slower, it can damage your heart just as well. Please, let me finish?"

Dikembe shook his head and sat on the ground. Olawu joined him, placing a gentle hand on his shoulder. "InDuna. Now is not the time to falter."

He looked up at her. She was using his words against him. She did not fight fair. He turned away from her with a near imperceptible nod. He held his tears at bay, for his men's sake. Then, blessedly, it was over.

The rain slowed to a drizzle as Olawu wiped his wound clean. She placed a salve on top and covered it with bandages. Dikembe sat bare-chested as she cleaned the blood from his kaftan.

The burning in his chest dimmed, and Olawu helped him dress and reattach his armor, tightening the straps with strength he did not know she had.

"Loose armor cannot protect your vital organs half as well." She smiled. "Now you are battle ready, InDuna!"

Dikembe grabbed Olawu by the shoulders and looked her in the eyes. "Stay close to me, udokotela. Do not leave my side, eh?" His gaze lingered, communicating unspoken words. Then he released her.

WHEN DIKEMBE GAVE THE signal, they advanced. The Oloko village stood strangely quiet as Dikebe warriors trampled the grass and sloughed through the muddy earth. When the first cries of battle rang out, the world exploded. Oloko warriors scattered from their huts with spears and swords, fighting with ferocity as the Dikebe swarmed around them.

Olawu remained on her horse and close to Dikembe, her staff clenched tightly in one hand and the reins in another. An Oloko warrior approached Dikembe, and he smashed his spear into the man's skull. Two more approached from the sides, and Olawu bent backwards, barely avoiding a tossed spear as she rolled off of her horse. She landed on her feet, staff in hand as she crouched down between the horses.

Dikembe joined her on the ground as the bottom dropped out of the sky. Torrential rain hammered Oloko and Dikebe alike, adding to the chaos and confusion of the dark. Dikebe warriors screamed and chanted war cries as they sliced through the Oloko.

Dikembe and Olawu continued to travel towards the center of the village. A large courtyard filled with warring men soon filled with still bodies. A behemoth of a man, wearing the hide of an ibhubesi, roared as he cut down two Dikebe warriors.

"Hondo! The Chief!" Dikembe signaled towards Hondo, who leapt from his horse and joined him on the ground, clearing a path between Dikembe and the Oloko chief. Dikembe ran forward, curved blade in hand. The chief swung his double-edged spear. Sparks flew as the metal tips of their weapons met. Dikembe's blade danced in the moonlight as he pummeled it against the chief's spear.

The Chief proved a worthy opponent for Dikembe, matching blow for blow. His spear nicked Dikembe's face, slicing his cheek. Olawu kept her eyes sharp as she stood in the courtyard. An Oloko warrior approached, swinging at Olawu with a machete. Olawu blocked each blow and delivered a hit to the warrior's chest. She brought the staff down hard over the warrior's ribcage, shattering bones. Olawu brought the staff to the warrior's face and froze. A woman's face stared back at her. Her eyes grew wild as she stared down the length of Olawu's staff.

She took a step back and looked around the courtyard. The Oloko warriors battled fiercely with blades, staffs, and spears, but there were not only men among them. There were women. Olawu stared in awe as a female Oloko warrior smashed spears with Boku, screaming with fury as she advanced.

Olawu glanced back at Dikembe, who bore down on the Chief with his blade. The Chief threw Dikembe back and pierced his shoulder with his spear. Dikembe pulled out the spear and thrust it through the Chief's hand, pinning him to the ground.

Olawu turned at the sound of hooves approaching. A group of Oloko riders armed with bows and ropes began fanning out. Led by a woman with long dreads and a hyena hide draped across her shoulders, they took out several Dikebe warriors, capturing others and dragging them behind their horses.

Olawu screamed for Dikembe, but he could not hear her over the sound of the rain and thunder. She ran towards him as the Oloko woman reared back with her bow. Dikembe dealt a fatal blow to the chief just as the bow released. Olawu threw her body over Dikembe, and the arrow pierced her middle. She gasped and Dikembe turned.

His blood-soaked face twisted in anguish. "Olawu?"

A rope tugged at her throat, pulling her away from him. One of the Oloko riders had her tethered to their horse. She clutched at the rope around her neck, gasping for air as the rider dragged her through the mud. Dikembe began to give chase, but he stumbled, clutching his chest where the spear had pierced him. He looked towards her, agony in his eyes as he pushed himself forward.

"Olawu!"

Chapter Forty Two

B usinge blocked a blow from an Oloko warrior before slicing through another. He swung his spear around him, clearing the space before charging forward. He smashed one Oloko warrior to the side and kicked another before stabbing a third. He heard the Oloko riders as they approached the courtyard.

"Utata!" He heard an Oloko woman cry out as she readied her bow. Businge deflected a blow and tossed his spear at the closest rider before they could send an arrow into Yero. The spear hit its mark and Businge followed the riders. He picked up another weapon from the ground and followed the Oloko woman on the horse. When she pointed her arrow, he spotted Dikembe.

"InDuna!" Businge shouted, rushing towards him. The arrow flew through the air and Businge screamed as it pierced Olawu's body. When another rider carted her away, Businge changed directions, flying after Olawu and the rider.

He shoved past Oloko and Dikebe warriors alike, pushing against his growing panic as the rider dragged Olawu through the village. The rain slashed at his face, and the mud gripped his feet, but Businge clenched his jaw and kept his eyes on Olawu. Another rider flanked him and tried to catch him in his rope. Businge grabbed the rope and pulled, bringing down rider and horse.

"Olawu!" Businge shouted as the sky popped and cracked. The riders began shouting at one another and took a hard left, shifting east. Businge shifted as well, but slipped in the slick mud. He rolled several feet before he was able to stand again, but a monstrous wall of earth descended on the valley. Businge turned as the mountainside buckled. Mud, earth, and trees crashed into the Oloko village, submerging it.

The mudslide continued its path of destruction, crashing towards him, and Businge ran towards a grove of trees. He climbed the thick branches until he reached the top. The earth consumed the trunks, snapping the trees like twigs. Businge flew from his perch and landed hard on the ground, crying out as his ribs snapped.

The earth finally grew still, though the rain continued. Businge rolled over to his stomach and pushed himself off the ground. He searched the eastern horizon, but saw no trace of the Oloko riders.

"Olawu!" Businge screamed her name with no reply. His tears mixed with the rain as he let out an agonized cry. She was gone.

Businge spit blood from his mouth and turned back towards what was once the Oloko village. Little could be seen in the dark, but much of the village was submerged. He walked back, ignoring the pain in his side as he scanned the ground for any signs of life. The rain began to subside, and Businge caught sight of a hand sticking out above the ground near a large, uprooted tree trunk. He approached with caution, not knowing whether the hand belonged to an Oloko or a Dikebe.

"Hello?" Businge called out. There was no point trying to rescue a corpse. A muffled shout rang out below the dirt, and Businge began to dig. When the hand connected with an arm, and the arm finally connected with a face, Businge slowed.

InDuna Dikembe gasped.

"InDuna!" Businge continued to dig until he was free from the soil. Dikembe looked at Businge from the ground, eyes filled with anguish.

"Where is Olawu?" he croaked.

Rage brewed inside him, but he shoved it down. "She was taken by the Oloko."

Dikembe shook his head. "We must go after her. We must find her!" Dikembe stood, but Businge pushed him back down.

"No. InDuna, she is gone."

"But we must protect her. If she is left to the Oloko-"

Businge snapped. "Dikembe! You are the son of InDuna Dike, and it is your duty to see to your men. We must look for survivors!"

"But Olawu-"

"Olawu is gone. It cannot be helped. But just as I found you, there may be others. We must go!"

"You said that you cared for Olawu."

"I do!" Businge growled, shaking him. "I care with everything in my being. Do not think that you are the only one suffering. It pains me to know we cannot help her. But she was not the only one who risked her life to stand by your side. Look for your men!"

Businge released him and turned away. They needed to find survivors. If he were left alone with Dikembe now, only one of them would make it back to camp.

DIKEMBE FOLLOWED BUSINGE towards the Oloko village. Though it broke his heart to think of Olawu, Businge was right. He had to find his men.

They dug through the mud and earth in search of survivors, but as time wore on, their hopes dwindled.

They had arrived in the Oloko village four hundred strong. When they left, they had but twenty men. More than half of their horses were lost, and those that remained were used to carry those who could not walk.

Dikembe walked beside Yero, Hondo, Boku, and Ibawa. Gamba, Gebo, and Yurin were dead.

Businge walked alone.

Chapter Forty Three

The Dikebe warriors arrived at their camp exhausted and disheartened. They'd lost brothers, akina baba, friends. In the span of several months, they'd lost more than half of their numbers. In the blink of an eye, they were down to a mere fraction.

Dikembe sat around a fire that evening with what remained of his guard. Yero sat among them, though he was no longer a guard. Their numbers were so small, rank hardly seemed to matter. Only four Chiefs had survived the mudslide, and they were all in the infirmary.

Boku's arm hung from a sling. Blood and earth covered every man's face. Businge sat away from the group, his torso wrapped to stabilize his broken ribs.

Dikembe felt as though he would suffocate in the humid night air. "Yero."

Every eye looked up.

"Yes, InDuna?" Yero asked.

"I need you to track someone."

Yero sipped the broth in his cup. "Who do you wish me to find, InDuna? The Oloko?"

"I want you to find Olawu."

Hondo gave Dikembe a strange look. "Is she not in Borimbe, Dikembe?"

"She was captured by the Oloko."

Businge lifted his head from where he sat.

"When?" Hondo asked.

"Today, as we were fighting. She was taken by the Oloko, dragged off by one of their riders."

"How could she be here?" Hondo's confusion remained. "Was she hiding in your tent, Dikembe?"

"She was the udokotela, Hondo. Ola was Olawu."

Boku's eyes lifted in surprise. "But how did she manage it? She had no hair and a flat chest!"

"That is not important now!" Dikembe growled. "Yero, I need you to find her."

"InDuna, I do not think this thing is possible."

"Yero, you are our best tracker. Surely if you try you can find her in the eastern valleys?"

"It would be difficult if it were just the rain and mud, but the mountain fell down on top of us, InDuna."

"What was Olawu doing in the valley?" Hondo asked. "Did you know about this?"

"War is no place for a woman." Boku sniffed. "You should know better, InDuna."

"Watch your words, Boku!" Yero barked. He glared at him, daring him to speak again. Boku held his tongue. Yero placed his hand on Dikembe's shoulder. "I am sorry about Olawu."

"What will they do to her?" Ibawa asked. Hondo gave him a warning glance.

Dikembe left the group with glassy eyes and a heavy heart. His feet found their way to the infirmary, and he sat next to InDuna Dike.

"Baba." Dikembe kissed his hand. His baba stirred and looked at him.

"My son has returned." He gave a tired smile. "Did we obtain victory today?"

Dikembe's lip quivered, and he shook his head. "Forgive me, Baba. I failed."

"Tell me what happened."

"I should have seen that the rains were too great. I should have called a retreat. We lost most of our men to the mountain. Four chiefs, over three hundred men, gone."

"Where is the udokotela?" he asked.

"He is tending the wounded."

His baba shook his head. "The other udokotela. *Your* udokotela."

"Captured by the Oloko." Dikembe lowered his head and wept.

His baba sighed. "I know you cared for Olawu, Dikembe. But if she is alive, it won't be for long. The Oloko will get what they can from her, and when she is no longer useful, they will dispose of her. It is the way of war. She is lost to you, my son."

Dikembe looked up at his baba, surprise on his face. "You knew?"

His baba nodded. "Do not worry. You will soon find another girl to warm your bed."

"Baba, I loved her."

InDuna Dike coughed again. "Even so."

Dikembe left the tent. His feet dragged through the thick mud as they carried him to the pond. He fell to his knees and looked up at the sky.

"Why?" he whispered. "Why her? Why take Olawu from me? It should have been me!" His heart filled with grief, squeezing the air from his lungs. He could not go on without her.

He stared at the water, stared at his reflection. Dirt and blood caked his face. He thrust himself forward, submerging his head into the water. He screamed until the air in his lungs left him. When water rushed into his nose and mouth, he welcomed it. It burned and squeezed the life out of him, but he didn't care. He wanted to die.

A hand at his back pulled him from the water, and Dikembe sputtered on the ground. Businge hauled him to his feet, eyes ablaze.

"Businge?" Dikembe rasped. "Leave me be."

"No." Businge shook him.

"I wish to die!" he cried. "I cannot live without her!"

Businge glared at him. "You must."

He shook his head, whimpering. "I cannot!"

"Coward!" Businge cried. "You were supposed to protect Olawu, and you failed." Businge's eyes were raw with tears. Dikembe looked away, unable to bear the anguish in Businge's face. It too closely mirrored his own. Businge's voice softened, but the pain in his voice remained. "You failed, Dikembe. And that pain you feel now? You will bear it."

Dikembe shook his head. "I cannot."

"You will. As your punishment, you will bear it. You will live with the knowledge that you, great and proud InDuna, are capable of failure. You are not God. You cannot control every outcome. Olawu put her faith in you, and now she is gone. Live with that truth. Let it humble you. Let it make you a better man."

Businge released him, and Dikembe fell once more to his knees and wept.

"You were not the only one who loved her. Remember that."

Businge left Dikembe on the bank. He cried until the first rays of morning light danced across the pond. His heart ached, and his conscience weighed heavy. But once again, Businge was right. He would bear it.

Dikembe returned to camp and looked for Hondo and the others. He found them all gathered around a fire, sharing a loaf of bread. Businge sat among them, quietly staring at the flames.

"Hondo."

Hondo looked up at him, eyes filled with worry. He stood and greeted Dikembe with his arm raised. Dikembe returned the gesture with a sad smile.

"Assemble the men. We will return to Borimbe in three days."

"Have you spoken with InDuna Dike and the Chiefs?" Hondo asked. Dikembe shook his head.

"The Chiefs are still recovering. It is for their sakes that we do not leave tonight. If we stay here, our supplies and our numbers will only dwindle further."

"But what of the Oloko, InDuna?" Boku asked.

"What about Olawu?" Ibawa asked. Hondo smacked him on the back of the head and gave Dikembe an apologetic look.

Dikembe took a deep breath. "Those captured by the Oloko must be considered lost to us. If we do not wish their deaths to be in vain, we must return to Borimbe and continue with our plans." Dikembe looked to Businge. "Will you return to Kanakam?" Businge nodded quietly. "Good."

"What plans, InDuna?" Boku looked confused. "Will we return to the eastern valley with more men during the dry season?"

"No." Dikembe shook his head. "Businge, how quickly will the plans at Kanakam be complete?"

"The dam should be finished by now. We will continue working on the reservoir systems and block off the river where it flows to the eastern valley. Once that is done, the Oloko's water supply should dry out in a year, maybe two."

Dikembe nodded. "The Dikebe villages that lie on the eastern side of the river will be vulnerable to Oloko attacks. We will construct outposts and fortify those villages in the coming months. Once their water supply runs out, the Oloko will slowly starve. If they travel west to the river, we will be ready for them. With no other resources, they will die by our sword or relocate to the eastern mountains. That is our plan, Boku."

Hondo nodded. "I'll inform the men now." Boku, Yero, and Ibawa followed, tapping their arms against Dikembe's as they left. Businge continued to sit by the fire.

"Businge?"

Businge stood at attention, locking eyes with him.

"Thank you for your words." Dikembe raised his forearm, and Businge stepped forward.

"Do not raise your arm in brotherhood to me. I follow you because I must, but I am not your brother."

Businge walked away, and Dikembe lowered his arm. He stared after Businge with narrowed eyes. "Have it your way, Businge. We part as enemies. Pray our paths do not cross again."

Part Three

Oloko Ekhaya

Chapter Forty Four

Olawu opened her eyes to a world of pain. Blood caked her neck, her entire backside felt as though it had been scraped away, and the arrow still piercing her gut remained a constant source of agony. She couldn't breathe without agitating some bruised part of herself.

She blinked and turned her head. A row of other Dikebe warriors sat beside her, lined along the inner walls of a small hut. Light peeked through the spaces between the straw, illuminating the mangled faces of the men around her.

She heard a female voice growl. "Where is the Dikebe camp?"

"Oloko scum!" was the reply. A sword ran through flesh, followed by a groan. Then silence.

"Where is the Dikebe camp?" The question came again, but this Dikebe warrior chose to spit. Things didn't fare well for him, either. Down the line the Oloko warrior went, until she finally reached Olawu at the end. She recognized the woman as the one who pierced her with an arrow.

"It seems you are the last." The woman bent down in front of her. "Tell me where the Dikebe camp is, and I shall put you out of your misery quickly."

Olawu shook her head. "Even if I knew, I would not tell you."

The woman narrowed her eyes and looked down at the arrow protruding from Olawu's gut.

"You have something that belongs to me, Dikebe." The woman yanked hard on the arrow's tip, pulling it through her stomach.

Olawu shrieked in pain, and the woman took a step back. She reached for her dagger and sliced through Olawu's armor. She continued to cut through Olawu's kaftan, exposing the wrapping around Olawu's chest. She cut through that as well. The Oloko warrior looked down at her in surprise. "You are a woman?"

The warrior's lips continued to move, but Olawu no longer heard her. Succumbing to the pain, all went silent and black.

OLAWU WOKE ON HER SIDE, surrounded by light. Her back tingled with a dull ache, and it seemed she'd swallowed all the sand in the valley. She tried to clear her throat and choked, invoking a fit of coughs. Her stomach twisted in pain, and she remembered the arrow. She reached for her abdomen, but her fingers met only bandages there.

Olawu looked down at her naked frame. She tried to sit up, gritting her teeth against the pain in her stomach, but she was unable to stand. Her head spun, and she vomited on her feet. The ground grew as she tumbled forward, but two firm hands caught her.

"Easy there," an elderly, feminine voice soothed. She steadied Olawu before laying her back on her side.

"Where am I?" Olawu worked her jaw with effort. The muscles in her face were tight, the skin bruised and chafed. "Who are you? Where are my clothes?"

"You must be very brave, Dikebe." The woman wiped Olawu's mouth. "I will summon Kioli, now that you are awake."

"Who is Kioli?" Olawu asked.

The woman ignored her questions. "You must not try to stand. You are not strong enough."

Olawu placed her hands on either side of the bed to get her bearings. The arrow was gone, but the wound still fresh. Her back was sore, but not raw. She looked up at the Oloko woman.

"How long have I been here?" she asked.

"Nearly a week now." The woman finally answered. "I will get Kioli."

Olawu absorbed the information as the woman left. Nearly a week since she was dragged away from the Oloko village. Olawu placed a hand on her neck where the rope had been. It was tender, but the skin had scabbed over in most places. Other than the wound on her stomach, she was mostly healed. Why was she alive? Why were they keeping her?

She looked around the straw hut, hoping to find something to use as a weapon. She spied a table in the corner with small bottles and a mortar and pestle. If they meant to torture her, she would not make it easy for them. She sat up once more, waiting as long as she dared for the nausea to subside. She pushed herself slowly from the bed to the floor, grimacing as her fingers touched the foul puddle gifted by her stomach.

On hands and knees, she crawled from the bed to a table, then pulled herself up. Her movements were slow, a futile effort to counteract the dizziness that played at the edges of her vision. She grabbed a mortar and pestle just as a pair of feet entered the room.

"What are you doing?" a voice boomed.

Olawu whirled around in what she hoped seemed a threatening stance, mortar and pestle raised in defense. Though her body stopped, the room continued to spin, and Olawu's eyes rolled back. She collapsed to the floor, landing hard on her side.

"Foolish girl," the voice muttered. "Chausiku, get her back to the bed."

Chausiku lifted her from the ground. She winced at the woman's touch, the skin at her back still sensitive. Olawu's stomach twisted, threatening to revolt, but Chausiku was ready for her, placing a large basket in front of her as she retched. With a few swift motions, Chausiku had her on her side once more.

Kioli pulled up a stool and sat across from her "What is your name, Dikebe woman?"

"Olaw-" She stopped herself. How much should she tell this Oloko woman? "My name is Ola."

"Do you know why you're alive, Ola?" Olawu shook her head and Kioli smirked. "Because you are not a man. Which is strange. The Dikebe do not allow women into their armies. They do not allow their women to do much of anything, really. I hate many things about the Dikebe, but it is their treatment of women which I despise the most. So, I am curious. How did you come to be in a Dikebe army? Have the Dikebe changed their ways?" Kioli laughed. "No, that cannot be it. Dikebe do not change. You must have joined their ranks in secret. But why would a Dikebe woman do such a thing? Are you not all mindless sheep, doing as your husbands tell you?"

Kioli rubbed Olawu's head as one would rub a dog's fur. Tiny curls had grown where once there was only skin. "You fascinate me, Ola. And the chief as well. We wish to know more of your story. One thing is certain. You are very unusual."

Olawu's brows crinkled in confusion. Had the chief survived? She'd seen Dikembe cut him down with his sword.

"Your Chief? He lives?"

Kioli's eyes narrowed. "*She* is alive and well, Ola."

Olawu's mind reeled. She? Their chief was a woman? "But the man with the ibhubesi hide, was he not your chief?"

Kioli stood, eyes dark and stormy as she glared at her. "The man with the lion's hide was not my chief. He was my utata. And you, Dikebe scum, came upon our village in the dead of night, like thieves, and stole his life from him!"

Olawu looked away. She knew well the pain in Kioli's eyes. "I am sorry for your loss, Kioli."

"Keep your empty words, Ola. Dikebe do not feel for anyone." Kioli turned to Chausiku. "The Oloko will gather in a few days' time. When she is well enough, clothe her and bring her to the Chief."

Chapter Forty Five

O lawu did not know what to expect for her first meeting with
the Oloko Chief. Chausiku led Olawu into the Chief's hut,
her limbs trembling with excitement as much as fear. A woman
leading an entire tribe? Such an exhilarating thought.

The Oloko Chief filled her with awe at first sight. She stood tall,
with a lean, muscular frame. Her weathered skin belied the strength
of her gaze, which pierced Olawu to her core. Silver, braided hair
flowed down her back, kissing her ankles. She wore a brown kaftan
overlapped by a colorful robe of purple and gold threads. Gold bands
pierced her ears, which stretched down to the base of her neck. She
walked up to Olawu and gave her an appraising look.

"Kioli has told me much about you, Ola."

"I have been told nothing about you, Chief of the Oloko."

The Chief chuckled. "That is Kioli's way. My niece does not
trust easily." The Chief looked down at Olawu's kaftan, a simple, tan
colored dress that came down to her shins. "Have you recovered well,
Ola?"

"Better than any prisoner could expect, I imagine."

"You do well to remember you are a prisoner. Though, perhaps,
if we speak more, that relationship will change."

Olawu scoffed. "For the better or the worse?"

"That remains to be seen," the Chief quipped. "You may call
me Chief Umfazi. Come, Ola." Olawu followed Chief Umfazi and
Chausiku out of the hut and into the heart of the village. Olawu
watched with keen interest as Oloko families gathered in the street

in brightly colored kaftans and robes. They all headed in the same direction, towards the center of the village. A large pillar stood high, surrounded by a circle of people.

"This pillar was constructed by my utatomkhulu." At Olawu's confused expression, the chief smiled. "I believe the Dikebe say the baba of your baba, yes? He built it after the first great conflict between the Oloko and the Dikebe tribes. At the end of a battle, the Oloko from every village would come here to celebrate those who died. We've continued the tradition until now."

Olawu watched as dozens of Oloko circled the pillar, singing and dancing and twirling. It was a strange sight, seeing so much joy in the midst of their pain. She remembered the day they laid her ubaba to rest. There had been no joy then. Just grief and profound sadness.

"Why do you not wail and mourn?" Olawu asked, curious. "Why would you sing when you have lost so much?"

Chief Umfazi smiled at her. "Ola, do not misunderstand. Those who have died will be missed, and there will be many tears. But this celebration is not of their death, but of their life. We rejoice in the memories we carry of our loved ones. The food and laughter shared. The stories and friendships. The passionate love, the birthing of children, the connections between Oloko. Death interrupts our lives, but it does not end them. So we celebrate and show how grateful we are for the gift of life, and through our celebration, we encourage one another to continue to live and fight for each other."

Olawu nodded in understanding. It was a beautiful thought. Chief Umfazi joined in the celebration, twirling and laughing with Chausiku. Olawu watched them in wonder. She had never heard of anything like this. The stories of the Oloko were always of their treachery and coldhearted ways. Could this be the same people?

Kioli stood beside Olawu, watching her closely. "Dikebe." Kioli turned her way. "Tell me why you did it?"

Olawu swallowed a lump in her throat. "Did what?"

"You jumped in front of my arrow. I had that inyoka dead to rights. You got in the way. Why?"

Olawu kept her eyes forward, but the ache in her heart was no doubt plain on her face. What had happened to Dikembe?

Kioli squinted her eyes, searching her face, then smirked and raised her head. "I think I have my answer. Ola, did you join the Dikebe army for a boy?"

Olawu's eyes widened. "No! Kioli, I-"

"I am actually a little disappointed now." Kioli shrugged. "I had thought perhaps you were different from all the other simpering Dikebe women. Turns out you are the worst of them. Sacrificing yourself for a man who would not do the same for you?" Kioli scoffed.

"I did it because of my ubaba!" Olawu blurted the words.

Kioli looked at her with one brow raised. "Your ubaba? Is that the man you saved? He looked too young."

Olawu shook her head. "My ubaba was an udokotela in my village. He was a good man. He helped anyone who came to his door, even if they could not pay. He would never turn anyone away. He taught me everything he knew, though he had to do it in secret. When InDuna-" Olawu thought over her words. She would need to choose them carefully. "When InDuna Dike became ill, I knew he would need a skilled udokotela to help him. The Dikebe men would rather die than stay home from war. So, I joined the army in secret to treat him."

"Why was the InDuna ill?" Kioli asked.

"He was injured by an Oloko assassin. She stabbed him with a poisoned dagger."

"Hmm." Kioli narrowed her eyes. "And the man you took the arrow for?"

"I saw you point your arrow at him, and I reacted instinctively."

"It is your instinct to throw yourself in front of arrows, Ola?" Kioli laughed. "You are fascinating. A Dikebe woman who is a secret warrior *and* udokotela? That is something." Kioli laughed again. "Alright, udokotela Ola. Come! Let us see if you are truly as skilled as you say." Kioli dragged Olawu through the streets until they came to a small hut outside the village.

"Why am I here?" Olawu gave the hut a wary glance and swallowed.

"This is where we keep our lost causes." Kioli opened the door to the hut. Flies swarmed above their heads as they entered. Olawu covered her nose at the smell, but Kioli seemed unbothered by it. Three Oloko lay on cots inside. Two men and one woman.

"What's wrong with them?" Olawu asked.

Kioli shrugged. "That's for you to find out, daughter of the udokotela."

"What about Chausiku? Has she not seen to them?"

"Chausiku is not an udokotela. She is a healer. And this is your test. Revive them, and you will live. If they die, so will you." Kioli left the hut, leaving an open-mouthed Olawu standing alone in the humid air.

Olawu looked back at the three Oloko. The first cot held a man in soiled clothes. Great drops of sweat fell from his gaunt face. His eyes were unfocused. His bones hung from his skin. Olawu suspected dysentery. She'd need to separate him from the others.

The second man stared at her with angry eyes that followed her around the hut. "What is your name?" she asked.

"Dikebe intaka!" The man cursed. "What does it matter? You will kill us, anyway."

"Can you tell me what is wrong with you?" she asked.

"Stay away from me!" he cried.

Olawu noted the way his fingers curled at his sides. "Can you move your fingers at all?"

The man shook his head, suddenly weepy. "Please help me," he whimpered. "I cannot see the light. It's so dark in here!"

Olawu placed her hand over his head. It burned with fever. "Has an animal bitten or scratched you recently?" she asked.

The man groaned. "My dog, Inja Ebomvu. He bit me. He never did that before."

"How long ago was that?"

"Four days ago. He died next day. Then I could not see. I became dizzy. They say I hit a man, but I don't remember. Now I cannot move my hands." The man's eyes grew wild, and he shrank away from Olawu. "Dikebe scum! Get away from me!"

She'd seen this behavior before. A man had brought his son to her ubaba after he was bitten by a dog. The boy was delirious and disoriented. He couldn't keep anything down, and his hands had curled in paralysis. Amarabi is what her ubaba had called it. Rabies. The child had died a day later. The man in front of her had been suffering four days already. There was little she could do for him, except make him comfortable. Those who suffered from amarabi rarely recovered.

She moved on to the third Oloko. The woman was young, possibly Olawu's age. A hint of recognition passed between them and she gasped. She had met this woman before. During battle she had shattered her ribs with her staff.

"Have you come to finish the job, Dikebe?" The woman smiled bitterly. Dried blood rested at the sides of her mouth, and her chest fluttered. Olawu's blow had been brutal, but not fatal. She creased her brow in thought.

"Can you tell me what is wrong with you?"

"I cannot move, and it is hard to breathe."

"Can you move your neck?" The woman shifted her head from left to right. "Can you move your fingers?" The woman wiggled her fingers. "How about your toes?" The woman shook her head. Olawu ran her fingers along the woman's leg. "Can you feel this?" Again, the woman shook her head. "What about here?" Olawu pressed her sides, and the woman cried out in pain.

"Can you describe what happened to you?" Olawu asked.

"Before or after you crushed my insides, Dikebe?"

Olawu turned away from her scowl. "After."

"I tried to stand and fight, but I could not hold my spear. So, I hid. One of the riders saw me and tried to help me onto a horse, but then the mountain came down. There was no time. He pulled me by my arm, but I could not get a grip on the horse. I was half dragged until we reached Oloko Ekhaya. When he brought me down from the horse, I could not walk."

This was all new information to Olawu. "What do you mean, the mountain came down?"

"You were there, were you not, Dikebe? The mudslide? Do you not remember?"

Olawu did not reply. It must have been after she was captured. Her thoughts returned to Dikembe. He had been injured. What had happened to him? Had he survived the mudslide? "What of this Oloko Ekhaya? Is that what you call this place?"

The woman nodded. "It is where the Chief resides. And where all the Oloko gather in times of war. But wherever our Chief resides becomes Oloko Ekhaya. It does not matter where. Just who." The woman winced as Olawu pressed her side again. "Oloko Intaba was home to the Chief's brother. It was my home as well. I cannot believe it is gone!"

Olawu swallowed the lump in her throat and continued on, assessing the damage to her ribs. Her torso had been wrapped and seemed to be healing, for the most part.

"What is your name?" Olawu asked.

"My name is Bolanle."

"Bolanle, I am going to remove your wrappings and look at your chest and back."

She nodded in consent, and Olawu began undoing the wrappings. When they were completely removed, she continued her examination on the front side of Bolanle's chest, then gently turned her to her side to check the back. As she studied Bolanle's back, she noticed a large protrusion near her spine. Olawu massaged it with her fingers and frowned.

"Bolanle, have you always had this bump on your back?" Olawu asked.

"No. There is a bump on my back?" Olawu moved Bolanle back to her original position and began looking around the hut for supplies. There were fresh cloths and a few instruments in the corner, but not much else. Olawu wiped the sweat from her brow and grabbed a cloth. She covered Bolanle from the neck down and left the hut. Breathing in the fresh air, she allowed herself a moment of frustration.

"I do not wish to die here, ubaba," she whispered into the wind. She sniffed and wiped away her tears before having a look around the area. Everywhere she turned there were high grasses and low lying trees. If she ran into the bush, she might be able to elude capture, but where would she go?

"Planning your escape already?"

Olawu whirled around. Standing before her was a very short woman with waist length dreads and a large smile. "Who are you?" Olawu asked as she quieted her nerves.

"I am Fayola! Kioli sent me to be your guard. But you can pretend I am your helper."

"What is it you will be helping me with, Fayola?"

"I will help you to find your hut at night and your breakfast in the morning. And if you try to escape, I will help you come to your senses." Fayola grinned as she cracked her knuckles, but Olawu did not find her words humorous.

"Can you help me with my work, Fayola?"

She shrugged. "What work is that, Ola?"

"I need fresh water and soap to clean out the hut and wash the soiled cloth. I also need proper tools for surgery, but everything inside the hut has a dull or blunt end. Is that something you can help me with?"

"You wish to have soap, water, and weapons, Ola?" Fayola shook her head. "I can help you with the first and second. For the third you must speak to Kioli."

"Where is she?"

"She is with the Chief. Today is a day of remembrance. The Dikebe have killed many Oloko, but the mudslide destroyed Kioli's home."

Fear twisted her insides as she asked the next question. "Were there any survivors?"

"Scouts were sent to the village some time ago. They returned with no survivors. At least we know that many Dikebe died alongside our brothers and sisters." Fayola spat and gave a satisfied grunt.

Olawu closed her eyes as her tears dripped down to her kaftan. She had sacrificed herself for Dikembe. If he had perished in the mudslide, it had been for nothing.

"What is it like for a Dikebe woman?" Fayola suddenly asked. "I have often wondered. Do you walk with chains around your necks?"

"What?" Olawu looked up in surprise. "No. Fayola, why would you say such a thing?"

Fayola shrugged. "I could never understand the Dikebe ways. The women are told they cannot go here or there, or do this or that. If you are not in chains, why do you obey such things?"

Olawu shook her head. Borimbe was worlds apart from Kanakam in its treatment of women. "In Borimbe, women are allowed to buy and sell just as the men. They can read and write and learn a trade as well."

"We do those things in Oloko. But if I wish to cook, I can cook. If I wish to fight, I can fight. If I wish to farm, I can farm. If I wish to sell, I can sell. Nobody stops me. Nobody says, 'eh, Fayola! You cannot do such things because you are a woman.' It is nonsense! Here, we Oloko work as a community, everyone doing their part. If we were to say only men can fight, we would never win any battle. For many of the men are not able to fight, and there are many more Oloko women. I would rather have Kioli fighting beside me than my brother Dingwali. He is very good with cooking, but he cannot hold a staff. And Kioli smells better."

Olawu understood Fayola's words, but she still felt the need to defend the Dikebe. "There are many places where women have it much worse, Fayola. In my village, a woman could not buy or sell without a man. She could not read or write or learn a trade. She could not be an apprentice or work for wages. She could only be at home. And if she were poor, she was sold in the market to her husband. This is not so in Borimbe."

"Ach! What village are you from, Ola? Are you not Dikebe after all? Kioli will be glad to hear this. She intends to kill you. She could not avenge her utata, and you are to blame. But if she learns you are not Dikebe, she will spare you, perhaps. Oh, I should not have told you so much." Fayola laughed, but again, Olawu could not see the humor.

"I know Kioli intends to kill me. She gave me an impossible task."

Fayola watched Olawu for a moment. She looked up at the sky and sighed. "It is getting late, Ola. Come, I will show you where to get some food. It is hard to work on an empty stomach, yes? Then we shall find Kioli and grab soap and water. No weapons, to be sure!"

Olawu followed Fayola to a section of the village bustling with activity. The smell of smoked meats and spiced rice wafted through the air. Olawu's stomach growled with envy. Fayola placed a bowl of rice in her hand and topped it with a string of meat and vegetables.

Olawu inhaled the food in minutes, drowning it with a steamy cup of jasmine tea afterwards. She did feel her spirits lift a bit. Fayola told her jokes as she ate, and stories about the Oloko. It was fascinating to hear another perspective. They were not as she had expected. And there were no strangers. Everyone knew Fayola by name, though at least a dozen Oloko passed by. They greeted one another as though they were family.

A heavy sadness washed over Olawu as she thought of Ugami and Kimani. Would she ever see her sisters again?

Chapter Forty Six

"Hard at work, I see?" Fayola bit into a papaya as she watched Olawu haul out a basket filled with soiled cloth. With help from one of the Oloko, she managed to move all three of her patients outside so she could clean the hut. Her first patient, Ashembi, was kept far from the other two. He looked much weaker than he had the day before, and Olawu worried he would die before the day ended. She had given him small amounts of water every hour or so to keep him hydrated, but the gaunt man was truly at death's door.

Kwame, the other male patient, fared much better in the sun than in the dark hut. He slept most of the day and only had a few episodes of delirium. Olawu had the hardest time with Bolanle, who groaned in pain each time she was lifted. It would have been easier to help her slowly walk on her own, but she had no feeling in her legs. Moving her had been a painful and slow experience.

Olawu wiped her forehead and made a face at Fayola. "Perhaps you would be willing to help?"

"Perhaps you would be willing to die," Fayola quipped. "I have no interest in mopping up Ashembi's waste."

"That part is done with, anyways. Fayola, are there more papaya nearby?"

Fayola nodded and pointed to a grove of trees in the distance. "There you will find many papaya, Ola! Shall I fetch some for you?"

Olawu nodded. "Please? I have an idea for Kwame. My ubaba used to make a stew out of papaya and ginger and feed it to patients fighting off infections."

"Hm, perhaps you should feed it to Ashembi also?"

"Oh no! It's meant to drive out the infection through the digestive system."

"Udokotela Ola. You are speaking gibberish to me."

"It will make him go. Ashembi is already going too much."

"Ah. But sometimes it is necessary to let things go, eh?" Fayola laughed heartily at her joke, and Olawu chuckled too. She walked back into the hut and scanned the floor for any spots she'd missed. It smelled a thousand times better now.

"Not bad, Dikebe!" Kioli whistled as she entered the hut, startling Olawu. "I see you've taken your test seriously. I suppose you value your life after all."

"Why would I not value my life, Kioli?" Olawu spoke the words with an edge.

Kioli shrugged. "By your own admission you, daughter of the udokotela, like to step in front of arrows meant for other murderous intaka."

"You speak of murder, but what are the Oloko? They've killed many Dikebe! How can you say you're any better?"

Kioli grabbed Olawu by the arm, squeezing until her skin chafed beneath her fingers. "They started this war. InDuna Dikebe came into our village. He raped our oomama and children. He slaughtered our ootata and sons. He burned our homes and crops and killed our livestock. And why did he do that to the Oloko? Because we would rather be free? Because we were not willing to live as the Dikebe do?

"Because we would not bow to his tyranny, he murdered us in our sleep. He robbed us of our homes and paraded us naked among the Dikebe villages to shame and humiliate us. He enslaved our sons and daughters. We tried to make peace, but the Dikebe did not want peace. So now we fight back, Ola. How are we the monsters? Are the Oloko conquering villages and forcing them to become like us? Are we taking men and women from other tribes and making them our slaves? Everything we do, we do for each other. This is not so for the Dikebe. InDuna Dike, like his utatomkhulu before him, fights only for himself."

Kioli released her with a scowl and removed a dagger from her waist. She set it down in front of Olawu.

"Fayola said you needed this. If you use it for anything other than helping your patients, Fayola will kill you without hesitation."

Olawu nodded. "I only need it for Bolanle."

"Why do you need it for her?" Kioli asked.

"Come see for yourself." Olawu walked outside to where Bolanle rested and leaned over her. "Bolanle? I'm going to turn you to the side, alright?" Bolanle nodded sleepily and Olawu gently turned her sideways, exposing her back and the bulbous bump that seemed to be growing. Olawu placed the dagger over an open flame to sterilize it. "This is going to get messy." Olawu made a small incision in the center of the bump and immediately blood and fluid began to drain. Whenever the draining stopped, Olawu gently massaged the hole, encouraging more fluid to leave.

"I thought all night about Bolanle." Olawu shared her thoughts. "She could not feel anything in her legs and feet, but she could feel the pain in her ribs. Her bones seemed to be healing to me, but the area has been a source of discomfort to her. Stranger still is the nature of her injury. It was not an immediate paralysis, but a gradual one. She could walk before, but not after her journey to the village. Then I saw this bump. It was not hard to the touch, but soft and pliable. I suspected it was full of fluid. You see her spine here, Kioli? It is part of a network of nerves that control the movement of the body. Bolanle was half dragged for miles with her arms outstretched, which pulled at her spine for an extended period of time. While the spine was stretched, fluid from her injuries began to build up here. That fluid pushed against the nerves of her spine, altering her ability to walk. This is what I suspect. If I am correct, then Bolanle should soon be able to walk."

"What if you're wrong?" Kioli pressed.

Olawu shook her head. "Then I must continue to search for answers for Bolanle." When all of the fluid drained from Bolanle's incision, Olawu bandaged her wound and turned her once more. "Bolanle, can you tell me if you feel this?" Olawu ran her fingers along Bolanle's legs. Bolanle looked at Olawu and smiled slowly.

"Udokotela, I can feel it!" She laughed, and Olawu ran her fingers along the other leg.

"What about now?"

She nodded and smiled. "Yes, Udokotela! Does this mean I will walk?"

"I think so. But we will need to start slowly. And there is a chance that fluid will try to build up again near your spine. I will watch you the next few days, and we will see."

Kioli gave Olawu an appraising look. "Well done, daughter of the udokotela. Perhaps I will not kill you after all."

"Kioli." Olawu turned towards the woman. "You placed me here to care for three lost causes. Bolanle will likely recover, but I'm not so sure about the other two. Kwame has a severe case of amarabi. Very few survive it, especially at this stage. Ashembi was deteriorating even before I arrived. It would take a miracle for him to recover."

"Then pray for a miracle." Kioli shrugged. "Return my dagger now."

Olawu glared at Kioli and slowly placed the dagger in her hand.

Chapter Forty Seven

Olawu had just sat down from a day spent tending to Kwame and Ashembi when Fayola grabbed her by the arm and pulled her towards the courtyard.

"Come, Ola!"

Olawu wiped the sweat from her brow and leaned forward as Fayola all but dragged her. The woman moved with lightning speed, weaving her way through bodies as they rushed into the village.

"Where are we going, Fayola?"

"To my brother's wedding." Fayola grinned, and Olawu crinkled her brow. They crossed the courtyard, passing the pillar, and stopped just past the outskirts of the other side of the village. Rows of mango and papaya trees stretched across the valley. Below the branches of one large tree were two very happy Oloko dressed in white kaftans.

A crowd surrounded them, and Chief Umfazi stood between them. Fayola released Olawu and ran to her brother, who was a good deal taller than her. She jumped on his shoulders and kissed him before joining the other villagers.

"Brothers and sisters!" Chief Umfazi began. "We are here to celebrate the joining of Dingwali and Akua on this glorious day that God has made. Dingwali, do you promise to love Akua and fight for her with all that you have?"

Dingwali grinned and nodded. "I do."

"And you, Akua? Do you promise to love Dingwali and fight for him with all that you have?"

"With all of my heart!" Akua cried.

"And you!" Chief Umfazi looked out at the crowd. "Do you promise to help them and fight for them with all that you have?"

"We do!" The Oloko responded with cheers and hoots.

"Then it is settled." Chief Umfazi smiled. "Dingwali and Akua, join your hands and hearts together, and let us rejoice in their union."

The Oloko cheered, throwing flowers at their feet as Dingwali and Akua approached. The men slapped Dingwali on the back, and the women kissed Akua on the cheek.

Next, Dingwali's family slaughtered a cow, and Akua, having changed into a dark orange kitenge, gifted several large quilts to each of Dingwali's family members. She then placed two gold pieces inside the cow's belly.

A feast ensued as many Oloko brought bowls of fruit, steaming pots filled with savory stews, and a spicy drink that made Olawu's head feel light.

Olawu had never seen such a display before. In Kanakam, marriages were private matters between families. A bride price was paid, and then the man took his wife home. Only the merchants held wedding parties, and Olawu had never been to one.

Many gifts were laid at Akua and Dingwali's table, including baskets, dried meats, and kitenge cloth. The level of affection doled on the young couple struck her with its beauty, and Olawu's mind drifted back to the day of the Choosing. Only the men had smiled that day. But Dingwali and Akua both looked so happy. She wondered if she would ever have something like that.

Fayola yanked her brother down and placed him in a headlock before kissing his forehead. Olawu laughed as Fayola raised a fist in triumph.

"Such a glorious day! I've finally gotten rid of Dingwali!" Those closest to Fayola congratulated her and even gave her kisses, too. Things truly were different among the Oloko.

"Daughter of the udokotela."

Olawu sighed and lowered her head. "What is it, Kioli?"

"Chief Umfazi wishes to see you. Come when the sun sets." Olawu turned, but Kioli had already disappeared into the crowd.

OLAWU ENTERED CHIEF Umfazi's hut just as the sun vanished behind the western horizon. She found her brushing the fur of her ibhubesi hide.

"Good evening, Ola." The Chief smiled at her and continued her work.

"You called for me?"

"Kioli tells me many good things about you, Ola. It seems we have been blessed with an udokotela in Oloko."

"I try my best, Chief Umfazi."

"You have been in Oloko Ekhaya for nearly half a year. I want you to consider something."

"What is that?"

"Becoming one of us." Olawu raised her eyebrows in surprise. "We have been watching you, Ola. Fayola speaks very highly of you, as does Kioli. They are both impressed with your skill and your character. Chausiku has also expressed her delight in you."

Olawu took in her words. Chausiku was always kind, but Kioli despised her. And Fayola was, well, Fayola. What would the Oloko gain by accepting her? And what would she have to do?

"I'm sure you have questions, Ola." Chief Umfazi gave her a knowing glance. "But first, I have questions for you."

"What questions do you have for me, Chief Umfazi?"

"Who are you, really?"

Olawu hesitated, unsure how to respond, but Kioli entered Chief Umfazi's hut at that precise moment.

"Another village was attacked!"

Chief Umfazi stood. "Where?"

"Oloko Umfula. The Dikebe sent a band of men south of the river and torched it. Gehizi is here, but he's badly wounded."

"Take me to him."

Chief Umfazi followed Kioli, who grabbed Olawu on the way. "We may need your help."

Olawu ran with them until they reached Chausiku's hut. Gehizi lay inside, half his body black with burns. A deep gash in his leg left a pool of blood on the floor.

"Chief." Gehizi spoke in between pants. "Umfula is gone. My children, Amila and Yamba-"

"Save your breath, Gehizi," Chief Umfazi soothed. "We will do what we can to help you. Rest now." She looked up at Olawu. "Can you do anything for him?"

"I am not sure."

Chief Umfazi pleaded. "Whatever you can do, please do it quickly."

Olawu nodded and looked at Chausiku. "First we must stop the bleeding in his leg."

Chausiku handed Olawu bandages, which she pressed against Gehizi's leg. He barely flinched, though it should have caused him great discomfort. A sinking dread lodged in her stomach.

"Kioli, how long ago was the attack?"

"Two nights ago," Kioli replied. "I fear he will not make it."

Olawu agreed. His shallow breaths grew more labored, and she knew he would die soon.

"He delivered the message to us." Chief Umfazi placed her hand on Gehizi's forehead. "You did well, Gehizi."

He reached for the chief and smiled. As the light faded from his eyes, his hand fell to his side. Olawu watched the others. All eyes were on Gehizi. Not one of them dry. The Oloko mourned even those from different villages.

She sniffed and willed away her own tears. She had no right to mourn him, but still, she felt a kinship to him. To all of them.

In that moment, Olawu realized that she no longer wished to be an outsider. She wanted them to kiss her cheek and celebrate with her as a sister. To share and build with them, even fight with them. She wanted to be an Oloko.

THEY RETURNED TO CHIEF Umfazi's hut with red eyes and somber faces. Kioli spoke first.

"Chief Umfazi, we must respond."

"Kioli, sit down." Chief Umfazi spoke with a calm voice that belied the tension behind her eyes.

"No. I cannot sit. I cannot rest while our brothers and sisters are slaughtered. Umfula was mostly farmers and hunters, and miles away from the nearest Dikebe tribe. Why would they burn a village that posed no threat?"

Chief Umfazi shook her head. "They've never attacked us so far south before. It does not make sense, Kioli, but we cannot react without a plan."

"It's that intaka Dikembe!" Kioli snarled.

Olawu's head snapped up at the mention of his name.

"Now that he is in power, he seeks to make a name for himself at the expense of our people. Mark my words, he will be ten times worse than InDuna Dike."

Olawu looked from Chief Umfazi to Kioli. "InDuna Dikembe? He's alive?"

Kioli stopped her pacing long enough to stare at Olawu. "Yes. What do you know of him?"

Olawu's mind reeled. *Dikembe is alive.* "But what of InDuna Dike? Did he not survive?"

"He is alive." Kioli gave her an odd look.

Olawu's gut twisted as a risky idea formed in her head. "Chief Umfazi? I accept your offer, and I have an idea I wish you to consider."

"Offer for what?" Kioli's eyes darted from Olawu to Chief Umfazi.

"Ola, we have not yet discussed your becoming an Oloko." Chief Umfazi held up a hand at Olawu's protest. "And you have not yet answered my question."

"I am ready to answer you now." Olawu took a breath. "I think there is a way to make peace between the Oloko and the Dikebe."

Kioli scoffed. "Make peace? Did you not hear me? That bloodthirsty savage will not rest until all of us are wiped from the earth!"

"That bloodthirsty savage is not who you think he is." Olawu sighed. "He is calculating and exacting, but he is not a monster. If he believed peace were possible with the Oloko, he would consider it."

"How do you know, child?" Chief Umfazi's eyes grew intense.

Olawu sucked in a breath. "I know because he is my husband."

Kioli's jaw dropped. "Your what?"

"My name is not Ola. It is Olawu. And InDuna Dikembe is my husband."

Kioli's eyes lit up. "The arrow you took for him?"

Olawu nodded. "Yes."

Kioli had a dagger to her throat in seconds. "The man who took my utata's life? Who slaughtered an entire village of innocent Oloko just days ago? He is your husband?"

"Kioli, don't!" Chief Umfazi warned.

"I consider this a stroke of good fortune, Chief Umfazi. We have something of value to InDuna Dikembe." Kioli dug her dagger into Olawu's neck. "Perhaps if I send him your head, he will feel just a fraction of the pain I feel. Do you think so?"

"Kioli, enough!" Chief Umfazi gave her a second warning.

Kioli released her, with reluctance, and Olawu wiped the blood from her neck. She steeled her nerves and continued. "If I could communicate with InDuna Dikembe somehow, let him see that peace is possible with the Oloko, I believe he would consider it."

"The second you leave this valley your life will be forfeit." Kioli growled. "Do you think us stupid? You would lead Dikembe right to Oloko Ekhaya!"

"Then what do you propose, Kioli? The Dikebe are too numerous for the Oloko to defeat. You cannot win against them."

"We do not need to defeat their armies. We only need to defeat InDuna Dikembe."

"What do you mean?" Olawu turned towards Kioli, but she ignored her.

"Chief Umfazi, we had a good plan. The Dikebe tribes are only united because of the InDunas and their sons. If they are no longer around, the tribes will scatter and squabble among themselves. I say we cut off the head of that inyoka, once and for all."

"We tried that, Kioli, but it did not work." Chief Umfazi shook her head.

"Because no Oloko could get close enough. Now we have Olawu. She could enter InDuna Dikembe's bedroom if she wished." Kioli finally looked at her. "You want to become an Oloko? Start there. Kill InDuna Dikembe."

Olawu shook her head. "It does not have to come to that. If I could just send him a letter-"

"You seem so confident." Kioli scoffed. "Tell me? How often did your husband consult you on matters of war? Did he come to your bed at night seeking counsel? Did he treat you as his equal?"

Olawu did not reply. She could not.

"Foolish girl. You overestimate your importance to InDuna Dikembe. If you are so special to him, why has he not come for you?"

Kioli struck a nerve. Now that she knew he lived, Olawu wondered the same thing. Perhaps he thought her dead. But still . . . Olawu lowered her head, resenting the pity in Kioli's eyes.

"I see my words have hurt you, Olawu. When will you realize that InDuna Dikembe is the son of his utata?"

Olawu looked to Chief Umfazi, eyes glassy with tears. "No. Chief Umfazi, do not ask me to do this."

Chief Umfazi looked at both women. The quiet in the room stretched on and on. Then she cleared her throat and placed a gentle hand on her shoulder. "Write your letter, Olawu. We will send a messenger to Borimbe and see what InDuna Dikembe says."

"Thank you!" Olawu cried.

Kioli scowled and shook her head. "Chief Umfazi, I must object-"

"Kioli. If there is a chance for peace, should we not take it? So many of us have died at the hands of the Dikebe already. Even a small chance of peace is worth the risk."

Kioli tightened her fists and dipped her head. "As you say, Chief Umfazi. I will send a messenger to Borimbe with Olawu's letter."

"I think it best you go, Kioli. We cannot risk a messenger being followed back to Oloko Ekhaya. I know you will be careful."

Kioli nodded. "I will. Olawu, write your letter. I will leave for Borimbe in the morning."

Chapter Forty Eight

Olawu gave Ashembi another spoonful of broth as he lay on his cot. Though his cheeks still hugged the bones of his face, he'd gained control of his bowels and his appetite had improved.

Kwame fared much better as well. He spent most of his day outside in the sun, and the papaya and ginger soup she'd been feeding him seemed to be working. The paralysis had eased, allowing his fingers to regain their dexterity. Their recovery was nothing short of a miracle.

"Olawu." Fayola greeted her as she hopped onto a stool, but no humor graced her face.

"Kioli still has not returned?" Olawu asked.

Fayola shook her head and scowled. Kioli had been gone nearly two weeks. She should have returned by now. Fayola's greetings were civil, but Olawu knew that she blamed her for Kioli's absence. Olawu prayed she would return safely to Oloko Ekhaya, and minded her words around Fayola.

"Rider approaching!"

The warning sent Olawu to her feet. Fayola took to the ground and ran. Olawu followed close behind, a bundle of nerves as they rushed towards the rider.

"It's Kioli!"

Olawu was too far to see her clearly, but even from her distance, she could tell something was wrong. Kioli had to be helped from her horse, and she couldn't walk on her own. Two men carried her to

Chausiku's hut. Fayola went in with her, but when Olawu tried to enter, she couldn't.

Mbomba, one of the village guards, raised his hand to stop her. A reminder that she was not one of them. Not yet. "Chief Umfazi will see her first."

Olawu understood, but it still stung. Living so long with the Oloko, she had almost forgotten. She returned to her patients, making sure they rested comfortably before returning to Chausiku's hut. She waited outside until Fayola walked out.

"How is she?" Olawu asked.

Fayola glared at her with red, swollen eyes. "Barely alive, no thanks to you." She spat at Olawu's feet. "You Dikebe are animals. Irhamncwa elibi. Not fit for life. Not fit for anything but the end of my spear!" Fayola took a step towards her, spear clenched in her fists.

Olawu stepped forward, arms extended. "I'm sorry, Fayola."

Fayola shook her head, and Olawu took another step forward. She leaned down and wrapped her arms around her. The woman melted into sobs, weeping against Olawu's shoulder.

"I'm so sorry." Olawu repeated the words over and over. Fayola smashed her fists against her, but her strikes lacked any strength.

Chausiku stepped out of the hut. Their eyes met, and Chausiku cleared her throat. "Olawu? Chief Umfazi would like you to come inside."

Olawu looked down at Fayola, who sniffed and wiped her nose. "Go on, Olawu. I'll be fine."

"I'll stay with her." Chausiku gave Olawu a reassuring look and pushed her inside.

Olawu sucked in a breath at the sight of Kioli beneath a sheet. Her armor lay in a heap on the floor. Her left arm bent too far the wrong way. Purple welts and swelling made her face twice the size. A blood-soaked kaftan lay across a stool.

"I failed." Kioli rasped. She tried to open her eyes, but the swelling prevented her. "I wore my armor. I waved my flag. I stopped my horse and bowed. I shouted my intentions." Kioli licked her lips. Her words came out stilted in between breaths. "Dikebe warriors patrolled the river. I told them who I was and why I came. But they did not see me. They did not see a warrior or a messenger. Not even an Oloko. They saw a woman. And they-" Kioli shook her head, fighting back tears. "They did not even take the letter, Olawu. They beat me and tossed me in the river."

Olawu remembered her own encounter with the guards at the gates of Borimbe. What would have happened if Businge had not intervened?

"Forgive me, Kioli." Olawu leaned down and kissed her forehead.

Kioli's swollen eyes grew wet with tears. "How? How can you defend such animals?"

Olawu sniffed and wiped away her tears. "Rest now, hm? Chausiku and I will take good care of you."

"Olawu." Chief Umfazi stared at the wall.

Olawu could only guess what thoughts plagued her mind.

"We've tried it your way, and we've paid the price for it." Her anguish was clear, though Olawu could not see her face. "If you wish to be an Oloko, you must let go of InDuna Dikembe. When you are ready to make that sacrifice, we will welcome you with open arms. Think long and hard, Olawu. You much choose, and there is no turning back."

Chief Umfazi kissed Kioli on the cheek before leaving Chausiku's hut. Olawu sat on a stool and wept.

Chapter Forty Nine

Olawu's hair blew in the wind as a gust rose up around her. She wore it in dreads these days, cropped at her shoulders and tied at the top when she sparred. She shielded the book in her hand, a gift from one of the elders who traded along the coast.

"Udokotela!"

Olawu set down the book and stood. Kwame ran towards her, a look of panic on his face.

"What is it, Kwame?"

"Come quick! To the courtyard!"

Olawu dropped her book and followed Kwame to the center of the village. The courtyard swelled with people. Many turned to her with pensive faces as she approached, sending worry up her spine. Had something happened to the Chief? Why did everyone stare at her?

The crowd parted and Olawu looked up at the pillar. Chief Umfazi stood in front of it, dressed in a golden kaftan. She smiled at Olawu and held out her arms. Olawu slowed her pace and looked around the courtyard.

"Ola! Step forward, my child, and take my hand." Olawu did as the Chief commanded and stood next to her in front of the pillar. "People of Oloko! Three years ago, Ola came to us as an enemy. But today we welcome her as one of us. Mark this day as one of great rejoicing. For we have gained a precious daughter. Many of you have benefited from her skill as an udokotela, sparred with her as a sister at arms, and shared your griefs as friends."

Chief Umfazi looked down at Olawu and smiled. "Ola, you have proven yourself worthy of our trust. Today is a very special day. For today I accept you not only as a daughter of Oloko, but as my own flesh and blood."

A cheer went up at Chief Umfazi's words, and Olawu looked around her, dazed. Her eyes landed on Kwame. He winked at her and smiled.

Chief Umfazi squeezed her hand. "I have no daughters of my own. The only blood relation I have is Kioli, and she and I are in agreement, as are the elders of our people. Olawu, you will lead the Oloko when I step down. Do you accept your place as my daughter and as future Chief?"

She looked out at the Oloko. They had accepted her and adopted her as one of their own. They truly were a united people. Not once had she heard a man refer to a woman as inja, and no man struck a woman without being punished for it. Men and women cooked, cleaned, crafted, and fought side by side. They saw each other as equals. How many times had she longed for that very thing?

"I accept."

Chief Umfazi began to sing, and the crowd followed her lead. Olawu smiled, but the moment grew bittersweet as she thought of Dikembe. Of what might have been. Of what she must do.

Even if he loved her, she knew Dikembe did not truly see her as an equal. He was a Dikebe through and through.

When she learned he had survived the mudslide, she'd hoped he would come for her. She remembered clearly the words he had spoken to her in his tent. *I will always come back for you, Olawu. Promise you will always wait for me?*

Olawu had waited. Even after Kioli had been brutalized, she held out hope. But he never came for her. It had taken many months to come to terms with even that.

InDuna Dikembe only seemed interested in making life more difficult for the Oloko. And as the months went on, their troubles grew. The stream that supplied water to their homes and land had slowly dried up.

It had not been noticeable, at first. The water levels dipped, then returned to normal during mvuli and masika, the rainy seasons. But with each season the levels dropped further and further, until one day, there was no water. The Oloko tried going to the west towards the Kanak river, but the Dikebe built fortifications all along the banks and drove out any Oloko who came near.

If nothing changed, they would soon starve. Their crops had already failed twice, and Olawu could not bear to see the Oloko children go hungry. The Dikebe continued to terrorize Oloko villages, plundering, pillaging, and burning homes to the ground. The Oloko grew more desperate with each passing season.

Chief Umfazi had held a meeting with the elders the night before, inviting Olawu to join them. Hearing the depth of their troubles had grieved her to her core. Borimbe was so plentiful already. What right did the Dikebe have to block them from the river?

"Olawu." Chief Umfazi had addressed her. "It is time to make your choice. We cannot wait any longer. If we do not end the oppression of the Dikebe, our people will starve. There is not enough water for crops or livestock. Our horses are dying! Our people are dying! Our children are going to bed and waking up hungry. We cannot allow this to continue."

Olawu looked at Chief Umfazi and Kioli. She saw their hearts. Even though she was not one of them, they had treated her with kindness. They fed and clothed her and let her be their udokotela. She wished to give back to them.

Dikembe had already let her go. It was time for her to do the same.

"I am ready to become one of you," she'd said. "I will return to Borimbe, and I will kill InDuna Dikembe."

THE PLAN WAS SIMPLE. Olawu would return to Borimbe, reunite with InDuna Dikembe, kill him, and return to Oloko Ekhaya. For several weeks, scouts had observed when and where Dikebe warriors guarded the river.

She gathered with Kioli, Fayola, and Bolanle in the Chief's hut to discuss the plan in detail. They mapped out the areas of the river with the fewest number of guards and came up with a plan to sneak Olawu across the river. It was clear riding from there to Borimbe.

"But what if you're spotted by someone on the road?" Fayola asked. "You saw what they did to Kioli."

Olawu snapped her fingers. "Kioli, do you have any of the Dikebe armor?"

"I should." Kioli nodded.

"If I am wearing my armor, they will assume I am a man at first glance."

"You will still need to clear the gates," Bolanle added.

Olawu nodded her head. "I will have to break in."

All three women looked at Olawu. "Break in?"

"If I can reach Dikembe in time, it will be fine."

"But what if you do not reach him in time?" Bolanle asked. "What if they catch you?"

"They won't catch me."

"But what if they do?"

Olawu grew quiet. This part of the plan was completely out of her control. She could not sneak past the guards at the gate, and the journey from the gate to the fortress held many opportunities for failure.

"I'll need our fastest horse," Olawu finally replied. "And plenty of padding beneath my armor. In case I get an arrow in the back."

Kioli winced, but Olawu gave her a sideways smile. "Do not worry, Kioli. I'll be fine."

"So, you get to the fortress, you see InDuna Dikembe, and then what happens?" Bolanle asked.

"I wait for an opportunity to kill him, and I-"

"Drive this into his heart?" Fayola presented Olawu with a long, serrated dagger. "For maximum results, plunge and twist!"

"Do not be so insensitive, Fayola." Kioli chided her with a nudge. "She took an arrow for this man, remember?" Kioli gave her a wary glance. "Are you sure you will be able to do this, Olawu?"

Olawu swallowed the lump in her throat and nodded. "I am sure."

"Remember, once you've finished the deed, you need to get out of there as soon as possible." Kioli met her eyes. "Do not linger, and do not take too long to do it. It is harder to hide in the daylight. We'll meet you at the northern bend here." Kioli pointed to a place on the map. "It is the best place to cross quickly, since it is very slippery and hard to patrol."

"Remember what to do if you don't see me by daybreak." Olawu gave them all hard looks. "You return to Oloko Ekhaya without me."

"Got it!" Fayola nodded with more enthusiasm than Olawu liked.

Olawu looked at the women surrounding her. Kioli, Fayola and Bolanle all volunteered to travel with her. Their first plan was to sneak across the river undetected. Bolanle would scout ahead while Kioli and Fayola stayed with Olawu. If that failed, their next plan was to distract the Dikebe guards while Olawu rode on to Borimbe.

If all went according to plan, they would return to Oloko Ekhaya in a few days.

Chapter Fifty

Olawu slowed her horse nearly a mile away from the gates of Borimbe. Her heart pounded in her chest. She took several deep breaths to silence it and tightened her grip on the reins. There was no turning back.

She coaxed the black steed into a gallop. The gates soon came into view, guards standing on either side. They grabbed their spears at the sight of her, shouting threats, but they moved too slowly. She kicked one guard down as she passed, bracing herself for a blow from the other. His spear grazed her arm, and she kicked it from his hands, sending the weapon to the ground.

Olawu cleared the gates and kicked the steed's hide. She raced through the streets of Borimbe as shouts rang out from the guards and night watchmen giving chase. The air whistled near her cheek as an arrow flew by. She took a detour and guided the horse through narrow streets and up back alleyways to throw off her assailants.

She silently blessed Naomi for guiding her through Borimbe all those years ago. She knew every inch of the city. She avoided the main road and continued through the back alleys, upending tables and lines of laundry as she passed. She could no longer hear the guards, but that didn't mean the coast was clear.

She continued to ascend the rocky terrain of Borimbe until the fortress came into view. The night watchmen sounded an alarm. She needed to get to Dikembe, and fast.

"InDuna Dikembe!" Olawu shrieked at the top of her lungs, repeating his name over and over.

The fortress guards lined up along the courtyard, swords and spears drawn. Men with arrows stood on the walls. Dikembe's personal guard stood out front, and Olawu recognized Hondo. She halted her steed and jumped from her horse.

"Hondo! I need to speak to InDuna Dikembe." Olawu fell to her knees and held up her hands as several guards grabbed her. Hondo stepped forward with a curious gaze. His eyes widened in recognition.

"Olawu?" He signaled for the guards to release her and Olawu stood.

"Hondo! I need to see InDuna Dikembe!" Her volume increased. "InDuna Dikembe, I must speak with you!"

Hondo stepped aside, and Dikembe stepped forward. He wore a black, full length kaftan and grey tunic that fluttered behind his legs as he walked. A thick beard, neatly trimmed, descended from his chin. Eyes dark and cold, he walked as one without fear.

As their eyes met, Dikembe's demeanor changed.

"InDuna?" Olawu whispered.

He walked towards her with slow steps, disbelief in his expression. "Olawu? Is that you?"

She nodded. "InDuna, I am here."

He cupped her face in his hands, searching her eyes, shaking his head. Finally, he pulled her into his arms. His beard tickled her neck as he tilted his head inward. "You're alive! My Olawu is alive!" He held her closely, crying into her hair as he spoke. "I did not think I would lay eyes on you again." He pulled back and looked at her. "How did you come to be here?"

"I escaped. Dikembe?" Olawu searched his eyes for something familiar. Dikembe seemed not to breathe as he watched her. He placed his hand against her cheek, and she leaned into his touch. He lowered his face, but stopped inches from her mouth, waiting.

Olawu closed the distance between them, pressing her lips hard against his. Dikembe pulled her forward, his kisses desperate. She wrapped her arms around his neck, and he drew her even closer, running his hands up and down the small of her back.

"InDuna." Hondo cleared his throat and Dikembe pulled away.

He looked at her, eyes hungry. "We should go inside."

Olawu followed him through the fortress halls until they arrived at the dining hall. He sent a servant to the kitchen with orders and pulled out a chair for Olawu. She sat slowly and stared at the table, wondering how many meals had been eaten there without her. Resentment tugged at her, but she held it at bay and offered Dikembe a bright smile.

Dikembe sat beside her, taking her hands in his. "I truly cannot believe you are here. Are you a ghost?"

"No, Dikembe. I am truly here."

He kissed each of her fingers, then rubbed them gently with his thumb. "My Olawu," he whispered.

Food arrived, and only then did he let her go. Olawu nodded gratefully and ate everything in front of her. Fayola and Bolanle had already gone over this scenario with her. She had to play the part of a prisoner of war. Being ravenous was one of the parts.

Dikembe waited until she finished to ask her more. "Where have you been all this time?"

"I was held prisoner by the Oloko." The best lies were wrapped in truth, and she and Fayola had practiced what she would say. "They kept me alive because I was a woman. They thought I might be someone of importance, since the Dikebe do not allow women in their army. After a few years of keeping me prisoner, they decided they would ransom me in exchange for some sort of river agreement. They thought I was a mistress to InDuna Dike, or to you. But their messenger never returned. When I overheard them saying that I was of no use to them, I knew I had to escape. I had never caused them any trouble, so they let their guard down. I found my armor, stole a horse, and came to Borimbe."

Dikembe lowered his head. "Did they hurt you, Olawu?"

"Only at first, when they tried to get information from me. After that, they treated my wounds and tried to befriend me. I was still a prisoner, but they let me have some freedom. Everywhere I went they had a guard with me, and I could not leave the village." Olawu's resentment rose again. This time, she could not shake it. She had to know. "Dikembe? Why did you not come for me?"

He lifted his head and frowned. "Olawu," he began.

"You promised." Olawu sniffed. "You promised you would always come for me."

Dikembe shook his head. "I'm sorry, Olawu. I thought you were lost to me. The Oloko do not hold prisoners for long. And after the mudslide, we lost so many men. We could not track you, and I truly thought you were dead. Please forgive me?" Dikembe kissed her hands and lowered himself to his knees. He placed his head in her lap. "I'm sorry I failed you."

Olawu wiped the tears from her face. "I understand." She placed her hands on her lap, and he kissed them again, lowering his face into her palms. Olawu let out a slow breath as her body reacted to his touch. "Dikembe, I am tired."

"Of course."

Dikembe stood and guided her to her room. She could have gotten there on her own, but he would not let her go. Two guards stood on either side of the door, and Dikembe dismissed them. Olawu stared after them as they took their leave.

"Have you had the doors to my room guarded this whole time?" she asked.

"I sleep here now." He cleared his throat. "It reminds me of you."

Olawu nodded and sat on the bed. Dikembe crouched on the floor in front of her and began removing her armor.

"It is very loose, Olawu," he scolded.

"I had to put it on myself."

Dikembe shook his head and sighed. "I suppose it could not be helped." He removed the armor and looked at her, longing in his eyes.

"Dikembe?" She spoke his name softly.

"Yes?" The word came out in a rasping breath.

"Will you help me with my kaftan?"

Dikembe nodded, gently tugging the top half of her kaftan up and over her head. He chuckled when he saw the miles of wrapping underneath it.

"Must you still wear this?" he asked.

"I could not wear my armor without it. It was not made for women." Olawu looked up at him. "I missed you, Dikembe."

He slowly removed the wrapping around her torso, stopping at the scar on the upper side of her abdomen. He touched it gently. "You bear a scar because of me." He spoke the words with bitterness.

"It does not hurt anymore," she whispered.

"Olawu?" He spoke her name in a haggard voice. Her pulse quickened as he placed his hands on both sides of her face, abandoning the wrapping altogether. "I will never let you go again. I swear it."

Olawu kissed him softly, closing her eyes and reveling in the feel of his lips against hers. Dikembe lifted himself from the floor, deepening their kiss. Heat passed from his fingers to her skin as he grazed her sides. He kissed her lips, her chin, her neck. When he returned to her lips again, he paused. He looked at her, waiting for her permission to continue. Olawu nodded her consent, but still he hesitated.

"I want you, Olawu. All of you."

Olawu gazed into his eyes and smiled. "I want you too, Dikembe."

She gave herself to him, feeling vulnerable in his arms. He spoke to her with soothing words and showered her with kisses. As the night drew on, they held each other. Olawu's head rested on his chest as he stroked her back.

"I love you, Olawu," he whispered as he kissed the top of her head. Olawu's chest squeezed in agony. The last man to speak those words to her had been her ubaba. As Dikembe drifted off to sleep, Olawu cried, clinging to the moment they had shared.

When Dikembe's breathing slowed to the rhythm of deep sleep, Olawu crept out of bed and dressed herself. She grabbed her armor and felt for the dagger taped to the inside near the back. She removed the dagger and struggled into her armor. After a few tries she managed to slide it on. She quietly tightened the straps as her heart thumped loudly in her chest.

It was a simple plan. Get in, kill him, get out. Olawu unsheathed the dagger and raised it high above Dikembe's chest. The Oloko would starve because of him. She had to do this.

Her eyes traveled to the scar on his chest, left by the arrow that had nearly taken his life. Ubaba had saved Dikembe all those years ago. Had he been saved just to die at her hands now?

Things were not so simple after all.

She lowered the dagger and wiped the tears from her eyes. She could not do it. Not even to save the Oloko. It was not Ubaba's way. And if she wished to be like him, it could not be hers.

Olawu sat on the stool near the table by the bed, her head full of frustrations. There had to be another way. Perhaps she could convince Dikembe to consider a truce with the Oloko. Now that she was here, she could speak to him directly.

But Dikembe had a temper. He would likely lock her in her room once he learned she had lied to him, and he wouldn't listen to a word. She would lose his trust the moment she confessed.

Olawu stared absently at the maps laid out on top of the table. Her eyes drifted towards a red circle drawn around Kanakam. She looked more intently at the map, and at the lines and crosses marking places along the Kanak river.

She turned to the map underneath, which was not a map at all, but plans for construction. She stared at the parchments in front of her, the wheels turning in her head. A deep, red line began at the Kanak river and headed east, following the stream that led into the valleys. The stream that fed water into the Oloko villages. The stream that had dried up.

Were the Dikebe behind the drought in the eastern valleys? Olawu looked again at the plans. She recognized the signature in the corner. Businge.

Olawu knew what she must do. She grabbed the parchments and folded them neatly before stuffing them inside her armor. She took a final glance at Dikembe before leaving the room.

The guards had not returned, but that didn't mean she would not be watched. She moved quickly to the stables and found her horse happily drinking from a trough.

"Time to work again, my friend." Olawu mounted her steed and clicked her tongue, riding back down into the streets of Borimbe. She moved quickly through the alleys until they reached the right house. She banged on the door several times until it opened.

"What in God's name are you-" Businge froze as he looked up at her. "Olawu?" His eyes softened at the sight of her, and he stepped outside. "You're alive?"

"Businge." Olawu had no time for pleasantries. "Do you remember when you promised to take me wherever I needed to go if I needed you?"

Businge nodded absently. "I can't believe you're here."

"Businge, I need your help!" Olawu's voice cracked as she spoke. That got his attention.

"What do you need me to do?"

"I need you to take me to Kanakam. Right now. I can explain everything on the way."

"Alright, just give me a few minutes." Businge closed the door and returned in his riding clothes. They grabbed his horse and headed to the eastern gate. Olawu averted her gaze as Businge spoke to the guards.

"Where are you headed this late, Businge?"

"Kanakam," he replied. "I have an emergency there." The guards glanced at Olawu and waved them through. As soon as they cleared the gates, Olawu sent her horse flying forward.

"Olawu!" Businge called after her, kicking his horse to match her speed.

"We've got to get to Kanakam!" Olawu shouted as she raced on. After a few miles at that pace, Olawu grabbed her side and groaned.

"Olawu?" Businge brought his horse closer. "Olawu, are you alright?"

She groaned again and pitched to the side, careful to roll as she landed to soften the blow.

"Olawu!"

Businge pulled his horse to a halt and dismounted. She continued her groaning as he approached. He gingerly touched her side, eyes full of genuine concern.

"Olawu, what's happened? Are you injured?"

She felt a twinge of guilt at her ruse. But it could not be helped.

"Olawu? Can you speak?"

Businge continued to look over her, desperately searching for the source of her agony. Olawu found a large rock and swung it hard against his head. He fell over, unconscious.

She whistled for her horse and it returned to her. "Forgive me, Businge." She lifted him onto his horse, tying his arms and blindfolding him as she tethered him securely to the brown mare. She abandoned the main road and headed towards the river.

When she neared the rendezvous point, she heard the familiar whistle of Bolanle. Olawu stilled, waiting for the all clear. When Bolanle whistled again, she crossed the river, Businge in tow. The women embraced as they descended from their hiding places among the trees.

"Is it done?" Kioli asked.

Olawu shook her head. "Not here. Let us return to Oloko Ekhaya."

They traveled quickly under the cover of darkness, stopping only when they were well into the eastern valleys. Businge stirred and Fayola stared at Olawu. She shook her head. They needed him alive.

When they crossed into Oloko territory, they made camp, tying Businge to a tree. He growled in protest when his feet were tied. Until that moment, he had been very quiet.

"Who are you people?" Businge snarled. "Are you bandits? Show yourselves!"

Kioli, Fayola and Bolanle all looked to Olawu. She placed a finger to her lips and shook her head.

"The woman I was with? Where is she? If you've harmed her, I swear I will kill you!" Kioli made a face at Fayola. "Show yourselves!" Businge screeched.

Olawu moved closer to Businge, examining the bloody knot on the side of his head. It gave her no cause for concern. He would live. And he was fully in control of his faculties.

She placed a bowl to his lips, startling him. Businge shook his head in protest, rattling his limbs in their restraints. Olawu waited for him to tire himself out, then placed the bowl to his lips again. Businge drank grudgingly, then hungrily. When the bowl was empty, Olawu gestured to the other women, and they followed her to an area out of earshot.

"Who the hell is that?" Kioli asked.

"An old friend," Olawu replied. She stared at each of the women surrounding her, making eye contact as she spoke. "I did not kill Dikembe."

Fayola scowled. "I knew it!"

"Olawu." Bolanle shook her head in disappointment.

"What happened?" Kioli asked.

"I won't lie to you. I could not do it." Kioli's eyes flashed in anger, but she did not speak her frustrations.

"And why have you brought your friend along with us?" Kioli asked.

"Because of this." Olawu pulled out the plans she'd found in Dikembe's room. She showed them the areas marked for construction. "If these plans are what I think they are, the Dikebe are responsible for our water supply drying out. It appears they've built a dam in Kanakam which is controlling the flow of water to the valley. See this name at the bottom?" The women looked at the plans, following along where Olawu pointed.

"This signature belongs to Businge. He and his ubaba are craftsmen. They've worked for InDuna Dike for a very long time. They're responsible for the construction of the citadels in all the Dikebe villages, and it looks like they've also drawn the plans for the dam. That," she pointed, "is Businge. I brought him here to tell us what he knows so we can find a way to bring water back to the valley."

"That wasn't the plan, Olawu." Fayola shook her head. "You were supposed to kill Dikembe!"

"Killing Dikembe won't matter if they've found a way to cut off our water supply, Fayola. You've seen with your own eyes how the Kanak river is guarded. Even without Dikembe, do you think the tribes will just willingly allow the Oloko to come and go as they please? We need to destroy this dam, and the only way to do it is through Businge."

OLAWU

"Why would he even help us?" Bolanle asked. "Does he not hate the Oloko as much as any Dikebe? How will we know he is telling us the truth?"

Olawu sighed. "I have a plan."

Chapter Fifty One

Dikembe opened his eyes and smiled. Olawu had returned to him. He had thought the pain in his heart would never leave, but seeing her last night had filled him with warmth and light, soothing the anguish away.

"Olawu?" He whispered her name as he turned towards her. But she wasn't there. He sat up and looked around the room. There was no sign of her clothes or armor. Had it been a dream?

Dikembe dressed himself and left the room, calling for his guards. Ibawa and Boku approached quickly.

"Yes, InDuna?" Boku spoke first.

"Olawu. Have you seen her?"

"No, InDuna."

"Did she leave the room this morning?"

Boku hesitated before speaking. "You sent us away last night."

"Is everything alright, InDuna?" Ibawa asked.

Dikembe clenched his fists and walked towards the courtyard. He found Hondo training with a group of Dikebe warriors. Hondo halted their exercises when he saw Dikembe approaching.

"InDuna!" Hondo bowed and crossed his forearms in greeting. Dikembe tapped them, his irritation growing.

"Hondo, have you seen Olawu?"

"No, InDuna. I can interrogate the fortress guards if you wish?"

Dikembe nodded and Hondo dismissed the Dikebe before heading off to the fortress walls. Dikembe looked out at the courtyard, apprehension growing. Where had Olawu gone?

"InDuna?" Ibawa approached him with a tentative step. "InDuna Dike is asking for you."

Dikembe sighed. He was in no mood to visit with his baba. He needed to find Olawu. "Tell him I'll be along later, Ibawa. I have pressing matters to attend to." Ibawa nodded and left. Dikembe couldn't shake the panic he felt. Things had gone well last night, hadn't they? They'd been closer than ever. Had he done something wrong?

"InDuna." Hondo returned, his face pensive. "The morning guard saw Olawu leave on horseback just after midnight."

Dikembe frowned. "Bring me my horse, Hondo. We'll head to the eastern gate. Send Boku and Yero to the south. If she's left Borimbe, I want to know."

"Yes, InDuna." Hondo left quickly.

Dikembe swore as anger pooled in his chest. How could she leave without a word? He paced the courtyard until Hondo returned, and they traveled down through Borimbe until they reached the eastern gate. The guards were just about to change when Hondo stopped them.

"You there, were you watching this gate after midnight?" Hondo asked one of the guards.

"Yes." The guard replied with a nervous glance towards Dikembe. "I was here with Bukuli." He pointed at the other guard.

"Did a woman pass through these gates after midnight?" Hondo asked. "She would have been riding a black horse."

"Oh, we do not let women pass without an escort." The guard eyed Hondo. "It is forbidden, as you know, so we would not have let her pass."

"She would have had dreads about to here and Dikebe armor," Dikembe cut in. "Whether she was with someone or not, did anyone like that pass through these gates?"

The guard seemed flustered, being addressed directly by Dikembe. "InDuna Dikembe, I do not think-"

"Yes, I remember!" Bukuli snapped his fingers. "Businge left for Kanakam this morning with a woman matching your description."

"Businge?" Hondo looked from the guard to Dikembe. "Are you sure?"

"Yes, I spoke with him. He said he had an emergency in Kanakam."

Dikembe's blood grew cold. Olawu had left with Businge?

"What time was that?" Hondo asked.

"Eh, around the first hour," Bukuli replied.

Hondo turned to Dikembe. "Do you wish to ride to Kanakam?"

Dikembe shook his head. If he rode to Kanakam now, he would kill them both. It was better to wait until he'd cooled down. Olawu had some explaining to do. He'd give them three days. If she did not return, he would drag her back to Borimbe himself.

Chapter Fifty Two

Kioli and Fayola both protested when Olawu suggested bringing Businge back to Oloko Ekhaya.

"If you do not wish him dead, you cannot bring him there!" Kioli cried.

"He won't make trouble," Olawu said. "He'll be too concerned with me to try anything."

"There you go again, Olawu. You overestimate your importance to these Dikebe!"

Olawu tried to ignore the sting of Kioli's words. "Businge has never let me down," Olawu insisted. "Not once."

"But what happens afterwards, Olawu?" Fayola frowned. "If he knows where Oloko Ekhaya is, we cannot let him go. He will lead the Dikebe straight to us!"

"Not if we keep him blindfolded," Olawu replied. "If he does not know the way, he cannot lead the Dikebe. And when we release him, we will take him far from the eastern valleys first."

"So you do plan to release him?" Bolanle asked.

"Once we have what we need, yes."

"I say we just kill him." Fayola shrugged. "Friend or not, he is still a Dikebe. Get what you need, Olawu. Then I will take care of him."

"You will do no such thing!" Olawu growled. "Control yourself, Fayola."

"What is Businge to you?" Kioli asked, eyes keen. "He must be more than a friend?"

"A lover?" Bolanle offered.

"I thought that was InDuna Dikembe?" Fayola grinned. "Oh! Olawu, you are a woman of many talents!"

"No, nothing like that." Olawu shook her head.

"Hang on a moment." Fayola scratched her head. "When we were in Oloko Intaba, one of the Dikebe men chased my horse. He followed us clear into the valley, and I thought I might have to cut you loose, but then the mudslide happened. Was that Businge?"

All three Oloko women looked back at Businge, new admiration glowing on their faces.

"You were the one who dragged me on your horse, Fayola?" Olawu touched her neck as though the scars were still there.

Fayola shrugged. "Kioli shot you with an arrow, but you focus on Fayola? If it weren't for me, you would have died in the mud!"

"Olawu, I am confused." Bolanle crinkled her brow. "Businge followed Fayola's horse through fighting Dikebe and Oloko, through the mud and the rain and into the valley, where he was stopped only by the crushing force of a mudslide, and he is *not* your lover?"

Kioli and Fayola joined Bolanle in their bewildered looks. Olawu opened her mouth and closed it. Businge had chased after her?

"I've changed my mind." Fayola grinned. "I will not kill Businge. I will marry him!" Fayola laughed and Kioli shoved her hard. Bolanle nodded her head in agreement.

"We need to stay on track." Kioli scowled.

Olawu agreed. "We will bring him to Oloko Ekhaya and continue with our plan there. Are we all agreed?"

All three women nodded their heads.

"Bolanle and Fayola, go on ahead and make the preparations. Kioli and I will bring Businge."

OLAWU

BUSINGE COULD NOT SEE where he was. He could only tell that it was dark. His body ached all over after walking for days tied behind a horse. He had no idea where Olawu was. They'd gagged him after his outburst, and they never spoke to him. Not a word. Once a day they fed him some kind of broth, but that was all.

As far as he could tell, he sat alone in the dark. He'd been this way for hours, possibly days. He was too disoriented to tell. His head throbbed, and he had an itch he couldn't reach, but his arms, legs, and eyes were still bound.

Businge tensed at the swishing sound of a door. It was followed by the thump of something landing hard on the ground. He heard a voice cry out in pain. It sounded like . . .

"Olawu?" Businge called out into the air. A heavy groan was the reply. "Olawu, is that you?"

"Businge?"

Joy crept into his heart at the sound of her voice. She was alive! He had so much to tell her, so many questions to ask. Where had she been all this time? What had happened to her after the mudslide? How had she ended up in Borimbe that night?

The door opened again. Businge tensed again as he felt the warm breath of a person near his ear.

"I have no patience, so I will only say this once. Give us what we want, and we will let you and your friend go."

"And if I refuse?" Businge growled and tugged against his restraints. He couldn't move forward more than an inch or so. The footsteps retreated and Businge heard Olawu cry out in pain.

"Stop!" Businge cried. "Do not hurt her!" Olawu's cries continued and Businge roared. "I said stop! Just tell me what you need. Please!"

"The dam in Kanakam. Did you design it?"

"Yes."

"What is it made of?"

"It is made of many things." Businge heard a loud slap and Olawu yelped. "Clay and cement!" Businge cried. "With wood for the levers."

"And who guards the dam? Dikebe warriors?"

"A few. But mostly men from Kanakam."

"How many guard the wall?"

Businge hesitated, and his blindfold was suddenly removed. It was hard to reorient himself to the dim light coming in through slits in the bamboo hut, but he made out Olawu easily enough. A dark Oloko woman with long dreads held her by a rope tied around her wrists. Blood stained her lower lip, and purple bruises marked her neck and shoulders.

The Oloko woman held a dagger to her throat. "I see you wish to see your friend die!" She snarled.

"No! Please!"

"How many?" she repeated.

"A dozen, sometimes more, depending on the time of day. Olawu, are you alright?"

"Businge." Olawu moaned his name, then collapsed into the dirt.

"Olawu!" Businge tugged at his restraints to get to her. Another woman entered the hut with parchments in her hands. She handed them off, then dragged Olawu out. "What are you doing?" Businge asked. "Where are you taking her?"

The woman crouched down with the plans, shoving them towards Businge. "Here's what happens next. You will show me exactly where the guards are positioned on this dam. You will show me where to find the controls, and you will answer every question I have. If you do not, you will never see your precious Olawu again."

Businge clenched his jaw and nodded. "I will tell you whatever you need to know. But please, do not hurt her. She knows nothing of this."

"Start talking."

Chapter Fifty Three

Olawu sat with Chief Umfazi in her hut, waiting for Kioli to return.

"Do not worry." Fayola gave her arm a reassuring squeeze. "Kioli is very good at interrogations."

Olawu shook her head. "Are you sure she'll be able to do this? Maybe I should go instead?" Olawu stood, but Chief Umfazi waved her back to her seat.

"This was your idea, was it not, Olawu?"

She nodded. It was. But she had not expected to see such anguish on Businge's face. She felt guilty for treating him this way.

"I think we've got what we need!" Kioli grinned as she walked in. Olawu stood, staring at Kioli as she laid out the plans on a table. Chief Umfazi, Olawu, and Fayola joined her. "Businge was very detailed in his descriptions, and we can send scouts ahead to verify the guard numbers. Olawu, look! This blockade is built almost entirely out of clay and stone. It was a separate project from the dam, and the area around it couldn't handle the weight of cement. There are weak spots here and here. If we can smash it, then it should restore the flow of water to the valley."

"But won't the Dikebe just build another?" Fayola asked.

"Fayola's right." Olawu frowned, tapping the plans. "We have to destroy the dam."

"It took nearly two years to build it, Olawu." Kioli shook her head. "It's as sturdy as the mountain rock it's sitting on. How would we destroy something like that?"

"Here." Olawu pointed to the plans. "You see the release gate at the center of the dam? It's held in place by mechanisms that are controlled there. If we can focus on destroying these cement pins that are holding the release mechanism in place, the water behind the dam should do the rest."

Kioli studied the plans. "Those cement pins are a few feet thick, Olawu. We're going to need something pretty strong to break them."

"What if we did not break them?" Chief Umfazi asked. "What if we could remove them instead?"

"If we had something slick to loosen them, we could pull them out." Olawu nodded. "But we would need lots of whatever that something is."

"Leave it to me," Chief Umfazi nodded.

"What about the rest of the dam?" Fayola asked. "Will they be able to rebuild the gate if it is blown off by the water?" They all looked to Kioli.

"I'll ask Businge. Any other questions?"

"Is he alright?" Olawu asked. Kioli raised an eyebrow. "I mean did you have to-"

"I did not hurt him, Olawu." Kioli gave her a pat. "Do not worry. I am not like Fayola. I can control my impulses."

"Ach, you are always picking on me!" Fayola scoffed. "Olawu gave him the goose egg on his head, why is she fretting so much? If Kioli has to rough him up a bit, he can bear it."

"How much time will we need to prepare?" Chief Umfazi asked.

Kioli and Olawu exchanged glances. "We don't have time to wait," Olawu answered. "If water is not restored soon, the Oloko will starve. And if Businge is missing too long, suspicions will arise. Is a week enough time for you to prepare, Chief Umfazi?"

She nodded. "For the sake of the Oloko, it will have to be enough time. You've done well, Olawu. I am proud of you." Chief Umfazi looked at Kioli and Fayola. "All of you."

Chapter Fifty Four

Dikembe pulled his horse to an abrupt stop before he entered Kanakam. Hondo pulled up beside him with Yero, Boku, and Ibawa close behind. Three days had felt like torture. He spent many sleepless nights wondering if Olawu was with Businge. If he were holding her, kissing her, removing her kaftan to-

"InDuna?" Hondo looked at him, waiting for further instruction. Dikembe grunted. Once he entered Kanakam, there was no deterring him. There would be no second chances for Olawu if he caught her with Businge. He stayed at the threshold, considering his heart.

Could he really harm her? What if Businge had tricked her, somehow? But how did Businge even know she was in Borimbe? She'd come straight to the fortress. She had to have sought him out. Unless she had been in communication with him all along. Had Businge known Olawu was alive?

"Should we ride to the citadel, InDuna?" Hondo asked.

Dikembe shook his head. He knew where he would go first. If Olawu were in Kanakam, she would not be at the citadel. She would be with her umama. Dikembe needed an explanation. He wanted to know why. Why did she leave him? Why did she go with Businge? What had he done wrong?

"Fan out." Dikembe finally answered. "Search the marketplace. I will go to her umama's home."

The guards did as he commanded. All except Hondo. He grabbed Dikembe by the arm, halting him.

"Dikembe." Hondo looked him in the eyes. "What will you do if you see Olawu here?"

It was the question he'd been wrestling with for days now. The truth was, he didn't know.

Hondo released his hold. "InDuna, I know your feelings for Olawu. I would ask that you exercise restraint. She has just returned to you. If you move in your anger, you may regret it later."

Dikembe nodded and turned his horse towards Olawu's childhood home. When he arrived at the small hut, he knocked on the door. Olawu's sister Kimani answered, a shy smile on her face as she welcomed him.

"How can I help you?" she asked.

Dikembe could not remember the last time he saw Kimani. She had been much smaller than the blossoming youth he saw before him now. Dikembe cleared his throat. "May I speak to your umama?"

"She is sleeping now." Kimani started to close the door, but it was halted by another hand.

"Kimani, who are you talking to-" Ugami's eyes widened at the sight of Dikembe, and she fell to the ground. "InDuna Dikembe!"

"It's been a long time, Ugami," Dikembe muttered.

"Thank you for your kindness, InDuna." Ugami remained on the ground, pulling Kimani down to join her.

Kimani kneeled with a grumble. Dikembe detected some of the same fiery defiance that had been prevalent in Olawu. It made his heart hurt.

"What brings you to our door, InDuna Dikembe?" Ugami asked.

"I am looking for your sister, Olawu."

Ugami's head snapped up in surprise. "Olawu?" Ugami stood, confusion on her face. "But isn't she . . ." Ugami placed her hand on her head. "Was she not captured by the Oloko, InDuna?"

Dikembe sighed. So, she wasn't here. It dawned on him that he had not sent word of Olawu to her family. "Who told you this, Ugami?"

"Businge." Ugami leaned against the door, overcome with emotion. "Is it not true? Is my sister alive?"

Dikembe's temper flared, despite her tears. What business did Businge have telling Olawu's family anything? He had always overstepped where it concerned Olawu. It made his blood boil.

"Tell me, Ugami? Do you speak to Businge often?"

"Of course, InDuna Dikembe. He is my husband."

Dikembe's eyes grew wide with shock. "Your husband?"

"Yes." Ugami smiled. "We were married last year."

"Have you seen Businge recently?" Dikembe pressed.

"Not since he left for Borimbe about a week ago. He should have returned by now." An infant began to cry from somewhere inside, and Ugami bowed. "Forgive me, InDuna, but my son is hungry."

"Is Olawu alive?" Kimani looked up at Dikembe. "My sister? Is she alive?"

"I don't know," Dikembe answered with a frown. "But if she comes here, you must send a message to me at the citadel." He looked from Kimani to Ugami. "I'll be there waiting. If you see her, you must come to me right away."

Dikembe got back on his horse, his thoughts swirling like a sandstorm. Businge had a wife and child to care for, and yet he had ridden off in the night with another woman. If it had been someone else, Dikembe would have merely been disgusted.

But Businge was with Olawu. His Olawu. One thing was certain. He would make Businge answer for himself.

KIOLI HELPED OLAWU into her armor, Fayola grinning beside them. The Oloko used a similar material as the Dikebe, but it was painted black while the Dikebe armor bore a natural brown. It also covered more than just her shoulders and torso. The armor ran the length of Olawu's arms all the way to her wrists. The Oloko custom-made each piece of armor, fitting it to the wearer. She was glad for it. She did not have to wrap her chest to wear it.

"You almost look like a warrior, udokotela." Kioli smiled. "There is just one thing missing."

"Missing?" Olawu looked from Fayola to Kioli.

Chief Umfazi walked into the hut, carrying the hide of a leopard.

"Long before it became the symbol of the Dikebe, the leopard was a symbol of cunning and strength. As you lead us on this quest, Olawu, go with the knowledge that all of Oloko stands behind you. This gift is for you." Chief Umfazi draped the hide around Olawu's shoulders. There were loops built into the armor for just such an adornment. Olawu bowed in front of Chief Umfazi.

"Thank you."

Chief Umfazi looked to Kioli and Fayola. "The jars are ready and being loaded up with the horses. Chausiku has seen to it. Mbambo will be riding with his strong masons. He knows the plan."

Olawu stood and Chief Umfazi held her gently by the shoulders. "You've done well, Olawu. May God be with you all. Are you ready to make your address?"

Olawu nodded even as her stomach twisted in knots. She would be responsible for taking thirty Oloko across the valley and into Dikebe territory. If all went according to plan, they would get in and out with minimal casualties. But Olawu was no fool. They could not plan for every contingency, and there were bound to be some unforeseen obstacles.

Olawu would ride with Kioli to the forest just east of the dam. They would wait until dark to take out the guards and sneak inside the dam's control area. Fayola would rendezvous with the strong masons from Oloko Intlambo, who lived further west, and they would tear down the secondary dam blocking the streams.

Even if they were able to avoid detection, they still did not know how long it would take to break the dams. The longer it took, the more they ran the risk of being discovered. Olawu prayed they would be successful.

She walked with Chief Umfazi to the front of the pillar. She looked out at the faces of the those who had welcomed her and made her part of their tribe. Far too many were thin and hungry. They were desperate. They needed hope.

"Oloko men and women! When I first came to you, I was ignorant. I had heard stories of the Oloko, but I did not know you." Olawu took a deep breath. She needed to open her heart to them, as they had opened their hearts to her. She needed them to know why they mattered so much to her.

"My name is Olawu. My ubaba was an udokotela in the village of Kanakam. When InDuna Dike and his son took over my village, they began building a citadel. While he was tending to Mama InDuna, my ubaba was crushed under the weight of a broken tower. Because I was a woman, I was not allowed to help him. He was carried to a room full of men with no knowledge of how to help him. And he died."

Olawu's voice cracked and she paused.

"In my village, a woman could not survive without a man. I was not allowed to work to care for my family, or even buy and sell in the market. We had to rely on the kindness of our neighbors. But our neighbors were not as kind as we had hoped. We became Pootagi, which meant that we were as low as slaves. Pootagi women could be purchased during a time called the Choosing and sent home with a stranger to live out their days as less than nothing. Those who refused were crushed and beaten. That was what I knew. That is the place I came from."

Olawu saw some shake their heads. Others cried, placing thin hands over their mouths.

"My ubaba loved me. He taught me that I had value, no matter what anybody said. When my ubaba died, I thought I would never feel such love again. But when I came to Oloko Ekhaya, it was as if my ubaba lived in each of you. You are my ubaba. You are my family. You are my home. And I will fight for you until my last breath!"

They cheered in front of her, as did the Chief beside her. Kioli, Bolanle, and Fayola clapped their hands and shouted. Olawu lifted a fist in the air and began to sing. The crowd did the same, dancing and swaying and raising their fists. They had to succeed.

Their survival depended on it.

Chapter Fifty Five

Olawu stared at the dark hut housing Businge. After today, she would likely never see him again. Bolanle would care for him while they were away.

She wiped a tear from her face. Businge had been loyal to her from the start. She hated betraying him in this way. But she had to protect the Oloko. Her people.

Olawu stepped inside. Businge remained blindfolded and tethered to a post. His head turned at the sound of Olawu's footsteps.

"Who's there?" he called out. "Where is Olawu? What have you done with her?"

"Businge."

He stilled as he recognized her voice. "Olawu? Are you alright? Did they hurt you?"

"Forgive me, Businge." She spoke the words softly as she bent down beside him. She placed her hand on his cheek.

"Olawu? What's going on? I heard shouting earlier."

She silenced him with a kiss. Though it was soft and brief, Businge seemed disoriented by it. "I wish there were another way. Forgive my deception, and know that you will always be my friend."

"Olawu?" Businge spoke her name with a longing she had not expected. She considered kissing him again. He seemed to want her to. She leaned forward, but thoughts of Dikembe made her withdraw.

She stood to leave. "Goodbye, Businge."

"Olawu? Wait." Businge shook his head, then grew still. A heavy silence filled the space between them. She witnessed the moment he realized the truth. His face twisted in pain, twisting her heart with it. "Are you one of them? Olawu? What have you done?"

She left the hut as Businge screamed her name. The betrayal in his voice followed her. Guilt as heavy as stone wrapped around her shoulders and she stumbled. She should not have gone to see him.

Kioli grabbed her arms, hauling her up from the ground. "Olawu? Are you alright?"

She nodded, though it was a lie.

"We're ready to move out." Kioli studied her. "Do you need a moment?"

Olawu needed a lifetime, but she straightened herself, steeling her resolve. "No. I am ready."

"Olawu." Kioli grabbed her arm, the intensity in her gaze frightening. "What will you do if you see Dikembe there?"

"He will most likely be in Borimbe, Kioli. Why?"

Kioli's expression grew bitter. "I hope to see him in Kanakam. I wish to put an arrow through his heart!"

Olawu's chest flooded with heat, and she pulled herself from Kioli's grasp. "Unless it is necessary, you will not kill anyone."

Kioli glared at her in disbelief. "What did you say?"

"No killing."

Kioli scoffed. "How do you expect us to defend ourselves with such restrictions?"

"If you must, then do what you need to do, but if it can be helped-"

"What difference does it make if we kill a few dozen Dikebe along the way? It's one less animal to deal with later!"

"Kioli, I know you hate the Dikebe, but-"

"No, you do not. You have no idea the pain I feel, Olawu. How many brothers and sisters I've lost to the hands of those monsters.

You wish to tell me that their lives are not forfeit in my presence? They killed my family. Your precious Dikembe killed my utata!"

"Yes, Kioli! Dikembe killed your utata. And the Oloko gutted his baba and killed his guards. Before that, the Dikebe murdered Oloko children as they slept. Before that, the Oloko burned down a Dikebe village. How many Dikebe have you killed, Kioli? How many obaba? How many sons? How many brothers? How many women did you widow? Dikebe and Oloko go round and round in circles, but when does it end? Hm?"

"When the last Dikebe is dead!" Kioli spat.

Olawu shook her head and took Kioli's hands in hers. "I understand your pain, Kioli. But you must let go of your hatred. Focus your energy on fighting for your Oloko brothers and sisters, not fighting against the Dikebe. There is a difference. One way leads to peace, the other does not."

Kioli grew quiet, then looked down at Olawu's hands. "I cannot promise not to kill anyone, Olawu. If I see another Oloko in danger, I will not hesitate to spill Dikebe blood. But I will try. And I will give your instructions to the others."

"Thank you." As Kioli walked away, Olawu sent a silent prayer to heaven.

Chapter Fifty Six

When the moon scraped against the top of Mount Kanagari, Olawu gave the signal for them to move forward. Fayola and the strong masons were already working on the smaller dam. If they succeeded, they would return water to the valley, at least temporarily. Olawu, Kioli, and a handful of others hid in the forest.

They would take out the patrol at the top of the dam, making way for Kioli's group to enter the control room. She and her team would disable the dam and use the jars of oil to remove the pins, which would, hopefully, compromise the rest of the structure.

Olawu's group would pour the rest of the jars of oil along the side of the dam. Archers hid in the forest, ready to let fiery arrows fly at Olawu's signal. Whatever the water didn't destroy, the fire would.

Olawu and her small band of warriors flew up the stairs, armed with staffs and spears. Though she had little love left for Kanakam, the thought of killing brought her no joy. Kioli and her group were on the opposite end closest to the control room. Most of her men carried jars of oil. Only a few held spears.

A shadow crossed over Olawu's face, and she paused as a guard walked near the top of the stairs. She nodded to Kwame, who stood beside her, spear in hand. He snuck up on the guard, jabbed him in the face with the butt of his spear, and caught him before he collapsed. Olawu signaled for the others to move forward. It was time to fight.

BUSINGE TURNED HIS head as Bolanle swung the hut door open. "Olawu? Is that you?"

Bolanle set a bowl of stew in front of him. "Do not kick your legs, or you will spill your dinner," she warned.

"Where is Olawu?" Businge asked. "I need to speak with her!"

"She's gone," Bolanle replied. "I will care for you in the meantime."

"Where did she go? What are you Oloko planning? Why have you brought me here? Why is Olawu . . ." Businge paused and shook his head, speaking through clenched teeth. "You Oloko are vile. Is it not enough that you are corrupt? Must you corrupt the innocent as well?"

"Corrupters of the innocent? That is one I have not heard before."

"Do not mock me, Oloko. You will pay for what you've done to Olawu!"

"And you Dikebe will pay for what you have done to us!" Bolanle replied with venom. "You speak of innocence? Do you know how many children starve in this village? Do you know how many have died at the hands of Dikebe warriors? Countless innocents taken by your greedy hands, and still you torment us. You have taken our very livelihoods, stolen our water from our valleys. Now we will take back what is ours."

Businge shook his head. "Your questions about the dam . . . you are not planning to build one, are you? You mean to destroy the dam in Kanakam."

Bolanle did not reply.

"That is impossible." Businge shook his head. "It is too well fortified. It would take weeks to destroy it, and by then you would certainly be caught. It is a fool's errand."

"We do not need to destroy the whole dam at once. Just the gate."

Businge frowned. "No, that's not . . ." His breath caught. "The pins."

"You catch on quick."

"You cannot!" Businge jerked forward, upsetting the bowl of stew in front of him. "Listen to me, please? You cannot destroy the dam!"

Bolanle sighed. "We are going around in circles now."

"No, you do not understand. If the gate is broken, the water from the reservoir will rush out."

"That is the idea."

"No! Do you not see? There will be no way to control the water, and it will flood the valley. Kanakam will be destroyed!"

She shrugged. "What do I care of Kanakam?"

"Please, you must stop this. My wife and child are in Kanakam. Olawu's sister and nephew will be killed along with everyone else near the dam!"

Bolanle ripped off Businge's blindfold. "What did you say?"

"Olawu's sister Ugami is in Kanakam. She is my wife. We have an infant son, Mbako, named after his babu. Her sister Kimani and her mama all live in Kanakam. If your plan is to break the dam, you condemn them all to death, as well as anyone below the walls. Please!"

Bolanle stood and rushed out of the hut.

BOLANLE RAN THROUGH the streets in a panic, searching for Chief Umfazi. She found her in the market sharing a meal with some of the elders. "Chief Umfazi! I just spoke to the prisoner, Businge. We need to reach Olawu!"

"Why, Bolanle? What has happened?" Chief Umfazi stood.

"The dam in Kanakam will flood the village and the valley once the gate is broken. We could lose dozens of Oloko if we do not reach them. Chief Umfazi, the prisoner says that Olawu's family lives in Kanakam! Her umama and her sisters. We must send someone to her."

"It is too late, Bolanle." Chief Umfazi spoke with sadness. "They have been gone three days already."

"But Olawu's family?" Bolanle sniffed. "We cannot do nothing."

"We have no choice."

Bolanle looked westward. "I will go."

Chief Umfazi shook her head. "Bolanle."

"I cannot sit by!"

"You will not reach them in time."

"I must at least try."

Chief Umfazi nodded her consent, and Bolanle rushed to the stables for her horse. She prayed she would not reach Kanakam too late.

Chapter Fifty Seven

O lawu watched from the top of the dam as her group poured oil over the outer walls. The last guard lay bound and gagged at her feet. They'd had to kill one of them to prevent an alarm from sounding, but the rest were tied up.

A loud crack sounded, and Olawu turned with a grin to the horizon. The small dam obstructing the valley stream fell away. Water gushed over the side, shimmering in the moonlight, pulling down what remained of the dam into the valley.

"We've done it, Olawu." Kwame grinned as he gripped her shoulder. "Soon this dam will break, and the water here will rush out."

She nodded and stared down at the flowing Kanak river. The main release gate was still closed, but draining grates released water from the dam into the river. A credit to Businge's talent.

Olawu turned and studied the reservoir behind the dam. Masika, the season of great rain, had just ended, and the reservoir swelled with water. It reminded her of a time when she was young and the Kanak river had flooded. The water levels rose so high that the river spilled over the bank. She had worried that it would reach Kanakam, but thankfully it hadn't.

Olawu stared at the reservoir, deep in thought. She looked back at the gate blocking the waters. A sickening feeling twisted her gut.

"Kwame. We need to go. Head back to the forest, and tell the archers to find higher ground."

Kwame nodded and led the others away. Olawu ran towards the control room. She found Kioli and the others burning the joints where the pins rested.

"Kioli!" Olawu screamed as she rushed forward.

Kioli turned towards Olawu, ready for a fight. "Have we been spotted?" She jumped down from a platform and pulled a dagger from her side.

"No. The water from the reservoir is twice as high from the rains. If we break down the gate, it will flood the whole valley."

Kioli's brow furrowed. "Fayola and the strong masons would not have left yet. They have only just finished their work."

"And they will be swept away if we do not stop now. Them and Kanakam." Olawu raised her hands to her head. Her umama and sisters. "My family. Kioli, my family is in Kanakam!"

"What do you wish to do, Olawu? Should we abandon the gate?"

Olawu trembled with indecision. If they did not destroy the dam, the Dikebe would simply rebuild the obstruction to the eastern valley, and they'd be right back where they started. But destroying the dam meant destroying her family along with it.

"Kioli, I don't know." Olawu shook her head.

Kioli placed her hand on her shoulder. "Olawu, we've already broken the dam blocking the valley stream. It is enough."

"But the Dikebe-"

"Will always find some way to attack us. If it is not this way, it will be another. But we are fighters, Olawu. We fight for our family, remember?"

"The first pin is out!"

Kioli and Olawu turned as a loud groan shook the ground beneath their feet. Samba and two others had been tugging on a rope tied to the pin on the left side. The gate swayed and bent as water pushed its way through. Another group of men tugged at the second pin, sliding it out inch by inch.

"Samba, wait!" Kioli cried. She turned to Olawu. "Go quickly. Find your family. We will try to fix it, but if we cannot, you must get them to higher ground."

Olawu hesitated. "Kioli?

Kioli smiled at her and kissed her cheek. "Go!"

Olawu nodded and rushed away, heart thrashing in her chest. She dashed down the stairs, and glanced back at the gate. If Kioli could not replace the pin, Kanakam would be lost.

She reached the ground and ran, following the trail of the river until she reached the familiar outline of her family's hut. She raced towards it, barreling into the bamboo surrounding the hut as she shouted for her sisters.

"Ugami? Kimani?"

Kimani ran out the back door, slamming into Olawu and knocking her from her feet. "Olawu!" Kimani cried as she squeezed her midsection. "Is it really you?"

"Kimani!" Olawu spoke in between pants. "We don't have time. We need to get you out of here."

"Kimani? Where did you go?" Ugami's hand flew to her mouth at the sight of Olawu. "Sister?" She ran forward and knelt beside Olawu, cupping her face in her hands and kissing her as she cried.

Years of anguish broke free at the sight of her sisters. She wept with them, hugging and kissing them, grieving the loss of time, so much time. She had missed them.

"What happened to you?" Kimani asked. "We thought you were dead."

Olawu wiped her face and stood. "I have no time to explain. We need to leave. Where is umama?"

"She is inside with Mbako."

Olawu hesitated. "Mbako?" Had her ubaba returned from the dead?

"Oh. Mbako is my son. Olawu, you remember Businge, don't you? He and I were married last year."

Olawu wanted to know more, but she needed to get them somewhere safe. Somewhere high up. "Come! We'll grab umama and Mbako and head towards the citadel."

"But why?" Kimani asked.

Olawu ignored her questions and rushed into the hut, searching for her umama. She found her sitting on the floor, her grandson in her arms. Ugami scooped up Mbako, and Olawu grabbed her umama, hoisting her over her shoulder.

"What is going on?" Her umama squalled as Ugami and Kimani followed them out.

"Olawu, please tell us what is going on?" Ugami asked.

"The Kanak river may flood at any moment! We must get to higher ground."

Ugami tied Mbako around her chest and grabbed Kimani's hand. They passed Olawu just as a groan sounded from the dam. Olawu turned in time to see the gate twist to one side. Water burst through, crashing down into the river. More water followed, bringing down trees as it moved towards Kanakam.

Olawu screamed. "Run!"

Chapter Fifty Eight

Dikembe jumped from his bed when he heard the sound. He looked out of his window, eyes wide with surprise as the trees near the riverbank toppled. Water rushed towards Kanakam at an alarming rate.

He left his room and headed towards the citadel wall, looking out at the dark huts of Kanakam. Then he saw her.

Olawu ran towards the citadel, her umama on her back. Ugami and Kimani ran in front of her. Dikembe called for Hondo as he rushed towards the stables. He mounted his horse and galloped down the hill. Hondo and Yero were seconds behind him.

Dikembe barreled down the hill towards Olawu, racing against the water, drowning out the voice in his head saying he wouldn't reach her in time.

Olawu stumbled, and her umama fell from her arms. Dikembe nodded to Yero and Hondo as he continued towards Olawu. They scooped up her sisters and turned back towards the citadel.

Dikembe pushed his horse harder, but as Olawu lifted up her head and their eyes met, he knew. He wasn't going to make it.

The water rushed in, slamming into Olawu and blocking her from his view. His horse reared back and he squeezed the reins to keep from being thrown. The water thrashed in the space between him and Olawu, crushing everything in its path. It went on for an eternity, and then suddenly, it stopped. As the waters receded, Dikembe forced his horse forward.

But there was no sign of Olawu.

"KIOLI!" SAMBA SCREAMED as he tried to push the pin back in place. "There's too much pressure. The pin cannot be replaced!"

Kioli ran towards Samba, soaked from the water spraying all around them. She looked at the angle of the gate, which had widened too far to be pulled back by their strength. Kioli ran a hand through her dreads, thinking. If they didn't get the water under control, Fayola and the others would be drowned downstream.

"There is nothing more we can do!" Samba shouted. "We need to go."

"No!" Kioli wasn't giving up. Not yet. She stared at the water pushing against the gate. "Dibali! Raise the gate!"

Dibali looked at her, confused. "But the other pin?"

"Forget about the pin. We need to raise the gate and use the stoplogs!"

Dibali nodded and ordered two men to help him turn the mechanism to raise the gate. The cement groaned as it rubbed awkwardly against the front sides of the dam, and the gate shifted at an odd angle.

"Samba! Quick!" Kioli called to him as she ran towards the secondary controls. "Businge created a failsafe in case the mechanism failed for the main gate. We need to release the stoplogs. There's a control on the other side there. We'll need to release them at the same time to make sure the distribution is even."

Samba nodded and ran to the other side. At Kioli's signal they turned the controls and the stoplogs rolled out. Kioli gritted her teeth as she turned the controls. The logs smashed against the gate, pinning it into place and stemming the flow of water. Kioli nodded to Samba, and he grinned. They had done it.

"What about Olawu?" Dibali asked.

Kioli's brow creased with worry. Had she made it to higher ground? "For now, we must find Fayola and the others and make sure they are safe. We will send a scout to find Olawu soon."

"But-"

"Olawu is strong. We will return for her later, Dibali."

Dibali seemed uncertain, but he obeyed her orders. They quickly retreated, meeting up with Fayola and the strong masons at the lower end of the trees that led into the valley.

Fayola bled from her arm, but the wound wasn't deep. She smiled wide when she saw Kioli. "Ah, did you see what we did, Kioli? We restored the stream! Now we shall have a good year. Do you not wish to thank Fayola for her sacrifice?" Fayola held up her bloody arm. "You see, Kioli? The archers could not see the marks in the dark, so I had to climb up and place myself in harm's way. One of the archers almost got me, and I fell and scraped my arm. But it is no matter. I did it for my people, and for my Kioli!" Fayola looked around Kioli, searching. "But where is Olawu?"

"There was a change of plans." Kioli scowled. "The reservoir was too high to destroy the gate. It would have flooded the valley and everyone in it. Including you, Fayola."

"Kioli!" The two women turned as Bolanle approached. Her horse foamed at the mouth as she pulled it to a halt. "Kioli! Do not break the dam!" She screeched as she flew off her horse. "The valley will flood!"

"Catch your breath, Bolanle. We already know."

Bolanle's haggard face lit up with relief. "Then I am not too late?" She spoke in between breaths. Kioli shook her head.

"But where is Olawu?" Fayola repeated herself.

Kioli looked back towards Kanakam. She wished she knew.

Chapter Fifty Nine

Dikembe could not hold his panic at bay. His horse tromped through the mud as he searched for Olawu. He called out for her, desperate to hear a reply. As he surveyed the broken wood and debris of the market, he grew more desperate. Kanakam was in shambles, dozens of homes washed away.

"Olawu!" Dikembe called her name again. He dismounted and sifted through every pile of debris in sight. "Olawu!"

He heard a cough nearby and rushed towards the sound. It was not Olawu, but an older merchant who had been sleeping in his cart, by the looks of it. Dikembe helped him up.

"Have you seen anyone else?" he asked. The old man shook his head and continued coughing. Dikembe scoured the market, then returned to his horse. He'd search all night and every inch of Kanakam, if need be. He had to find her.

OLAWU'S EYES BULGED as something hard smashed into her gut. She gasped, but it was cut short by another blow. Three pairs of feet met her on her way to her knees. Bright light sifted through the window behind her, illuminating the red and orange kaftans of her captors. Her mind cleared, and her pain gave way to panic. Where was her umama?

"Lift her head." A familiar voice spoke. A heavy hand yanked her head backwards. Her eyes focused, and she scowled.

"Batiko." The name left a bitter taste in her mouth.

"We meet again, Olawu." Batiko had grown a beard and was several pounds heavier. A necklace of teeth she had known since childhood hung from his neck. "I see you've been busy."

"As have you." Olawu wheezed. "How is it you have become the Chief of Kanakam?"

Batiko grinned. "My sweet Olawu. You are looking at the most wealthy merchant in Kanakam. When Chief Zulu and so many others did not return from war, I had no choice but to become Chief of Kanakam."

"I did not realize dogs could become chiefs in Kanakam."

Batiko chuckled. "I see you still have not learned your place. Hold her up."

The men on each side of her hoisted her up, and Batiko slammed his fist into her gut a third time. Olawu retched, spitting out blood as she emptied her stomach. She likely had a few broken ribs.

"I'm curious, Olawu. How did the wife of InDuna Dikembe get mixed up with the Oloko scum?"

"What business is it of yours?" Olawu rasped.

Batiko sucked at his teeth. "My guards were beaten and killed. The Kanak dam nearly destroyed. My beloved village flooded by a band of Oloko led by a woman with a leopard hide about her shoulders. Imagine my surprise when in the wreckage my men found *you*." Batiko lowered himself until their faces were level. "Do you know what the penalty is for defying the Dikebe?"

"I am sure you will tell me." Olawu wrestled her arms against the men at her sides, but they held her fast.

Batiko snorted with glee. "No, I will show you. Take her."

The men dragged Olawu outside and into the market square, which had been cleared away to make room for a large platform. It looked just like the one used for the Choosing. A tall, wooden pillory rested at the center of the platform.

288

Olawu fought against the men at her arms as they dragged her into the pillory and locked her head and hands in place. She had to stand at the tips of her toes to keep herself from choking.

Batiko watched her, the mirth never leaving his eyes. "The Dikebe have much better ways to break injas like you, Olawu. This device comes from Borimbe. Do you like it?" Batiko chuckled as Olawu struggled to breathe, then turned to the growing crowd.

One of the village men blew a loud horn, and more villagers gathered, whispering and pointing as they stared at her. She recognized some of them.

"People of Kanakam!" Batiko bellowed. "A great tragedy has befallen us! The Oloko have attacked us without provocation. They set out to destroy the great structure InDuna Dikembe and his ubaba before him built on the edge of Mount Kanagari. They sent a great flood through our village. And who did they send to do it? One of our very own daughters of Kanakam!"

Batiko stepped aside, allowing the villagers to see Olawu's face.

"It's Olawu!"

She spotted Auntie Morimbe in the crowd. More shouts followed as the people recognized her.

"You are angry, and rightfully so!" Batiko shouted. "Should this inja not be punished? Should this Pootagi not be put in her place?"

Angry shrieks rang through the air. Batiko stepped out of the way as rocks, sticks and refuse flew at Olawu. He allowed the abuse to continue for several minutes before stepping back onto the platform.

"In Kanakam, women should know their place. Those who do not should be broken. But what do you think, good people of Kanakam? Should we break her?"

"Batiko!"

The crowd parted as InDuna Dikembe walked towards the platform. "What are you doing with my wife?"

Batiko squared his shoulders and glared. "Great people of Kanakam. On the day Olawu was to be my bride, InDuna Dikembe interfered with our rituals and stole her away." Batiko looked to the crowd. "Because of his interference your homes are now flooded. Your children have drowned! Your livelihoods have been ruined! InDuna Dikembe says with his mouth that Kanakam is free to govern our own affairs, but his actions say otherwise."

"Watch your words." Hondo unsheathed his sword and lay it at Batiko's throat. Batiko winced, then sneered at Dikembe.

"Will InDuna Dikembe interfere again with the matters of Kanakam?" Batiko asked. "Will he go back on his word *again* and show us that he cannot be trusted?"

The crowd grumbled in protest, their eyes shifting from their InDuna to their Chief. As they grew more restless, Batiko smirked.

"What proof do you have of what you say?" Dikembe asked. "You call her a defector and a traitor, but unless you have evidence-"

"Look with your own eyes, InDuna. She wears the Oloko armor. Her shoulders bear an animal hide, signifying that she leads them. If that is not enough, I have eye witnesses. Seven of my guards, and three of your own can testify to the truth of my words. She is a traitor!"

The crowd festered with angry howls, chanting for her to be broken. They would be satisfied with nothing less.

Dikembe looked at Olawu with a torn expression. She knew he loved her. But he did not trust her. "Stand down, Hondo."

Hondo looked at Dikembe, sword still raised to Batiko's neck. "InDuna?"

Dikembe's jaw hardened, and he turned away. "Stand down."

Hondo lowered his sword and stepped away from the platform. Olawu searched Dikembe's face, but he would not meet her eyes.

Old resentments bubbled to the surface as the crowd continued their bloodthirsty chants. Her eyes traveled over their hate-filled faces, witnessed their scowls.

A young girl in the crowd watched her. Her large, brown eyes grew wide at Olawu's gaze. She recognized the fear in them. The girl's thin frame and distended belly told a troubling story. Another girl stood beside her, equally haggard and afraid.

And there were others. Women, young and old. Children. The most vulnerable in Kanakam watched her. In the glint of her eyes, the Pootagi saw a reflection of their own fates. Follow the rules, or be broken. They knew nothing else.

Her ubaba's words returned to her. "God would not let me sleep if I turned my back on one of His children."

Mbako knew something. Something Olawu had just begun to realize. The people of Kanakam wanted her broken. Had always wanted to break her. But she would not let them.

Olawu's resentment gave way as she finally understood. Her ubaba, udokotela of Kanakam, had given the people more than medicine. He had given them dignity and hope. An example of genuine love for everyone, not just for those in power. Olawu took a breath and lifted her chin.

"People of Kanakam!" She fought to raise her neck above the wood. She needed to speak every word clearly. "No matter what you take from me, know that you will never take the truth. You may break every bone in my body, but you will never break my spirit!"

Olawu's eyes locked with the young girl in the crowd. She spoke again, her gaze never leaving the girl's face.

"I am Olawu, daughter of Mbako, the faithful udokotela of Kanakam. I am the adopted daughter of the great Chief Umfazi of the Oloko. She has accepted me as her own, and I will not deny her.

"I am not an inja. I am not a Pootagi. I am not a lowly woman. I am loved. I am of great value. My sisters and brothers will fight for me, and I will fight for them."

The young girl's mouth opened in awe, and Olawu's heart lifted.

"It is time to break this insolent woman!" Batiko snarled. One of the village men handed Batiko a club. He walked back to the platform, leveling his face with Olawu. "Now you will learn your place, inja!"

Olawu smiled.

Batiko straightened and raised his club. A whistle rang out as an arrow cut through the air, piercing his chest. Several more arrows zipped by, and the marketplace erupted into chaos.

Hondo pushed Dikembe back, shielding him with his body. More arrows glided past them as the approaching horses sent dust swirling through the air. Batiko's guards scattered, abandoning his body on the platform.

Dikembe ran towards Olawu, broke the locks on her pillory, and gently lifted her from the wood. Olawu stared at him, surprised. He kissed her, long and deep, then pushed her into Kioli as she passed on her horse.

Kioli caught Olawu and secured her in front of her lap. Fayola stood on her steed, aiming her arrow directly at Dikembe. Kioli shook her head and Fayola smiled, then let the arrow fly. It landed at Dikembe's feet, and she laughed before taking hold of her reins.

Olawu stared at Dikembe, a bewildered Hondo at his side. Dikembe's eyes met hers, then he crossed his forearms and bowed his head.

Chapter Sixty

Olawu took a breath and stepped up to the pillar as the hum of thousands of Oloko surrounded her. Chief Umfazi stood before her, dressed in gold with her hair braided into a long, winding crown. Streaks of white paint ran across the top of her face and along her chin. She nodded at Kioli, who stood beside her with a garland made of leather and bone. Kioli stepped forward, and the humming stopped.

All was silent as Kioli placed the garland over Olawu's head. Chief Umfazi motioned towards Chausiku, who stood with a bowl of paint in her hands. As Kioli returned to her place beside Chief Umfazi, Chausiku stepped forward, streaking Olawu's face across her forehead, nose, and lips.

Chausiku took a step back, and Chief Umfazi finally stepped forward. Her keen eyes pierced the depths of Olawu's soul. When the chief smiled, Olawu released her breath.

"People of Oloko!" Chief Umfazi shouted, her eyes never leaving Olawu's. "Give honor to your new leader. Chief Olawu!" The chief bowed, and all of the Oloko did the same. Olawu looked out at them with tears in her eyes.

"Umntu ngumtu ngabantu!" Olawu quoted the proverb, knowing its truth. It was her connection with the people in front of her that allowed her to be her true self.

She lowered herself to her knees and bowed. First towards Chief Umfazi, then three more times towards the Oloko.

"Just as you pledge yourself to me, I pledge myself to you!" As she stood, the rest of the village stood with her, shouting and cheering as they welcomed their new Chief.

OLAWU SAT IN A LARGE pavilion set in the center of the tiny village of Uxolo. The villagers that passed smiled at her, admiring her golden poufed kaftan and headdress. She sat alone, but Fayola, Bolanle, Kwame, and Kioli kept watch nearby. She suspected that Yero would soon be among them, hidden in some undetectable spot.

She heard Bolanle's low whistle and smiled. He was here.

She folded her hands in her lap, admiring the intricate designs carved into the stone pavilion. Lionesses and leopards, elephants, monkeys, and exotic birds surrounded her. For a small village, Uxolo bore many surprises.

Olawu's pulse quickened, and she looked up. Dark, calculating eyes met hers and she smiled. "Dikembe."

"Olawu."

She looked past him and raised her eyebrows. "Where is he?"

Dikembe's face darkened. "You were serious?"

Olawu sighed. "InDuna Dikembe, the requests I made were clear."

"Chief Olawu." Dikembe's shoulders slumped. "Must we do this?"

"Do you like this place?" Olawu gestured to the landscape of Uxolo. "It aligns neither to the Oloko nor to the Dikebe, and it is more or less in between the two lands. Not too far from the river, and not so crowded as Borimbe. A perfect neutral territory."

"Mm." Dikembe nodded absently. "About your terms. Olawu-"

"They were quite simple, Dikembe."

"But haven't you . . ." Dikembe scowled and sat beside her. "Haven't I what?"

"Olawu, it has been nearly a year. Have you not missed me?"

She swallowed and shook her head. "I've been too busy."

"The message I sent you?"

"I got your message, InDuna Dikembe. I sent my answer."

"But would it not make sense, Olawu? For you to return to Borimbe as my wife, and-"

"And leave the Oloko?"

He sighed. "Olawu, I do not wish for you to leave the Oloko. I just wish for you to return to me."

Olawu scoffed. "You have not changed at all!"

"And you are as stubborn as ever!" Dikembe growled. "Olawu, I love you."

"Yes, Dikembe, you love me. But do you respect me? Do you value me? Do you see me as your equal?"

"I agreed to meet with you here. Can you not meet me halfway?"

Olawu stood. "Goodbye, InDuna."

"Olawu?"

She walked away, not once looking back.

BUSINGE WALKED WITH Ugami through the marketplace, their fingers intertwined. Mbako slept soundly in the wrap secured around Ugami's back, his chubby legs swinging at her sides. Businge kissed the back of her hand, and then her cheek.

"What was that for?" Ugami asked.

"I am grateful for you, Ugami." Businge smiled. "Do you think this would look nice on Kimani?" Businge showed her a piece of fabric and waited for her inspection. His time in Kanakam over, he had moved Ugami and her sister to Borimbe.

"She would look lovely in this color." Ugami's face lit up as she touched the cloth. "Businge? I'd like to visit my umama later, if that is alright?"

Businge's smile faltered. "Ugami."

"It has been so long since I have seen her. Can you not make peace with InDuna Dikembe?"

Businge frowned. InDuna Dikembe had taken Fadhila to Borimbe after Olawu's escape. Officially, her presence in Borimbe kept the Oloko from striking back at the Dikebe. Businge knew the real reason. Dikembe wished for Olawu to return to him. "InDuna Dikembe is too proud to make peace with me, Ugami."

"Perhaps it is you who is too proud, Businge."

Ugami turned, mouth widened in shock. She fell to her knees at the sight of Dikembe. "InDuna!"

Businge glared at Dikembe as he pulled Ugami to her feet. "What brings you here, InDuna?" His eyes and tone held a challenge. "Do you not have servants to go to the marketplace for you?"

Dikembe looked as though he might reply, but stopped himself and instead turned to Ugami. "You look well, Sister. How is Kimani?"

"She is well, InDuna. How is my umama?"

"She is comfortable." Dikembe shrugged.

"That is good to hear. Would it be possible for me to visit her soon?"

Dikembe raised his eyebrows. "Of course! I would never forbid a mama from her child. Do not tell me Businge has been keeping you from her?"

Businge bristled. "Just keeping her from *you*, InDuna."

Dikembe's mouth twitched. "What was that?"

"Desperate men do desperate things. How are your peace talks with the Chief of the Oloko?"

"Watch yourself, Businge." Dikembe took a step towards him, fists clenched.

"Forgive me, InDuna." Businge bowed. "I know that failure is a sensitive subject."

"And what exactly have I failed at?"

"Being the man she needed."

As sparks flew between the two men, Ugami stepped between them. "Businge?" Ugami placed a gentle hand on his shoulder. "I'm hungry. Won't you show me that place you promised to take me?"

Businge's attention returned to Ugami. "Of course."

He kissed her and took her by the hand. Ugami bowed awkwardly towards Dikembe as they walked away.

DIKEMBE CLENCHED HIS jaw as Businge and Ugami turned their backs to him. He hated Businge. Even more, he hated what he'd been tasked to do. But Olawu had left him no choice.

"Businge!"

He turned, raising himself to his full height as if readying for a fight. "InDuna?" His reply dripped with condescension, infuriating Dikembe further. Businge had never shown him proper respect. But for Olawu's sake, he would let it slide.

Dikembe clenched and unclenched his jaw and fists. *Damn Olawu for making me do this.*

"I need your help."

Chapter Sixty One

Olawu found herself in the village of Uxolo for the second time in as many months. Dikembe had asked to meet with her there, and she had agreed after expressing her terms.

She spotted Dikembe in the pavilion. Businge sat next to him. Their eyes met, and the muscles of her jaw twitched. She had not seen Businge since she had kissed him goodbye in Oloko Ekhaya.

He had returned to Kanakam to oversee the repair of the dam, but afterwards returned to Borimbe. Olawu watched him with worried eyes, hoping he held no ill will or resentment towards her.

Businge smiled as she stepped into the pavilion. "Olawu!" He greeted her. "Chief Olawu, I mean."

"It is good to see you, Businge." Olawu glanced at Dikembe, whose pout made him look almost adorable. "InDuna Dikembe, can you give Businge and I a moment?"

Dikembe opened his mouth in protest, then closed it. He bowed his head and stomped away.

Businge watched Dikembe leave, a glint of amusement in his eyes. Olawu grew quiet, unsure of how to begin.

"It is good to see you, Olawu. I brought you something from Borimbe." Businge pulled out a jar and opened it.

The smell of roasted fowl flooded her senses, and she grinned. "Businge, you brought me my favorite food from Borimbe?" Olawu accepted the jar, touched by his thoughtfulness.

"The jar is very cold, so the meat stayed fresh for the journey. The next time you visit Borimbe, I will take you there with Ugami. She loves it, too."

Olawu noted the way he smiled as he spoke of her sister. That was a relief. "I'm glad you and Ugami have found comfort in each other."

He nodded and took her hand. "Olawu, I love your sister, and I would not trade my life with her for another. But you are still very special to me. I hope you can be happy."

Olawu smiled, but couldn't stop the tears that followed. "I'm sorry, Businge." She sniffed. "You have always gone to great lengths on my behalf. I will always be grateful to you."

Businge wrapped his arms around her and kissed her cheek. "I never wanted your gratefulness." He chuckled sadly. "But I would not keep you from your happiness. And I know that you love Dikembe."

"I'm not sure that he knows it."

"Ach! Dikembe is stubborn and quick tempered. Olawu?"

"Yes, Businge?"

"Please know that I forgave you a long time ago. All the wounds you gave me healed. I promise there was no permanent damage done to my heart or my head. Do not let it bother you."

Businge's embrace lingered a few moments longer, putting Olawu at ease. When he released her, the weight she carried broke free as well.

"Thank you, Businge. I do have one favor to ask of you?"

"I am at your service."

DIKEMBE GLARED AT BUSINGE as he and Olawu spoke in private. Fury blazed through his insides, burning hotter with each passing second. If Businge dared touch her, he'd cut off the man's right hand and toss it to the dogs. He'd rip him to pieces. He'd. . .

Businge held Olawu's hand, and Dikembe reached for his blade. But he could not falter again. Olawu would not forgive him.

Olawu offered Businge a smile brighter than the sun, and they embraced. Dikembe turned away, deflated. Infuriating woman.

The longer she and Businge sat together, the more Dikembe's hand trembled at the hilt of his sword. But he would bear it. He loved Olawu, but it wasn't enough. She needed to see that he respected her as an equal. That he trusted her. But seeing his wife in another man's arms would never bode well with him. Equal or not.

Olawu finally called him back. Dikembe put his emotions in check, cleared his throat, and greeted them both with a nod.

"InDuna Dikembe, I think we are ready to discuss our truce."

"Of course, Chief Olawu. What do you propose?"

"Two things. The reservoirs that were built to supply water to Dikebe tribes. I want extensions built into the eastern valley as well."

Dikembe grimaced. "It would be very difficult to convince Dikebe men to build aquifers for Oloko tribes."

"I am not suggesting the Dikebe do the building. There are plenty of craftspeople in Oloko. So long as they have Businge's guidance, they will be fine."

"Alright. What is the other thing?"

"Lift the restrictions on women traveling from all Dikebe villages."

"Olawu."

"This is not negotiable, InDuna. If you were enslaved against your will, what would you do? Would you accept your captivity?"

Dikembe frowned and crossed his arms. "What does this have to do with anything?"

"Please answer the question, InDuna."

"I would not accept it. I would escape or die trying."

"And if you managed to escape and return to Borimbe, would you be accepted, even though you were once a slave?"

"Of course. Olawu, I do not see why this is-"

"The Pootagi women of Kanakam are slaves, InDuna. Many women in other villages are treated no better. They are beaten, broken, forced into labor through no fault of their own. If they wished to escape their bondage, how could you deny them? Dikembe, you are strong, but even you could not endure such a life. Why should anyone else be forced to accept it?

"If a woman wished to leave Kanakam and its cruelty, how could you not allow her? If I had escaped from the Oloko and returned to you, I would have been killed at the gates of Borimbe. Even now, I cannot enter any Dikebe village without a male escort. My female messengers are unable to bring letters to Borimbe or even the fortifications surrounding the eastern bank. You must lift the restrictions."

Dikembe sighed and scratched his beard. "These are your terms?"

Olawu nodded. "These are my terms."

"And what do the Dikebe get in return?"

"Peace, for starters. And open trade. The eastern valley is a vital resource for agriculture. That is the real reason why the Dikebe have coveted Oloko territory for so long. Trade between Dikebe and Oloko means access to hundreds of acres of crops."

Dikembe scowled. "Controlled by the Oloko."

"As they should be." Olawu glared. "We can negotiate trade agreements down the road if you wish, InDuna."

"Alright. You've stated your terms. Now hear mine." Olawu lifted her chin and waited. Dikembe sat beside her and took her hand in his. "Be my wife, Olawu."

"Dikembe."

"The only way to truly bring peace is to join the Oloko and the Dikebe tribes together. An agreement of words does not mean anything. But joining as husband and wife will secure peace for both sides."

Dikembe removed a box from his tunic and placed it beside her. He opened it to reveal the blue lotus barrette he'd had repaired in the market. "A long time ago, a young girl with curious eyes and long, braided hair was given this barrette by my mama. But a fool broke the barrette and her heart and left her alone in the world. He thought that he could make it up to her by keeping her behind him."

Dikembe looked up at her. "I am not a fool any longer, Olawu. I do not wish to have you behind me. I wish to have you beside me. Fighting with me, fighting for me, fighting for peace between the Oloko and the Dikebe. I cannot promise to be perfect. But I can promise that I will stay by your side. Please accept me."

Olawu sighed. "Dikembe."

"You do not have to answer now. But either way, this belongs to you." Dikembe placed the barrette in her hands and kissed her fingers. "I have no other terms. If you do not wish to return to Borimbe, I will accept it." Dikembe stood to leave. "If there is nothing else, Chief Olawu, I must get back." He gestured for Businge to follow as he left the pavilion.

Businge stood to leave, but hesitated next to Olawu. "Do you have a message for your sisters, Chief Olawu?

"Tell them that I love them and hope to see them soon."

Businge nodded and followed Dikembe to their horses.

OLAWU STARED FOR A long time at the barrette in her hand. As she considered what it meant, a slow grin broke out on her face. She stood, heart swelling, and ran out of the pavilion.

"InDuna Dikembe!"

Dikembe and Businge had already mounted their horses, but stayed their reins as she approached. "Yes, Olawu?"

"There is one more matter we need to discuss. I cannot lead the Oloko from Borimbe, and you cannot lead the Dikebe from the valley. What do you think of Uxolo?"

Dikembe set his cool, dark eyes on her and shrugged. "It aligns neither to the Oloko nor to the Dikebe, and it is more or less in between the two lands. It is not too far from the river, and not so crowded as Borimbe. A perfect neutral territory."

"Then we are in agreement. I accept your terms."

He jumped down from his horse and closed the distance between them. She watched him with a wary eye, sensing he was up to something. He stopped just inches from her and bent down, leveling his eyes at her.

"Chief Olawu, adopted daughter of the great Chief Umfazi of the Oloko and beloved daughter of Mbako, the faithful udokotela of Kanakam. You cannot be my wife."

Olawu reared back in surprise. "What?"

Dikembe sighed. "I take back my offer."

Olawu scowled. "You cannot. And, by your own admission, I am already your wife!"

"Are you? Did I eat your isitshalo? Did I pay a bride price to your family? Did you give your consent? Ach, Olawu! What do you take me for?"

"Dikembe, do not make light of my acceptance."

Dikembe smirked. "Olawu, I cannot accept you as my wife if it is not your will. I will not force you."

"These were your terms!"

He shrugged. "I changed my mind."

Olawu placed her hands on her hips. "Must you be so stubborn, Dikembe?"

"I prefer diligent, Olawu." She glared at him. That was the third time he'd used her own words against her.

"Would the two of you kiss already?" Businge yawned. "We are losing daylight."

Olawu scowled, eliciting a chuckle from Dikembe. He drew her close, then placed her arms around his neck. "My Olawu. I am yours. But I must know something?"

She looked into his eyes, recognizing his need. "I love you, Dikembe."

He smiled at her and she kissed him, pulling him closer. He wrapped his arms around her and lifted her into the air. Olawu laughed as he twirled her around and kissed her again.

He tried to kiss her once more, but she held a finger to his lips. "Dikembe?"

"Yes, my love?"

"I wish for you to grant me one request?"

"A request?"

"There is something I've wanted to do with you for a very long time. We have done it before, but-"

"Say no more." Dikembe's smile held a hint of mischief. "Just tell me when you are ready, and I will make the arrangements."

"I want to do it in Borimbe."

"As you wish."

"In the courtyard."

Dikembe raised his eyebrows. "The courtyard, Olawu?"

"Yes! And I want my guards Kioli and Fayola and Bolanle to be there."

"Olawu, I do not think-"

"And of course, Hondo. And Yero, Ibawa and Boku. Perhaps your parents as well? Or do you think that would be too embarrassing?"

"Olawu, what are you thinking?"

She looked up at him and grinned.

Epilogue

Olawu stretched her neck from one side to the other as she rolled her shoulders. She wrapped her fingers around her staff and signaled to Dikembe that she was ready. He scowled as he approached her, twirling his staff between his fingers.

"Take him down, Chief Olawu!" Fayola shrieked and whistled from her spot on the courtyard steps.

Hondo bristled and growled as her hand smacked his face. "Watch yourself, little one!"

"Little?" Fayola turned her fierce gaze on him and pounced, but Kioli held her back.

"Fayola, you know the Dikebe have no manners." Kioli chuckled. "You can spar with him afterwards, eh? For now, we must cheer Chief Olawu!"

Fayola wiped the spittle from her mouth and nodded in agreement. "I will deal with this inja later!" She feigned a strike at Hondo and hissed before returning to her seat.

Dikembe swung his staff and Olawu blocked, then returned with several short swings of her own. Her strikes were unrelenting as she pounded the wood of her staff against his. Dikembe blocked each blow, but each hit pushed him backwards.

"InDuna, do not falter!" Yero called out with a laugh. Dikembe nodded and took a step forward, pressing hard against Olawu's staff. She kneed him in his gut before shoving the end of her staff into his armpit. Bolanle gave a loud hoot as Kioli and Fayola shrieked in delight.

Dikembe's eyes grew wide as she continued her attack. She smacked his left leg before he could block, but he pulled his staff up in time to protect his face.

"Olawu!" Dikembe panted as she continued with another round of swift, hard attacks. "Do you mean to scar my face, my love?"

"Save your breath and focus." Olawu's attacks grew faster and harder, and Dikembe soon lost his staff. Her staff connected with his shoulder, and he rolled onto the ground. He retrieved his staff just before Olawu's foot struck his arm, and he tripped her. He quickly climbed on top of her, pinning her arms with his knees.

"Olawu, would you not rather engage in some other activity?" he teased. "You have never beaten me before."

"Before I was not Chief of the Oloko."

Dikembe bent down to steal a kiss, but his efforts came to nothing as his body left the ground. Olawu flipped him over her head, slamming him into the dirt. He groaned as Olawu's staff pressed against his chest.

"Do you yield, Dikembe?"

He shook his head. "We've only just begun."

He swung his staff, and she stepped back, swinging hers casually as she waited for him to return to his feet. Dust and rocks flew as their feet scraped the ground. The steady clap of wood against wood created a rhythm as they danced around each other, giving and taking.

The sky darkened as billowing black clouds covered the midday sun. Thunder rumbled and growled as the rain began. Slow at the start, the rain soon poured from the sky at a furious pace. It battered the courtyard, creating deep puddles as Dikembe and Olawu continued their battle. The steady pelt of rain against the ground added to the cadence. Lightning cracked in the distance, illuminating their dark faces, but no one moved.

Dikembe clenched his jaw, and their water-soaked hair clung to their necks and faces. Olawu dodged a swing from Dikembe, stepping into a puddle. Dikembe laughed, twirling his staff behind his back and into his other hand.

Olawu shook her head. "A delightful trick for children, Dikembe, but not for serious battles."

"Is this a serious battle, Olawu? I had not noticed."
Olawu charged him with a shout, hammering his staff with a swiftness Dikembe could not counter. He dodged and blocked the first hits, but was too slow to dodge them all. She clipped one shoulder, then his thigh, before sending the butt of her staff into his gut.

Dikembe doubled over and Olawu smacked his back, sending his face into the mud. She climbed on top of him and locked her staff beneath his neck, suspending his head in the air.

"Yield?"

DIKEMBE STRUGGLED TO move, but Olawu had him. His eyes traveled to his guards. Hondo and Yero fell over in fits of laughter. Ibawa and Boku at least had sense enough to keep their smiles hidden. Dikembe growled and closed his eyes.

"I yield."

Olawu's guards screamed and shouted her praise as she released him. Dikembe remained in the mud, sulking. Olawu extended her hand to him, but he pushed it away.

"Leave me."

She shrugged and ran to her Oloko guards, shouting and dancing. Hondo walked over to Dikembe and squatted beside him in the mud, chuckling. "I suppose it is settled, then."

"What?" Dikembe growled.

"We were not sure who would really be in charge when the Dikebe united with the Oloko. But now the lines are clear."

"What?" Dikembe sat up and stared at Hondo. "What are you talking about?"

"Ach, Dikembe! Sparring with Olawu was not a good idea. You should have known she would beat you. Now the whole world knows that your wife is the true InDuna of the Dikebe!"

"InDuna? Hondo, you are speaking nonsense."

"First it will be little things. You will tell your servant to bring you food, and your servant will say, let me see what InDuna Olawu says about that. Next, you will see your warriors offer you but one arm, and when Olawu comes, they will bow and offer her two!"

Dikembe laughed. "If it were not Olawu, I might be worried about such things."

Hondo chuckled and placed his hand on Dikembe's shoulder. "Still, you should not pout in the mud. If you were one of my men, you would be beaten."

Dikembe scowled, but Hondo was right. He stood with a sigh, then walked over to where Olawu danced with her guards.

"OLAWU?"

Olawu turned towards Dikembe, a glint of humor in her eyes. "Yes, my love?"

Dikembe bent down to his knees and crossed his forearms together. "Mama InDuna of the Dikebe, Chief of the Oloko. You have beaten Dikembe today. You fought well and did not falter. Please accept my congratulations."

"What is he doing?" Fayola tilted her head at Dikembe. "Why are his arms crossed like that?"

"It is a sign of respect, Fayola," Kioli explained.

Olawu smiled down at Dikembe. "Why do you extend your arms to me? Is this not reserved for your brothers in arms?"

"You are my brother in arms, Olawu. Did we not agree to fight for one another?" Dikembe's eyes rested on hers, and her heart beamed in delight. She nodded and tapped her forearms against his, then, pushing aside a loc pressed to his face, she bent down and kissed him.

"You've done well, Dikembe. Today I was your brother, but tonight, I shall be your wife."

Dikembe's broad smile warmed her through and through. He kissed her again, then left the courtyard with his guards. Olawu watched him leave, then turned to Fayola, Kioli, and Bolanle. Their presence in Borimbe was a miracle in itself. There was more work to do, but the healing between tribes had begun.

Olawu looked up as the rains subsided and the clouds began to clear. The warm sun kissed her skin and she smiled. Though she could not see him, she felt as though her ubaba was still with her. Somehow, she knew he would be proud of her.

She was Chief of the Oloko; Mama InDuna of the Dikebe. But at all times she was Olawu, daughter of the udokotela.

Isiphetho

Acknowledgements

The words "umntu ngumtu ngabantu" (a person is a person because of other people) ring true for the birthing of this book. I'll keep it brief, but I would be remiss if I didn't thank the people who helped me along the way.

Thank you to my wonderful husband, who always, always believes in me, and stops what he's doing when I need him to lend me a hand with something technical, or graphical, or when I need to run some random thought by him. Thank you to my beta readers, who offered their time and input. Thank you to my silent supporters, and the people who always ask what I write and where they can find it. A very special thanks to Donna, who's seen this story in its rougher times and read probably a thousand versions of blurbs, synopses, and all those frustrating writerly things that plague us indie wordsmiths.

Thank you to the Lord above, and the community of friends and fellow laborers that keep me moving forward.

Thank you to you, the reader. For taking a chance on Olawu, and on me.

Discussion Questions:

1.   There are 3 very different tribal representations in the story. In what ways are their cultures different? In what ways are they similar?

2.   The Olawu we begin with is not the same Olawu in the end. In what ways does she grow or change? What caused those changes?

3.   How do the women in the story show strength? Resilience? Wisdom?

4.   Olawu's relationships with the men in her life are all very different. What are your thoughts on her relationship with her father? With Batiko? Businge? Dikembe?

5.   Olawu struggles to reconcile her memories of the people of her village with the treatment she receives as a Pootagi. Can you relate to her struggle?

6.   Community is an important theme in the story. What role does community play in the situations and outcomes Olawu faces?

7.   There is a proverb in the story "a person is a person because of other people." What are your thoughts on the meaning of the proverb and its significance?

8.   In the beginning of the story, Olawu is seemingly oblivious to the plight of the Pootagi in her village. What does this say about her? How does her attitude change over time? Can you draw any parallels to present day forms of privilege?

9.   In what ways are Olawu's relationships with the women of Kanakam similar to the women of Borimbe and Oloko? In what ways are they different?

10.   How do the relationships Olawu forms with other women affect her choices?

11.   Were there any characters you felt a deep connection with, or that mirrored some of your own personality or ideals?

12.   There are three men with romantic interest in Olawu. Were you surprised by her ultimate choice? Who would you have chosen if you were Olawu?

13.   How does the setting play a part in the outcomes of the story?

About the Author

P. J. Leigh is a lifelong lover of stories and enjoys all kinds, from mystery to fantasy. Her biggest motivations for writing are the two beautiful girls she has at home, which is why her writing showcases female characters of color. Awards include 1st place in the WCPL Short Story Contest for "Take Me Away," 1st place in the Prose monthly challenge for "The Earth Sighed Seven Times," and 6th place in the Writer's Digest Short Story Competition for "The Shifter."

If she's not plotting and scheming, she's typically reading, crying over K-dramas or, inevitably, doing laundry. Learn more about her projects by scanning the QR Code below or visiting pjleigh.com.